Evil Intentions Come

Timothy J. Lockhart

INTRODUCTION BY RICK OLLERMAN

Stark House Press • Eureka California

EVIL INTENTIONS COME

Published by Stark House Press
1315 H Street
Eureka, CA 95501, USA
griffinskye3@sbcglobal.net
www.starkhousepress.com

EVIL INTENTIONS COME copyright © 2023 by Timothy J. Lockhart.
All rights reserved, including the right of reproduction in whole or in part in any form. Published by Stark House Press by arrangement with the author.

ISBN: 979-8-88601-024-4

Book text and cover design by Mark Shepard, shepgraphics.com
Proofreading by Bill Kelly

PUBLISHER'S NOTE:
This book is a work of fiction. Any references to historical events, real people, or real locales are used fictitiously. All other names, characters, places, and incidents are the product of the author's imagination, and any resemblance to actual events, locales, or persons, living or dead, is entirely coincidental. Without limiting the rights under copyright reserved above, no part of this publication may be reproduced, stored, or introduced into a retrieval system or transmitted in any form or by any means (electronic, mechanical, photocopying, recording or otherwise) without the prior written permission of both the copyright owner and the above publisher of the book.

First Stark House Press Edition: April 2023

EVIL INTENTIONS COME

When Pete Scarcelli agrees to represent sultry Justine Kingman in divorcing her husband Ben—the richest man in town—he has no idea what he's getting into. But he soon finds out that Justine has more plans than just divorce for her husband—deadly plans. When Pete initially refuses to go along, Justine reveals a secret from her past that changes his mind.

As he begins to plot with Justine, Pete also has to navigate around Sally Carruthers, a prosecutor and Pete's foe in the courtroom, but a potential lover outside of it. Her father, the chief of police, doesn't want Pete anywhere near his daughter. And then there's Jack Greese, a hardboiled private eye who's not above working both sides of the street.

As Pete is drawn deeper and deeper into blackmail and murder, he learns the hard way that only the devil stands between him and Justine. And the devil is a slippery fellow indeed.

Timothy J. Lockhart Bibliography

Smith (2017)
Pirates (2019)
A Certain Man's Daughter (2021)
Unlucky Money (2022)
Evil Intentions Come (2023)

"...a modern master of pulp espionage ..."
—Kristofer Upjohn, *Noir Journal*

"...this is quality pulp fiction. A thoroughly enjoyable read."
—Paul Burke, *NB Magazine*

"A riveting, page-turning thrill ride ... Ten thumbs up."
—Victor Gischler, author of *Gun Monkeys*

"...a great storyteller."
—*Ship & Shore*

DEDICATION

To Margaret Whitlock Mortimer and
In Memory of Louis Read Mortimer, Jr.,
Captain, United States Navy Reserve (Retired),
Mentors, Friends, and Godparents Nonpareil

ACKNOWLEDGMENTS

The author wishes to thank the following persons
who kindly read and provided helpful comments
on the manuscript of this novel:

Carmel Corcoran
Zhimin "Grace" Gong
Marie Gregory Griffin
Guy Holland
Lisa A. Iverson
Dena Lockhart Jackson
Bill Kelly
Warren L. Tisdale
Zhonglian WANG
Edward W. Wolcott, Jr.

And, as always, special thanks to
Greg Shepard
and the rest of the fine folks at Stark House Press,
who make the publishing process a pleasure.

INTRODUCTION FOR EVIL INTENTIONS COME

By Rick Ollerman

It's no surprise that when writers get together they often talk about books. Actually, I hope it's not a surprise—there does seem to be a rather large percentage of "aspiring authors" that don't appear to have done much actual *reading*. It's something I'll never understand, like radical politics or the both sweet and salty flavor of chocolate covered pretzels (pick one and choose the appropriate snack already). Many times the "non-reading writers" don't have the background to discuss book things in relation to other book things and the talk often turns to movies and what happened in a film as opposed to what happened in a book.

If you're going to write a crime novel, you should not only read and have read crime novels, you should read and have read *a lot* of crime novels. I don't know how to write a romance novel because I haven't read them and wouldn't have a clue where to start. I think I'd have a difficult time with a YA novel because other than reading Harry Potter to my daughter I don't have the background: I don't know the field and I fear I may not have the sensibilities for what it would take.

Anyway, it's a bête noire for me (another one is the phrase "pet peeve" so I choose possible pretentiousness with the French phrase—no one gets weird if you say "déjà vu", do they?) even though sometimes—*sometimes*—it's actually helpful. Even when it feels wrong (like those chocolate covered pretzels or—gasp—kettle corn). In Timothy Lockhart's *Evil Intentions Come*, it's immediately clear he's done the reading, not just the watching. You know Lockhart's not a noir dilettante from the jump. He's done the background.

"They threw me off the hay truck about noon." If you haven't read just that one line (and can't identify it now), you probably shouldn't attempt writing in the noir genre. On the next page, when James M. Cain writes, "Then I saw her," as the first sentence to a paragraph that ends with "…her lips stuck out in a way that made me want to mash them in for her." you kind of know what kind of ride you're getting on even though you're not quite sure if "mash" would be a good thing to do or a bad thing. Maybe something of both? I don't have the answer but talking about the genius of Cain's *The Postman Always Rings Twice* isn't the point but when people ask me to define noir fiction for them, I just point to that book and say, "Read that."

Fortunately, in this case, the 1946 movie with Lana Turner and John Garfield makes the same point as the book. Hell, even the Jessica Lange and Jack Nicholson recreated it in their 1981 remake but as usual, the original is better. Then there's the movie version of Whit Masterson's (one of Bob Wade's and Bill Miller's pseudonyms who were better known as "Wade Miller") *Badge of Evil*, which was Orson Welles' last film in America. He called it *Touch of Evil* and just like you know where you're going once you get off Cain's hay truck, you know what you're in for from the long, single-shot opening: close-up of unknown man arming a bomb before moving to a car and slipping it into the trunk.

Lockhart knows that ride, he knows how to lay that truck and get you on board. He's read the books and knows the movies. As a writer, Lockhart sets the table for this book and while we don't know how he's going to get *there*, we know we're on the way. And whether you know the books or have only seen the movies, the experience that Lockhart unfolds before you is, hopefully, just what you're looking for when you want to pick up a noir novel. He scratches that itch, he delivers the goods, he gets the rollercoaster underway.

I've been part of a lot of conversations about "What is noir?" and even, "Why call anything noir?" and my short answer to the first question is simply a book where the protagonist starts out screwed and ends up screweder. Many other people have tried to delve deeper and have formed lists of elements of common traits in noir stories, but they often sound as requirements or prerequisites for the label and I think formalizing art is a slippery slope. Some of the most common are that the protagonist must make bad decisions (happens across all forms of literature and helps create conflict, doesn't it?); there must be a femme fatale (could we get away with calling this simply the "love interest," though admittedly ones that tend to go sideways hard); the protagonist must end up, through his poor decision making, in a place worse than where he started (see my above "screweder" definition); and so forth.

Like all debates about art and literature, or what constitutes either, the beauty is often in the eyes of the beholder. And is there a point to looking for things to slap a label on, or should a book just be a book, or should we limit our classification of such to standardized categories like "crime," "romance," "literary" and "horror"? But then again, who would decide what label to apply and where? The publishers who put out the books? The bookstores that need to figure out the best way to present and sell the books? Amazon (gasp) so that they can optimize potential online shoppers' search results?

Leaving these giant and weighty issues aside, I'll say that Lockhart's *Evil Intentions Come* is a noir novel. Not just noir-ish, either, another label-ish attribute that gets bandied about. Read it as a crime novel and come away impressed by the noir elements; read it as a noir novel and feel satisfied as it scratches that particular itch; read it as a story that burns a few hours of daylight at the beach or night-light before bed—any way you like, whether labels serve or do not, read it as a story that propels forcefully from start to finish. And enjoy it for what it is, whatever you choose to call it.

January, 2023
Compass Lake, FL

....

Rick Ollerman is a crime fiction novelist, short story writer, editor and critic. He is the author of the essay collection, *Hardboiled, Noir and Gold Medals*, has recently edited *Down & Out: The Magazine* and is currently the Editor at Large for Stark House Press.

Evil Intentions Come

Timothy J. Lockhart

EPIGRAPH
"It is what comes out of a person that defiles.
For it is from within, from the human heart,
that evil intentions come:
fornication, theft, murder, adultery, avarice, wickedness,
deceit, licentiousness, envy, slander, pride, folly.
All these evil things come from within,
and they defile a person."
Mark 7:20-23

CHAPTER ONE

We are far from the sea here, and among the many things I miss are the tang of saltwater and the cries of gulls. But sometimes late at night, when the noise of the day has died and all is quiet except for the occasional cough or toilet-flush, I stare into the darkness and see again sails billowing against bright sky and hulls carving through dark water.

The vision lasts until I remember going out on his boat—the hungry fire, those terrible screams—and everything that came after it. Then the vision vanishes, and blackness closes in around me.

□ □ □

This is what I remember of that night.

When I got to the landward edge of the dock, I stopped. I stood there, watching and listening. I saw and heard nothing to make me think anyone was awake on the boat.

I walked across the dock, my boat shoes making almost no sound on the wooden planks. The tide was near high, so the deck was about a foot above the dock. I stepped up there slowly, partly to make sure I had my footing and partly to keep the boat from heeling suddenly under my weight. She was big enough not to have heeled much in any case, but I wasn't taking any chances.

None other than being there in the first place and doing what I was about to do.

I went to the main hatch, moving as softly as I could. The hatch was closed, but Justine had told me that Kingman didn't lock it when he was on board, and he hadn't. I eased it open and stood listening again. Still nothing.

The interior was almost completely dark, but my eyes had adjusted to the night, so the moonglow through the windows was all I needed. I went down the ladder one step at a time, pausing after each one.

At the bottom I stopped again. I'd thought I might hear Kingman snoring, but I didn't. I figured he must be sleeping too soundly for that.

Justine had said she'd be sure to fix his drink so that he'd pass out, and obviously she had. She was a strong-willed woman. Hell, she'd talked me into doing this awful thing, hadn't she?

I crept past the navigation station on one side, the galley on the other, and then through the salon. Kingman kept the spaces shipshape, and I admired the way she was laid out. He probably loved his boat as much as I loved mine, and I hated what I had to do to her.

Suddenly it struck me that I was more reluctant to kill the boat than I was to kill Kingman, and I didn't like what that said about me. But there it was, and I couldn't change it.

Or at least I wasn't going to.

The hatch to the main stateroom up forward was open. I tiptoed to the threshold and looked inside. In the dim light all I could see was that a figure lay on the double berth, turned away from me and covered almost entirely by a blanket. I would have thought Kingman would be bulkier lying there, but perhaps the mattress was soft. I strained to hear and finally detected the faint sound of breathing.

I closed the hatch, making a soft click that sounded loud to me in the silence. Then I went up to the bridge.

I pulled the flashlight from my pocket. After partially covering the lens with a finger, I pushed the switch to "on" and played the dim, yellow light over the instrument panel. Most power cruisers have similar controls, and Kingman's was no different.

The key was in the ignition, as Justine had said it would be. I'd checked online to make sure this model of boat used diesel fuel, not gasoline, so I knew I didn't have to run the bilge blowers before getting underway.

I started the engine, keeping it at idle. That sounded loud to me too although it was really a muffled noise about like that of a car running in a driveway. Maybe it would wake Kingman up, but I didn't think so. He seemed to be—I couldn't help thinking it—dead to the world.

I went back on deck and cast off the lines. The boat drifted a little way from the dock as I went back to the bridge. Then I eased the throttle forward, still keeping the engine noise down, and moved out into the river.

I debated whether to turn on the running lights and decided I'd better. That's what Kingman would have done if he were taking the boat out, and a darkened boat might attract more attention than one running normally. So I switched them on.

I motored slowly. I wasn't familiar with that section of the river, and I didn't want to hit a log or snag in the dark. The boat rode well, moving easily through the water, and any other time I would have enjoyed the cruise.

When I got close to where the river empties into the bay, I moved out to the middle of the river's broad mouth and put the wheel on autopilot. Then I ducked below to check on my passenger. Actually, "cargo" was probably a more accurate word.

The figure in the berth hadn't moved. Good.

I went back to the bridge, opened the throttle a bit, and headed out into the bay. Once I cleared the point of land to port, I turned that way and paralleled the shoreline until I was about a mile off the cove where I'd left my car.

I shut off the engine and left the boat drift. I looked all around but didn't see any other boats. There were a few lights here and there on the shore, but they were probably just security lights left on all night, and none of them was close. So I was alone on the water.

Alone except for . . . him.

Justine had told me that there were life jackets on board, and I found them in a locker beneath a bench seat. Taking a jacket was a risk but only a slight one—the police wouldn't know how many had been on board. I dropped it on the deck and went below.

I pulled the little plastic bottle from my pocket, opened the nozzle, and began squirting kerosene on everything readily flammable—cushions, paper charts, wood. When I had almost emptied the bottle, I looked at the hatch to the main berth. Should I open it and squirt some on the blanket?

Maybe. That might be the smart thing to do, but I couldn't bring myself to do it. I hated Kingman, sure, but I couldn't do that to anyone. He was going to die horribly as it was.

I squirted the last of the kerosene on the curtains and dropped the empty bottle on the deck. Then I took out the matches.

I scratched one into flame and lit the cushions. I used another to light the curtains. The fire spread quickly, much more quickly than I would have imagined. I backed away from the growing heat, dropping the box of matches beside the plastic bottle, and went up the ladder into the fresh air.

I shrugged myself into the life jacket and knotted the cloth ties in front. I did a full turn, looking again to see if anyone, any other boat, was around. I was still alone although soon the boat would be a bright beacon on the water and might attract attention. Might even draw someone to come out and investigate.

But if that did happen, I wouldn't be there. I went to the edge of the deck and stepped off into nothing.

It was a short drop to the water. I went in cleanly, sank below the surface, and kicked to get my head out. The kick and the jacket pulled me right up. The water felt cool but not cold although I knew I'd be cold later when I climbed out of the bay in wet clothes.

I started stroking for the shore. After I'd gone about a hundred yards, I began to see the shore more clearly because there was more light around me. I knew the reason and turned back to look.

The interior of the boat was a mass of flame, and devilish tongues of yellow and red were licking up from the main hatch. The fire threw off a cloud of thick, black smoke darker than the night sky. Across the water I could hear popping and crackling and then a louder *smash* when the fire blew out a window.

The sight was horrible, and I couldn't bear it long. I turned away and resumed swimming. Then I heard something else.

A scream. A scream of pure terror. The boat muffled the scream somewhat, but the fear in it came through clearly, and the sound was like nothing I'd ever heard. *That must be how the damned scream in hell*, I thought.

The scream didn't last long—it couldn't with a person in a small space next to a roaring fire. The sound, surprisingly high-pitched, cut off after a few seconds. Even then it kept ringing in my ears.

From that day to this I still hear it sometimes.

CHAPTER TWO

I guess I should begin at the beginning, with that really hot summer we had a few years ago. I think of it as the August everything went to hell. Not all at once, of course. But looking back, it certainly seems that things happened quickly.

When I heard the front door of our office open, I looked up from my desk and saw her just inside the little reception area, standing there hip-cocked and long-legged in a white tennis dress. The sight was so pleasantly surprising it made me want to laugh, but then I looked into her eyes and could tell she didn't like being laughed at.

"Hello," she said in a low-pitched voice. She used a wristband to daub at the sheen of sweat on her forehead. "I hope I'm not intruding."

I don't know whether she meant to look angelic—all in white, even if the dress was short and clung to every curve—or simply alluring. She certainly did look good, her light-auburn hair contrasting with the dark green of her eyes and complementing the fine dusting of freckles on her high-boned cheeks.

I learned later that she hated the freckles, which she usually concealed with a touch of makeup. She regarded them as an imperfection and had for them the contempt she held for anything imperfect—or weak. Anything that wasn't, as she was, solid steel.

And still later I wondered who, if anyone, was responsible for our meeting like that. Maybe Kris. If she'd locked the front door as she was supposed to when she left for lunch, maybe none of it would have happened.

Or me. I guess you could say I was responsible, because although I didn't think the lock clicked when I heard the door shut behind Kris, I didn't get up to check. I told myself I was busy—now I think I was just lazy. Or careless, the way I proved to be about so many things.

Or you could hold Justine herself responsible. For our meeting and most of what came afterward. If she hadn't shown up at my office that day, hadn't stood there in that short, tight dress . . . .

Sometimes I think about what my life would be like if I'd never met Justine—or at least never gotten involved with her. I have a lot of time for thinking now. I don't know what I'd be doing if we hadn't met— probably still practicing law—but I know I wouldn't be here, lying awake in the long, slow darkness.

That was on a Wednesday, just about noon. A few minutes earlier Kris had told me she was going to lunch, which meant I'd go when she got back and reopened the office. Kris is—was, I mean—my office assistant, a petite bottle-blonde young enough to work for the small salary I paid her and pretty enough for me to overlook her frequent typing and filing mistakes.

Not that Kris was dumb. She figured out pretty quickly that she could arrive a few minutes late, leave a bit early, and take long lunches if she helped me get the essential work done in a reasonably competent manner. She also figured out that the sexier she dressed, the less likely I was to say anything about the sloppiness of her work.

We'd gotten to where she was showing deep cleavage and creamy thighs on a daily basis. We hadn't fallen into bed together, but I figured it was just a matter of time.

In a way the prospect saddened me—I always lost assistants after I slept with them. Either they quit after they learned that, despite my denials, I was still seeing other women, or their possessiveness got to me and I fired them. A couple of times, to avoid facing claims of one kind or another, I'd had to make severance payments I couldn't afford.

Apparently the word had gotten around in our little legal community here in Kilmihil. Whenever I went to see other lawyers in their offices—with my shady clients and their weak cases I could seldom persuade opposing counsel to come to me—their females staffers gave me knowing and often disapproving looks.

But I never got to sleep with Kris because Justine showed up. Having to pay Kris severance later would have been cheap compared to what Justine cost.

Justine cost me everything.

"I'm sorry," the woman in the tennis dress said, daubing again at the sweat. "Perhaps this isn't a good time?"

I suddenly realized I hadn't said anything. I guess I'd been too busy taking in the sight of her. I'd never before thought of sweat on a woman as sexy, but she made me see the possibility. The exercise had pinked her cheeks and raised cords of muscle in her arms and legs. I thought of a lioness—one roaming the wild and eating what she killed, not one captured and locked in a zoo.

Not only was she stunning, I thought I'd seen her somewhere. Of course, in a small town like ours, with just over seven thousand people, you do see most folks from time to time. Even—or especially—the ones you want to avoid.

"Not at all. It's just that—"

She gave me a prodding look, which made me remember my manners, and I rose from my chair. "Excuse me. Please come in and sit down."

She stepped into my private office. "I was driving home from the club when I saw your sign. I noticed your girl going to lunch, and some impulse made me park and barge in." She smiled, a bright smile with flawless white teeth. Her gums were blood red. "I suppose I just hoped to be able to talk to you alone."

I stepped around the desk and held a chair for her. "Please. Have a seat."

"All right. If you're sure I'm not bothering you."

I wanted to tell her that any man who liked women would be "bothered" by her, but I said, "Not at all." I continued to hold the chair until she lowered herself into it. Despite the perspiration she smelled faintly of perfume, not at all like a locker room.

She looked up at me, still smiling. "Thank you. By the way, my name is Justine Kingman."

The coin dropped. Then I remembered—she was the wife of Benjamin Kingman, one of the richest men in town. He'd made his money putting up strip malls and office buildings. In some cases he'd had to tear down old houses to do it, houses that some said were historically or architecturally important and should have been preserved. Kingman had a lot of critics, but he never answered them. He just kept building things and making money.

I'd met him a few times at business lunches around town. Each time but the last he'd acted as though he'd forgotten our previous meetings. The next-to-last time I'd reminded him, pointedly, that we'd met before. So at our most recent meeting he'd said, loud enough for others to hear, "Oh, yeah, the ambulance-chaser with the good memory."

I forced myself to laugh, but I squeezed his hand as hard as I could, and I saw him wince. Then he squeezed back, and I had a hard time not letting the pain show. But I didn't.

I'd also met Justine. Just once, and she probably didn't remember—there was no reason for her to. Around Christmas of the year before, Kingman had held an open house at his offices and invited every businessperson in town. I was surprised to be included, especially after what he'd said to me that time, but I went. You never know where you're going to find your next client, and I was hoping to move up in class with mine.

Justine had been there, looking lovely in the proverbial little black dress. Her smile had appeared pasted on, and I could tell from her slight slurring that she was about two drinks ahead of me. We'd chatted for a couple of minutes—mostly I'd answered her questions, some of which had seemed at the time to be a little too probing—but I hadn't seen her since.

Now she didn't appear to recognize me, and I didn't want to embarrass her by reminding her that we'd met. So I said nothing about it.

That turned out to be a mistake. Just the first of many I'd make with her.

CHAPTER THREE

She held out her hand, and I took it. Despite the mugginess outside, the air in the room must have been dry, because I felt an electric shock when our hands touched. She didn't seem to feel it.

"How do you do, Ms. Kingman? I'm Peter Scarcelli." Everyone calls me Pete, but I'd learned that "Peter" could get away with quoting higher fees than "Pete" could.

"Yes, I know." She held my hand a moment, and I thought perhaps she did remember, but then she said, "I saw it on the sign—your 'shingle,' correct?"

"That's right although it's not a term lawyers use much anymore."

"Well, I think I need one. A lawyer, I mean."

Her statement surprised me, and I thought about it as I walked back to my chair. Her husband knew plenty of lawyers, all of them high-priced and therefore supposedly good.

"A lawyer? But doesn't Mr. Kingman use several—"

"Yes, he does." She didn't react to my knowing who her husband was—no doubt she was used to such recognition. "But this is about Ben, so I can't very well ask any of them to represent me."

"I see." I didn't, of course, but I've learned that clients like it when you look lawyerly and say, "I see." Building a church steeple with your index fingers is a nice accompaniment.

"Do you mind if I smoke?" she asked abruptly. She'd probably noticed the ashtray on my desk. I tried to keep the office aired out so the smell wouldn't betray me to nonsmoking clients.

"Not at all. In fact, I'll join you."

She dug her cigarettes out of her little white purse. I got the plastic lighter out of the middle drawer and went around to light her cigarette. She touched my hand and there was that shock again.

Back behind my desk I shook out a cigarette and lit up. She watched me, a sort of amused look in those green eyes. I didn't know what the joke was, but I was glad she was enjoying herself. I was enjoying looking at her legs, barely covered by the little skirt, and her breasts straining against the V-neck top. I didn't know whether she could play tennis well, but I knew she'd look damn good even playing badly.

We puffed in silence a few seconds. Then she said, "I've decided to divorce my husband. Can you handle it?"

I decided to play counselor, not shyster. "Divorce? Are you sure? That's a pretty big step."

She waved her cigarette. "Yes, yes, I know. I've thought about it a long time, and I'm very sure. He's seldom home and ignores me when he is there. He's verbally abusive to me and has even hit me a few times, usually when drunk. He's often drunk these days."

I knew where he probably did a lot of his drinking: the Lanchester Creek Yacht and Country Club, the most prestigious private club on Virginia's Northern Neck. At his party I'd overheard him talking about playing golf there.

Although I'd been to the club only once, I could still picture how the oak-paneled grill room looked out over the Chesapeake Bay, the breeze rippling the blue water and filling the white sails of boats from the club's marina as they tacked back and forth on a golden October afternoon. Sitting in the grill, seeing the polished brass everywhere and the trim, gray-haired men sitting over long lunches as discreet waiters moved quietly among them, I'd practically smelled the money in the room. And I'd wondered—I still wonder—how many deals were done over the dark-green tablecloths and the polished mahogany bar.

A lot, I figured. Deals that people like Ben Kingman and his friends could do but not a bottom feeder like me. I badly wanted admission to that world but knew I didn't have the price of a ticket and probably never would. Unless something unforeseen happened.

"I see." I'd have to be careful not to wear that one out. "Have you tried counseling?"

"No. What would be the point? He's cheated on me several times, including with some of my friends." She dragged angrily on her cigarette. "At least I thought they were my friends. Besides, he wouldn't go to counseling with me, and I have no intention of going alone."

"I understand. Are there any children involved?" I reached for a legal pad to begin making notes.

"No, thank God. I'm Ben's second wife, as you may have guessed."

I had but didn't say so. It's hard to figure out a well-tended woman's age, but she couldn't be much more than forty and Kingman was in his sixties. I didn't know much about women, but I did know better than to tell a woman my suppositions about her age or weight or anything else that had a likelihood of offending her.

"He has a son and daughter by his first wife, but they're both grown and gone. With Ben and me, well, after the first few years we stopped having sex often enough for me to get pregnant—or want to. For the last couple of years we've barely had sex at all."

I wondered why she felt she should tell me that, but I didn't say anything.

After a brief pause she continued. "So I've decided to end this sham of a marriage and move on." She stabbed her cigarette out in the ashtray and looked up at me. "Will you help?"

I should have told her no. I hadn't handled enough divorces to get good at it, and I didn't need to make an enemy of her powerful husband. But I wanted the work—the fees, I mean—and I liked the idea of going after a man who clearly disliked me and had openly insulted me. Plus I was intrigued by her.

I already wondered what she looked like underneath that white dress.

So I said, "I don't do a lot of divorce work—that goes mostly to people who specialize in it—but I'll be happy to help if I can."

She looked me in the eye. "You think you're good enough. Don't you?"

I met her gaze. "Sure, I think so. In fact, I know so." I held my pen over the pad. "Let me start getting some of the details."

She smoothed the short skirt over her tanned thighs and suddenly seemed to realize how she was dressed. "No, not now. As I said, I just stopped in impulsively. I need to go home and change. Why don't you meet me there this evening and we can discuss things?"

"At your house?"

"Yes, of course. Come by at six-thirty. I'm going out to dinner later, but we can have a drink and you can ask any questions you need to."

"What about your husband?"

"We won't be interrupted. Ben's out of town on business until Friday evening."

The arrangement sounded odd, but she was paying the bills. Or would be. "Okay, what's the address? And your mobile number, in case I get lost?"

She told me, and I jotted the information on the pad. Then she rose, and I walked her to the front door. Neither of us offered to shake hands again.

For some reason she glanced around the parking lot—three-quarters empty and drowsing in the late-summer heat—before stepping quickly to a late-model Lexus SUV that cost more than the total for my last three cars. She slid in and pulled out. She may have given me a short wave, but I couldn't be sure through the tinted glass.

I went back to my desk and sat there chain-smoking until Kris returned. Then I left for lunch. I was hungry . . . but not for food.

CHAPTER FOUR

I spent the rest of the long afternoon doing little work but lots of thinking about Justine Kingman. Sometimes I was even thinking about her divorce.

I was so distracted I barely noticed Kris's low-cut top when she came in to have me sign some bill letters. I scrawled my name on three before I glanced up and saw the top halves of her breasts a few inches from my nose.

I shifted my gaze higher and saw Kris smiling at me. Perhaps "smirking" is a better word. I signed the last two letters and watched as she gathered all of them, taking her time and leaning over my desk more than necessary.

When she finally straightened, I looked at my watch—4:07. "What else do we have to do today?"

"That's about it unless you've got something for me."

There were two ways to interpret her statement. I looked closely at her but didn't see any sign she'd meant the second one. "You opened a file for the Kingman matter, right?"

"Sure—'Kingman versus Kingman'. But I thought you weren't wild about taking divorce cases."

"I'm not. But I have to do a lot of things I'm not wild about to pay the bills, including your salary."

She put her hand on her hip. "Yeah, well, that's the first one you should pay. Always."

I'd thought she'd say something like that. "Sure, sure. Look, it's slow. Why don't you take the rest of the day off?"

Her eyes brightened. "Whatever you say, boss. See you in the morning."

As she neared the doorway I said, "By the way—that's a really pretty top you have on. Brings out the color of your eyes."

She turned and smiled. "Think so? Thanks."

She gave me a wink and went back to her desk. In less than a minute I heard the front door close behind her.

The office was supposed to be open until five o'clock, but one of the few advantages of being a solo practitioner is that you can close whenever you like—as long as you don't mind losing the occasional client because of it. I didn't think anyone would drop by this late on a stifling day in August, and the phone system would take a message from anyone who called. So

I switched off my computer, grabbed my sport coat, and left.

I was driving a black Miata then, a sporty little two-seater convertible with a stick shift. Considering the gear I had to haul to and from the boat, the car wasn't really practical, but it was fun to drive and women seemed to like it. Unfortunately, some jerk had side-swiped the Miata at a bar a couple of weeks earlier, leaving a long, ugly scrape that my high deductible and low bank account wouldn't let me fix right away.

For some reason I couldn't explain, I didn't go straight to the marina. Instead I drove out to the country club.

The club was on a large parcel of land at the mouth of Lanchester Creek, so it bordered both the creek and the bay. To keep out the undesirables, a white wooden fence paralleled the highway and ended in brick pillars flanking a wrought-iron gate at the entrance to the club. I ignored the prominent sign that said, "Private Property—Members and Guests Only" and went slowly down the long paved driveway shaded by huge oaks.

Despite the heat a number of golfers were out on the course, the Easter-egg colors of their clothing making them easy to spot against the emerald grass and beige carts. When I got to the parking lot I heard the *thock* of tennis balls on the courts and the cries of children splashing in the pool.

I drove past the clubhouse, a big white building that had been the home of the wealthy family that once owned all this land. I didn't know what had happened to the wealth or the family, but from my previous visit I knew the former house, with large wings attached on both sides and an equally large extension on the back, held the club's formal dining room, grill room, ballroom, bar, library, and offices. The building to the side that held the fitness facility was almost new but coordinated with the clubhouse down to their matching red-carpeted entrances.

Almost all of the cars in the paved parking lot were new and expensive. I figured the ones that weren't, grouped at the far end of the lot, belonged to the club's staff. I pulled into a spot but kept the engine on to run the AC.

I saw a few people walking around, mostly women, and they were mostly tall, thin, and blonde. They looked as expensive and well-maintained as the cars around me. Other than the fellows on the golf course, I didn't see many men. The husbands were probably still at the office, working to pay for all this.

That was a sexist thought, I knew. Undoubtedly some of the women members of the club had careers and worked hard at them. I'd been up against some women lawyers who were as dedicated as any men and better than most of them.

But these women reminded me of Justine Kingman. They all had careers too, worked hard at them, and made money—but not in the form of a paycheck. Part of their compensation was being able to relax here at "The Club."

As I was sitting there, thinking my deep thoughts, a uniformed security guard came over to the car and tapped on my window.

I ran it down and looked into his dark, impassive face. "Yes? What is it?"

"Excuse me, sir, but I don't see a club parking sticker on your car. Are you a member?"

I became annoyed. I was just sitting in my car not bothering anybody. I suppose the guard had noticed that my car looked as though it belonged with the staffers' vehicles.

"No, I'm not a member." I raised my chin and continued to look the guard in the eye.

"Then are you a guest of a member . . . sir?"

"Not at this time."

"Then I'll have to ask you to leave. This club is for members and guests only." He was still polite, but frost had come into his tone. Apparently my necktie wasn't enough to make up for my dented ride.

I knew there was no point in challenging him, but I didn't want to let him win so easily. "I'm looking for someone."

"Uh-huh. Who's that?"

"Justine Kingman."

His lip curled but so slightly I almost didn't see it. "Mrs. Kingman?"

"Yes, I have some business to discuss with her."

The guard thought about that a moment. Then he said, "I don't believe Mrs. Kingman is here at the moment. And if you got business with her, the place to do that would be your office."

I didn't say anything, just waited.

The man sighed and unclipped a mobile phone from his belt. "Sir, I don't want to call the police, but I will if you don't leave right now. It's up to you."

I didn't think he was bluffing, so I said, "All right," and pulled away slowly.

In the rearview I could see the guard watching me go.

☐ ☐ ☐

I drove to the marina where I kept my boat—a 36-foot sloop I'd renamed *Law Lass*. I knew renaming a boat was supposed to be bad luck, but I thought she deserved a new name after I found her squatting on jack stands in a weed-infested boatyard, a faded "For Sale" sign hanging from a limp lifeline.

I'd fixed her up with repairs, paint, and a new suit of sails, restoring her to life on the water. She wasn't the fastest boat on the bay, but she had good lines, responded well to someone who knew how to sail her, and, except during very hot or cold weather (when there was always the option of a motel), served as a reasonably comfortable place to live.

She was also catnip to the ladies, who smiled when I told them two things were better on the water and the second was sailing. I'd seen quite a few demure schoolteacher-types shed their inhibitions along with their clothes once we were at sea under a hot sun. Wanting "no tan lines" seemed to be a good excuse for a lot of things—especially after a few drinks.

And apparently making love on the water under a midnight moon is a pretty common fantasy for women. That the boat's original name, *Seaduction*, made things a bit too obvious was another reason for changing it.

I got some casual clothes—khakis, boat shoes, and a golf shirt—from the boat and then went to the marina's head to shower and touch up my shave. Like the rest of the marina, the head could have used cleaning and a coat of paint, but the owner claimed he saved money—and kept our slip fees lower—by not being "overly aggressive" about maintenance.

That was another way of saying the marina was seedy. There were a few other sailboats, ranging from a couple as big as mine down to daysailers, but most of the boats were stinkpots, small powerboats used for fishing, bigger ones used for cruising, and a couple of sleek, fast boats their owners said they used for "knocking down waves." With the careless disregard that some power boaters have for "rag hangers," they usually managed to knock down some of those waves too close to my boat, making her rock through their wakes and causing my female companion of the day to cover herself with a towel.

I didn't like either effect.

I went back to the boat, walking slowly because of the heat and perhaps just to savor the sight, sound, and smell of an old Chesapeake Bay marina in late summer. The bright boats barely moving at their slips beneath a bright sky, the slaps of water on weathered wood and halyards on aluminum masts, the hot, green stillness of the pine woods across the road, and the unmistakable scent of saltwater mixed with fainter aromas of fish, gasoline, and mud.

Something made me love it completely and absolutely. Although I hadn't reflected on it at the time, now I can see that spending all those summers at the Willoughby Spit marina down in Norfolk instilled in me a love of boats and the water that was as deep and hard as bone.

This marina certainly wasn't as shipshape as the one I recalled from childhood or the similar one at the Lanchester Creek Yacht and Country Club, but it made me remember the lessons about weather and knots and seamanship I absorbed from my grandfather. (My father's father—my other grandfather died before I was born.) I could still hear him telling me, in that softly rolling Tidewater accent you don't hear much anymore, how to tie a bowline: "First you make a hole. Then a rabbit comes out of the hole . . . ."

Back at the boat I put away my lawyer clothes and fixed a bourbon on the rocks with a splash of water—perhaps more to relax for my meeting than to enjoy the taste. I checked the Kingmans' address on my phone and studied the route to their house. Apparently they lived near the river at the end of what looked like a minor country road among some others just like it. Even with using my phone, the house might not be that easy to find.

But then something told me I'd be able to find it all right. *Oh, yes, you'll find her . . . that part won't be a problem.*

I waited, but the voice in my head didn't say anything else.

I sipped my drink and smoked a cigarette while sitting in the shade of the bimini top and looking out at the water. The sun was still above the horizon, but the shadows it cast were beginning to lengthen, and the western sky was taking on a rosy tinge.

Sailors' delight. Maybe that was a good omen. I could use some luck—good luck anyway. It seemed as though I hadn't had any of that in a while.

When I'd finished both drink and cigarette, I closed and locked the boat's main hatch. Then I got back in the Miata and drove away from the marina, headed for her.

CHAPTER FIVE

As I'd suspected, the Kingmans' house wasn't easy to find. The cell coverage outside town and near the river was spotty and kept fading in and out. When the map on my phone showed anything, it suggested that their place was in several acres of woods bordering the river upstream from the club.

I left the highway and took what I thought might be the right road: a narrow two-lane blacktop, sticky from the day's heat. The road twisted down past several houses, some new but most old, and a couple of small farms.

There were no house numbers, and some of the mailboxes by the side of the road were unmarked. The mail carriers must have learned the route over the years to the point where they didn't need any help finding the right houses.

When the road started to climb back toward the highway, I reluctantly decided I was lost and would have to call Justine for directions—assuming I could get enough signal to make the call. But then I passed a tree-lined, oyster-shell lane headed by a flat-black metal mailbox on which the word "Kingman" had been stenciled in neat white letters. I braked the Miata to a stop, backed up to the entrance to the driveway, and started down it.

Because of the heat I had the top up and the air conditioner on. But it was cooler under the awning of the big trees, so I turned off the AC and rolled down my window. I heard the tires crunching over the oyster shells, and behind me rose a fine dust as white and gritty as mausoleum marble.

The driveway curved and drew away from me through the trees, so I couldn't see its far end. Although I was moving, somehow I felt suspended between the road I had left and whatever lay in front of me at the end of the road I was on.

The driveway ended in a semicircle in front of an imposing ranch-style house that sprawled to the right and left. With its fitted stone and large picture windows, the house looked like something designed by a good architect who'd been given a big budget to work with and had used every penny of it.

I thought a traditional style—that of the original clubhouse, for example—might have looked better and certainly would have been more in keeping with the history and culture of the locality, but it was

Kingman's money. And apparently he had a lot of it.

To leave the driveway clear, I parked near the garage. The Lexus sat in front, carelessly angled across two of the three doors. I hadn't noticed the vanity plate in the office lot, but now I saw it read "KINGMN" as if to mark the car—or maybe its driver?—as his property. I shrugged and walked to the front door.

I rang the bell and waited. No one opened the door, and I didn't hear footsteps inside. I rang again and waited some more. I checked my watch. It was 6:36, so I wasn't early.

Just as I was trying to decide whether to ring again or simply leave, she opened the door. She wore an ivory linen dress that was snug but not tight. Her brown arms, bare almost to the shoulder, contrasted nicely with the dress. She wore little makeup and a few simple pieces of gold jewelry.

"Sorry to make you wait—the maid's left for the day, and I was still getting ready."

I wanted to say that the sight of her made the wait worthwhile, but I just smiled and nodded.

"Please come in." She made a graceful gesture, and I walked by her, catching again the subtle scent of her perfume.

"Thanks."

"No, thank you for coming all the way out here to talk."

"No problem. I always like to accommodate my clients if I can."

She smiled at that. "Good. I think you can accommodate this one better over a drink."

"That sounds fine."

She led me from the foyer through the living room and back to the study—both big rooms with polished oak floors largely covered by oriental rugs that picked up the Williamsburg colors on the walls, a different color in each room. The rooms were filled with just the right amount of art and antique furniture.

"You have a lovely home."

"Thank you."

"Did you do the decorating yourself?"

She laughed. "God, no—I wish I had that much talent. The first Mrs. Kingman did it, with the help of a professional, of course. I've just tried not to fuck it up."

The harsh word sounded both deliberately chosen and out of place in her beautiful home. I was to learn that, like a few other women I've known, Justine seemed to enjoy the contrast between her refined surroundings and her cynical view of them.

The color scheme in the study reminded me of the grill room at the country club, and I wondered how much money Kingman had made simply by sitting behind that big desk and talking on the phone. The room was lined with bookshelves crammed with books as though someone had read them, not arranged them for display. The wet bar built into one corner looked both well-stocked and well-used.

I liked what I'd seen of the house so far, and I wondered what the bedrooms were like—not that I was ever going to find out. Based on what she'd told me, I assumed they slept in separate rooms. Hers was probably feminine but not frilly and his probably masculine almost to the point of being overdone.

She walked behind the bar. "What would you like?"

"Bourbon with a splash of water."

"Ice?"

"Yes, please."

She smiled as she began making the drink. "I figured you for a bourbon man. Kingman drinks scotch, but you seem like the traditional Southern type."

Her calling him by his last name sounded odd. I'd heard a few other women occasionally refer to their husbands the same way, however, so maybe it wasn't all that strange.

"I'm just a redneck with a law license."

That brought a laugh. "I'm sure that isn't true."

Well, maybe not entirely true, but there was truth to it. Sometimes I felt I wore my background like a cheap suit. That sharp-eyed guard at the club had probably seen it—and seen right through me.

I wondered if Justine had also seen through me. And if she hadn't already, how much longer it would take.

CHAPTER SIX

She handed me the drink and poured herself a glass of white wine. She held out her glass, and I clinked it. "Cheers," she said before taking a sip.

"Better days." I tasted the drink, and it was perfect.

"Let's go out on the deck. There's usually a breeze this time of day, and we'll be cool enough if we sit in the shade."

"All right."

She picked up her phone, a pack of cigarettes, and a lighter and led the way through a sliding glass door to a large redwood deck. A large wooden table with an umbrella and canvas director's chairs was on one side, and a built-in hot tub, big enough for at least six people, was on the other.

A flight of stairs led to the manicured lawn, a smooth green carpet that sloped gently down to the darkening river, broad this close to the bay. An oval swimming pool with a low diving board lay in the middle of the lawn. Some wrought-iron tables and chairs sat on the concrete pool deck. A flagstone walkway led to the pool and then to the wooden dock beyond it.

A power boat, a fast-looking cruiser about thirty feet long, was moored to the dock. She had bright brass and flemished white mooring lines and blue trim that looked good against the gleaming white hull.

"Nice boat. What's her name?"

"Oh, that's Kingman's plaything. He named it *Loophole* as in 'tax loophole'. I think he takes a deduction for it."

I was sure he did, and it might even be legal, depending on the nature of the deduction. But I wasn't there to give tax advice.

"Let's sit down," she said, and we walked over to the table. I held her chair for her, and she thanked me with a smile. I sat across from her and pulled a pen and a small notebook from a pocket of my khakis.

"So, you want a divorce."

"Yes. I gave you the reasons at your office." She pulled out a cigarette, and I leaned across the table to light it for her.

I didn't think I could take notes and drink and handle a cigarette all at the same time, so I held up my palm when she offered me the pack. "No, thanks, not right now." I flipped the notebook open. "I remember the reasons, and they seem like pretty good ones. Still, as I said at the office, divorce is a big step."

"The voice of experience?"

"No, I've never been married. A good thing for some lucky woman."

"Oh, I don't know. You seem bright, and you're reasonably good-looking. Your manners aren't bad either."

That sounded almost flirtatious, and I looked closely at her. She kept herself up well, but she had to be six or seven years older than I was—maybe more. And whereas her husband was rich, I was barely scraping by. She couldn't want to get romantically involved with me.

"Thanks. You said the two of you have no children."

"That's right."

"So I guess you'd like to walk out of the marriage with half of the martial property."

"I'd like to, but that won't happen. I signed a prenuptial agreement that one of Ben's lawyers prepared. I don't think Ben would have married me if I hadn't."

"Did you have your own lawyer look at it before you signed? Advise you about it?"

"Yes—although I don't think he was very good."

"Maybe not, but under Virginia law a prenup is solid if each party had his or her own lawyer." I paused. "So, how much do you get under the agreement?"

"About one quarter. Say, three or four million. Something like that."

I made a note of the amount. "That's still a lot of money."

"Yes. Not half but still a lot."

"I'll need to see the agreement. Maybe he's breached it in some way and it won't apply."

She blew out a plume of smoke that twisted and curled in the warm wind. "I doubt that. His lawyer was very good."

In contrast to me? No, she couldn't mean that—otherwise she wouldn't have hired me. "I'll still need to see it—in the interest of due diligence if nothing else."

"All right. It's in the safety deposit box at the bank. I'll bring it to your office tomorrow."

"Fine." I had some of my drink while I thought about how to get into the next topic. "You said your husband has had affairs."

"Yes, quite a few of them over the years. In fact, I think he's seeing someone now."

"How do you know?"

"Oh, a wife usually knows. He's made a few slips here and there, little lies about where he's been and with whom. Plus a couple of my friends have seen him with other women and told me about it."

"Do you have any physical proof of these affairs?"

"No. I suppose it wouldn't be hard for a private detective to gather some, but that seems so . . . grubby somehow."

"Perhaps, but if Mr. Kingman is resistant to the idea of divorce, you may need some leverage, especially to get spousal support while the matter is pending. By the way, have you told him you want a divorce?"

"No, not yet. I wanted to consult a lawyer first."

"Good. You're going about this the right way."

"Thank you."

She drank some wine, looking at me over the rim of the glass. She'd said it would be cool there in the shade, but my skin felt hot. I hadn't had that much to drink, so I told myself it was just the weather.

"How do you think he'll feel about splitting up?"

"He won't like it—not if it's my idea. If it were something he wanted, that would be different. But I expect he'll fight me."

"Then I definitely think we should have some proof that he's been playing around. I know a private detective who can probably get some."

"All right, if you really think it's necessary."

"I think it's prudent. Better to have the evidence and not need it than not to have it if we do need it."

"I suppose so."

I made a note to call Jack Greese in the morning. "Have you made any preparations for the divorce? I mean, other than talking to me?"

"No. What sort of preparations?"

"Several things. You should open your own bank account and put as much money in it as you can without arousing your husband's suspicion. You should have at least one credit card account that's yours alone. You should get a private e-mail address and rent a post office box so that I can send you documents subject to attorney-client privilege."

"That sounds like a lot."

"There's more, like making copies of financial records—bank statements, checkbook registers, things like that. Inventorying and photographing everything of value in this house. And you should stay in the house—continue to live here, I mean."

"I guess I should be taking notes on all this."

"No, you don't need to. I can give you a checklist when you stop by tomorrow." I jotted another reminder for myself.

"All right." She finished her wine, and I took the hint, finishing my drink too.

"I guess that's all for now." I closed my notebook and stood.

She got out of her chair and stepped close to me. "Thanks again for coming out, Mr. Scarcelli."

"Peter, please. Or just 'Pete'—that's what my friends call me."

"And do you consider clients your friends?" she said, a playful tone in her voice.

"Some of them. The ones I like."

"Then I hope I'll be in that category, Pete."

Without thinking, I said, "You already are, Mrs. Kingman."

She smiled. "Good. And please call me 'Justine'."

"Okay, thanks . . . Justine." I liked saying her name and thought I could get used to saying it. I also liked the way she said mine.

She picked up the glasses and led the way inside. She put the glasses on the bar and picked up her purse. "I have to leave for my dinner engagement now. Let me show you to the door."

We walked back through the house, she slightly in front of me. I tried to think of something witty or at least polite to say, but I couldn't. Watching the smooth roll of her hips in that snug dress was a major distraction.

She locked the front door behind us and then turned to face me. For a moment I thought she might give me a friendly kiss on the cheek, but she held out her hand, and I took it.

"I'm so glad you're willing to take my case, Pete. I feel very comfortable in your hands."

"I'll do my best to keep you feeling that way."

She smiled again, this time a bit enigmatically, and waited as I walked to my car. I looked through my window as I started down the driveway, and this time I saw her wave as we parted.

CHAPTER SEVEN

For dinner I drove over to The Barge, a dive on the Rappahannock River that stood mostly on land but did have a barge out back where people liked to sit in nice weather. By the time I got there the evening had cooled enough for the barge to be comfortable, so I went out there and had a bourbon while I waited for my greasy chicken sandwich and fries.

I had another drink with the meal and was trying to decide between having a third or coffee when I saw the hostess leading Sally Carruthers and her father to a table. Sally noticed me and came over to say hello.

I stood, and she gave me a quick hug. "Hi, Pete. How're you?"

"Fine. You?"

"Good. It's Dad's birthday, and naturally he wanted to come here instead of someplace fancy."

"Yep, that's your dad."

"Have you finished dinner?"

"Yes. I had the heartburn special: the chicken sandwich."

Sally laughed, a pleasant, musical sound I'd liked since I'd met her four years earlier when I defended a man she'd charged with drunk driving. She was a good commonwealth's attorney, firm but fair, and we'd been able to reach a plea bargain that punished my guy, a first-time offender, but kept him out of prison. She was the sort of prosecutor who didn't regard all defense counsel as the sleazy lawyers that some of us are.

I didn't exempt myself from that category.

"If you're done, why don't you sit with us for a while?"

"Thanks, but I don't want to intrude on your birthday dinner."

"Oh, come on, just for a minute. Dad would love to see you."

I doubted that. Sally seemed to like me a lot more than her father did. Whenever our paths had crossed, he'd been professional, even polite, but always distant as though he knew something bad about me that hadn't become public.

I reluctantly let Sally pull me over to the table where her father was sitting. He didn't smile at me, but he did rise to shake my hand.

"Counselor, how are you?"

He was always that way with lawyers in private practice. I guess he didn't want to create a perception that he was overly friendly with any of us.

"I'm fine, Chief. I hope you are."

"Another year older, something I don't want to celebrate but Sally does."

"Of course, I do, Dad. This one's a milestone."

I wondered what she meant by that, but I figured if she wanted me to know, she'd tell me.

Chief Carruthers seemed embarrassed by her remark, and he covered it by saying, "Here, let's all sit down." I was struck, as I had been before, by how much the chief sounded like my grandfather. The chief's Tidewater accent was milder but definitely there.

"I can only stay a minute," I said. I caught the waitress's eye and made the signing motion for her to bring me the check.

We took seats, and the waitress brought water and menus for Sally and her father and the check for me. When she asked them if they wanted anything else to drink, Sally declined, and her father ordered ice tea.

If Sally's father hadn't been there, I would have gotten that third drink, but I didn't want him to see me consume alcohol and then drive. I knew that because of their jobs—her dad was our chief of police—neither Sally nor her father ever drank alcohol in public.

"And please bring this young man some coffee," he said.

I was surprised at his gesture but didn't protest. I didn't want to offend him, and I never minded spending time with Sally.

"So, are you working on anything interesting these days?"

"No, sir, nothing in particular. Just the usual."

"The usual, huh? Mostly criminal defense?"

"Some, but more civil suits."

"Slip and fall?"

"Some."

"I see."

His tone wasn't mocking, but his cold, steel-blue eyes were, and I could tell what he thought of me: not much. I regretted that he felt that way—I respected him, and I wished I had his respect in turn. But maybe in addition to his distaste for my kind of law practice he was afraid I'd try to date his daughter.

Sally had been in a short and apparently unhappy marriage before discovering that her husband, a not-too-successful real-estate agent, was cheating on her. He was also gambling away more money than they could afford. I thought his taking Sally to Las Vegas for their honeymoon probably should have been a sign, but I never pointed that out to her. The couple didn't have children, so Sally had quietly divorced him and, as far as I knew, had essentially been married to her job since then.

I'd made a drunken pass at her a couple of years earlier at a cocktail party during the Virginia State Bar's Annual Meeting in Virginia Beach. That hadn't been long after the divorce, and she'd gently turned me down. But she'd also forgiven me, and we'd become friends, having lunch occasionally and swapping courtroom stories.

Once or twice I'd thought about asking her out, but I knew I wouldn't get her into bed quickly the way I was able to with a lot of other women, and I also knew she'd want a true relationship, not just someone to sleep with. So for once I'd done the sensible thing and not screwed up a friendship with a woman just to get in her pants.

I'd never told her that, of course. The net result was that whenever we met socially, which happened fairly often in our little town, she always seemed to be waiting for me to ask her out. In contrast, her father, who knew about my reputation with women, always seemed to be holding back from warning me to leave his daughter alone.

I didn't blame him. If I'd been in his shoes, I would have wanted to do the same thing.

The waitress brought my coffee and took their orders. Sally asked for a salad with grilled tuna—she had a good figure and was careful to keep it—and her father ordered the same dish I had. He was solidly built, but the weight was mostly muscle, not fat. I'd heard he had a wicked right hook and hoped I'd never had to find out for myself.

After the waitress left, I asked Sally how work was going and then whether she found any time to ride Rusty, the chestnut stallion she kept at a local stable. Having a horse was her one indulgence—she was a gifted equestrian and had been on the riding team as an undergraduate at the University of Virginia.

She didn't say much about her job, but her face lit up when she talked about Rusty. While drinking enough of the coffee to be polite, I enjoyed watching her as she described their most recent ride. Her dark hair and eyes made a vivid contrast with her light skin that showed how much time she spent in her office and how little in the sun.

Suddenly I was conscious of my boat tan and wondered if it made me look lazy. Well, I was rather lazy, so if anyone thought so, I guess I deserved it.

When she finished the story, I took a sip of coffee, debating whether to ask her the question. Then I decided to plunge ahead.

"Sally, you travel in better circles than I do. What do you know about Ben and Justine Kingman?"

CHAPTER EIGHT

Sally gave me a quizzical look. "Not much. Why do you ask?"

"Business. I may be doing some legal work that involves them."

"Good for you. Clients?"

"I can't say—yet."

"I see. Well . . . ." She looked around the restaurant, probably checking to make sure no one would overhear her, and then continued, keeping her voice low. "They're a wealthy couple, of course. He was already well off when he married her, and he's made a lot more since then. He's into real estate mostly but owns some businesses too, a couple of dry cleaners and some car washes."

"All above board?"

"As far as I know. Oh, there have been a few rumors about money-laundering, but I've never seen any evidence of that. Probably those rumors come from people jealous of his success. Kingman has sharp elbows, and I'm sure he wouldn't hesitate to cut a few corners if he thought he needed to, but he doesn't appear to be any more dishonest than your usual businessman."

"Nice comment on our local business community," the chief said, smiling a little.

"Dad, when you've seen what I've seen, you can't help being a bit cynical."

"I understand. You wouldn't believe how many of the people I've locked up in jail have claimed to be innocent."

"Oh, yes, I would." She smiled back at him. "I prosecuted a lot of those people."

I should have kept my big mouth shut, but doing that has never been my strong suit. "Maybe some of them were innocent."

Both Sally and her dad looked at me. After a moment he said, "Maybe one in a thousand, or ten thousand, and they get out as soon as the mistake is discovered."

I didn't want to argue with him, so I didn't point out that "as soon as the mistake is discovered" might be—had been, in some cases right here in Virginia—several years. I just had another sip of coffee and then asked, "What about Mrs. Kingman?"

Sally seemed relieved that I wasn't going to argue with her father. "She does what a lot of second—or third—wives of rich men do. Raise money for charities, volunteer to help with civic events, and play a lot of tennis, maybe some golf. I don't mean to be catty, but that's just how it is."

"Sounds like a life you might enjoy," I said, teasing her a little.

"Maybe, if I knew a man rich enough for me to have it."

"That lets me out, but I'll let you know if I run across someone suitable."

"Do that."

Our repartee, even as innocent as it was, clearly made her father uncomfortable. I saw him look at his wristwatch—he was as old school as they come—and then at me. I didn't need any more hint than that.

I thanked Chief Carruthers for the coffee and said I had to go. I stood and the chief did likewise, shaking my hand again and saying goodnight. Sally held out her hand, and I took it, being careful not to hold it as long as I would have liked to.

As I approached the exit, something made me look back, and I saw her watching me go. That made me feel good and bad at the same time—something I wanted, or thought I wanted, but couldn't have.

I drove to the boat and went aboard. I opened all the hatches and turned on a fan in the salon. I changed into running shorts and a T-shirt and fixed a drink. Then I sat in the cockpit while the boat—and I—cooled down.

I lit a cigarette, but it tasted like straw, and I stubbed it out after a couple of puffs. I had some of the whiskey, listening to the quiet sounds of the night—the breeze running through the rigging, insects making their various clicks and clacks, and off in the woods an owl asking me "who-who?"

I didn't know who—in fact, I didn't know much of anything. Just that I was dissatisfied with my life. With myself. Sure, I was a lawyer but not a very successful one. Not even, if I was brutally honest, an especially good one.

And where was I headed? Already thirty-four and getting nowhere fast. I was just a low-rent lawyer with scuzzy clients faking injuries to suck a few dollars from insurance companies. The kind of attorney who runs ads promising people to get "all the cash the law allows."

Not exactly what I'd dreamed of when I went to law school.

I envied Sally. She was one of the good guys, using the law to make society better. Her father was very proud of her, and I understood why he looked down at me. I didn't blame him.

I thought of how she'd watched me as I was leaving. Maybe I was wrong not to ask her out. After all, the worst thing she could do would be to say no, and I'd heard that word before. Lots of times.

But I hated the idea that maybe later, afterward, we wouldn't be friends anymore. I didn't have a lot of friends—I was too self-centered for that—and I didn't want to lose one of my best ones.

I finished the drink, tossed the remaining ice over the side, and went below. The interior had cooled some, and I put the mosquito screens in place. Then I crawled into the main berth and turned on the light. I picked up the Daniel Woodrell novel I was reading and tried to get back into the story, something usually easy to do with his stuff.

But this time it didn't work. I kept thinking of Sally's smile, how she'd looked when she'd come over to me at The Barge. I'd never thought of her like that before, and I wondered why I was doing it then.

After reading the same paragraph three times, I put down the book and snapped off the light. In the close darkness the night sounds seemed louder, and I could hear them over the low hum of the fan.

I closed my eyes and settled myself into the berth. Then, for no reason I could explain, even to myself, I thought of Justine. I thought of how she'd looked in that short tennis dress, a bit hesitant while wiping sweat off her face, and how she'd looked later in the linen dress, relaxed but sophisticated and in control of the situation.

I knew I shouldn't think of a client like that, but I couldn't help it. Justine was a beautiful, sexy woman, and she knew it and obviously used that fact to get what she wanted. And of course being rich helped. That helped a lot.

From my college course on the American novel, one of the few classes I'd bothered to attend, I remembered what Fitzgerald said about the very rich: "They are different from you and me." I wasn't sure the Kingmans qualified as very rich, but they were certainly wealthier than I was ever going to be. So that was very rich as far as I was concerned.

I wondered if Justine was seeing someone. Could be, and maybe that was the real reason she wanted a divorce. I couldn't see her wanting one just because Kingman played around—she must have known when she married him that he'd almost certainly do that. She was the second wife, after all, the trophy wife. So putting up with some infidelity was part of the bargain.

Getting slapped around was something else, of course. I was surprised she'd let him do it more than once. Justine seemed like the kind of woman gutsy enough to have a gun handy the next time he tried it, the kind who'd show the gun and tell the man she'd use it if he hit her again.

Or maybe not. As I waited for sleep to find me, I told myself that I barely knew her, so I really had no idea what she was or wasn't capable of.

No, I didn't know then. But I found out.

CHAPTER NINE

I didn't sleep well. I had a dream about chasing someone—a strange, hooded figure, a person I didn't know—down a long hallway but never catching up. In fact, as I became winded, it seemed that the figure slowed so that I wouldn't fall too far behind. I woke in a tangle of sheets damp with my sweat and sat up suddenly, banging my skull on the overhead, something I hadn't done since shortly after moving onto the boat.

I got up and splashed my face. Then I took the screen off the main hatch and went to sit in the cockpit. The world was still, quiet, and black except for a few lights on shore here and there and the starlight reflecting in the water that was as smooth and dark as oil.

I sat there for a couple of minutes, feeling flat and tired, until the mosquitos found me. Then I went below and crawled back into the stale berth. I fell asleep again, and if I had another dream, I didn't remember it when I got up in the morning.

I made some coffee and then shaved, showered, and dressed in the marina's head. I drove to the diner near my office and had my usual breakfast of ham and eggs. I'd tried flirting with the pretty waitress a couple of times but hadn't gotten anywhere—working girls, often shrewder than their upscale sisters, could be immune to my supposed charms—so I kept things polite but not personal.

I read *The Washington Post* as I ate, noting that yesterday's problems were also today's and nobody knew any more about how to solve them than on the day before. *You're getting cynical, pal*, I told myself as I paid the check and left a tip large enough to ensure that although the waitress might, and probably did, think of me as a skirt-chaser, she couldn't call me cheap.

I went to the office, and for once Kris was there ahead of me. Today's outfit was a blouse so sheer I could have counted the whorls in her lacy push-up bra and a short skirt so tight that it constrained her steps. I gave her a smile and said good morning. Then I got more coffee, and went to my desk.

I had plenty of work to do—mostly minor-accident cases that would settle for relatively small amounts, yielding me even smaller amounts as my contingency fees. But I was reluctant to get started, so I lit the first cigarette of the day (I was trying, without much success, to quit) and sipped my coffee while I thought about my new favorite subject—Justine

Kingman.

She'd said she would stop by with her prenup, but she hadn't said what time. I didn't want to take the chance of being out when she arrived, so I decided to call her. I told myself I was simply being thorough, as any good lawyer would be, but even I didn't believe that.

I checked the time—9:12. A little early, maybe, but not too early. I stubbed out my cigarette, found her mobile number on my legal pad, and dialed it on the desk phone. After three rings I thought I'd get voice mail, but then she answered.

"Hello."

"Hi, it's me, Pete Scarcelli."

"Oh, hi. How are you?"

"Fine, thanks. Listen, what time do you plan to come to the office today? You know, to drop off that prenuptial agreement? I want to be here so I can give you the checklist I mentioned." Kris could have taken the prenup and given her the checklist as easily as I could have, but Justine didn't need to know that.

"Yes, I remember. As it turns out, I have a pretty busy day, so I'm not sure I'll have time to stop by your office."

That annoyed me, but the next thing she said made my annoyance vanish.

"If you're free this evening, why don't you come to my house for dinner? That way we can go over both documents, and I can ask you some questions I've thought of."

When had she said Kingman would be back? Tomorrow, right? Yes, tomorrow. So a working dinner tonight sounded like a good idea.

"That will be fine. Thanks."

"Good. Wear something light, and we can eat outside."

"All right. What time should I be there?"

"Let's say seven. That will give me time to fix something and still be presentable."

I didn't say that it was hard to imagine her being unpresentable. What I said was, "See you then."

After we hung up, I sat there for a long moment, savoring the idea of having dinner with Justine. A business dinner, sure, but I thought it would still be quite pleasant. Invited to the Kingmans' for dinner . . . maybe I was moving up in the world.

Talking to Justine made me remember that I needed to call Jack Greese. I looked up his contact information and dialed his mobile. As I could have predicted, I got his voice mail. Jack, never a morning person anyway, did most of his process-serving and surveillance work in the late afternoon and at night, so he was difficult to get on the phone early in the day. I left a message asking him to call me back after lunch.

Then I forced myself to dig into the crap that littered my desk, but it was difficult to concentrate. I kept looking up from documents, staring into the middle distance, thinking of . . . you know. I told myself I was acting like a stupid teenager, but that didn't help much.

Even Kris, not the most observant person in the world, eventually noticed my distraction. "Everything okay, Pete?" she asked when, about mid-morning, she brought me a pleading to sign.

"Sure, great." I scrawled my almost illegible signature on the document. "Just got a lot on my mind."

"I understand." She stepped behind me and put her hands on my shoulders, kneading the muscles. "You work too hard."

That wasn't true, and both of us knew it, but I didn't contradict her. I let her continue massaging my shoulders for half a minute and said, "That feels good."

"Well, that's my job—to make you feel good . . . about work."

If I hadn't met Justine the day before, I would have said, "Just work?" But I had met her, so I said, "Thanks," and after a few more seconds she took her hands away.

"Anytime, Pete." She gave me a smile, picked up the pleading, and left my office.

Hmm, I thought. It seemed that Kris was after a raise. But when I remembered how much her predecessors' "raises" had cost me, I decided to go slow this time. Maybe Kris would get that raise, and maybe she wouldn't. We'd have to see.

I plugged away for another hour, and when I took a break I made sure to get a copy of the divorce checklist from Kris so that I wouldn't forget to do that later. I also got the standard client-engagement letter she'd prepared for the Kingman matter. I slid both documents into my scuffed leather briefcase—a rare present from my dad when I'd graduated from law school.

Thinking of my father made me realize I hadn't seen him or even talked to him in a while. I felt guilty and told myself I should check on the old man.

I picked up the phone again and dialed his landline—he didn't have a mobile. I usually got voice mail, but this time he answered, his voice rough from last night's whiskey and this morning's cigarettes.

"Yeah?"

"Hi, Dad, it's Pete."

"Oh, hi, Pete. What's up?"

"Nothing much. I thought I might come see you, bring you something to eat. How would that be?"

"You don't need to do that—I got plenty of food here."

"Sure, Dad. I just thought we might have lunch together."

"All right—if you want to. Come on out."

"I'll bring some barbeque."

"Fine. And some beans, baked beans. I like those."

"Okay. See you in about an hour."

CHAPTER TEN

As my father always did, he hung up without saying goodbye. He'd never liked to talk on the phone, and that characteristic had grown more pronounced as he'd gotten older. My mother's death—breast cancer—six years earlier had also contributed to it. By then the only people he willingly talked to were me—once in a while—and the old men he hung out at The American Legion hall.

I told Kris that I was taking a long lunch. Then I drove to the grocery store and bought cigarettes, beer, and some food for my dad. Next I went to the state liquor store and got him some bourbon. My last stop was Big Poppa's Pig Pit—"Best Q in the Rivah Realm"—where I got two pounds of chopped pork barbeque with coleslaw, rolls, and, of course, baked beans.

I took the road, another two-lane blacktop, toward my father's place, the mobile home he'd lived in since selling the house right after Mom died. He'd never actually said it, but I think he couldn't bear the constant reminders of her after she was gone. Also—and he'd certainly never said this—I think he didn't want to bring the middle-aged women he hooked up with occasionally back to the home his wife had made.

In the Northern Neck you never have to go far to be out in the country, so soon I was driving between fields of corn and soybeans, the houses widely spaced and set back from the road. Big red barns marked the prosperous farms, and dilapidated gray barns, many collapsing on themselves, marked the rest, with the two types about evenly split.

After a few miles I turned off the pavement onto a rutted gravel road. I bounced down that for a mile or so, raising a cloud of dust behind me, as the woods closed in on either side. I came to a rusted mailbox with "Scarcelli" hand-lettered on it and turned onto my father's driveway—if you can call bare dirt a driveway.

Those last fifty yards were more rutted than the gravel had been, and I slowed to avoid banging the bottom of the low-slung Miata on the ground. I parked next to my dad's battered old pickup and got out.

I was always struck by how quiet the country was and how still. The air was so fresh it could almost make you high. But not, I remembered without a trace of nostalgia, as high as the crappy weed I'd smoked in high school. The whole landscape seemed to be slumbering in the hot sun, waiting for something. What that might be I didn't know.

Dad's mobile home sat at the edge of the woods, so it got shade most of the day. At one end of the structure my dad, who'd worked as a carpenter after he'd retired as a Navy chief petty officer, had built a picnic table, and a couple of benches and some chairs. He liked to sit out there in the morning, drinking coffee and reading the local paper, and then again in the evening, watching the sun go down as he drank beer. The whiskey he saved for nighttime, when he watched TV—sometimes with the sound off—and usually fell asleep in front of it.

About a quarter-mile down a gentle slope lay a large pond, shinning like burnished steel in the bright sun. Sometimes my dad went fishing there, catching bass or bluegill and frying them with hushpuppies flavored with onion. My mother had been a good cook, so he'd never had to do much in the kitchen, but he could cook a few things and cooked them well when he bothered to cook at all.

He didn't do it much these days, eating mostly canned or frozen stuff or fast food. When he first moved to the trailer, I offered a few times to take him to a restaurant, but he never agreed to go. He said he didn't want to dress up and watch me pay too much for food that was nothing special. So I'd compromised by bringing him something special once in a while as I was doing that day.

I got the three sacks out of the car and walked toward the front door. He must have heard my car because he opened the door before I got there. He was wearing his usual worn khaki trousers and a T-shirt that had once been white but would never be again. He hadn't shaved in a couple of days, and his eyes were more bloodshot than usual.

"Hi, Pete. Thanks for coming out."

"Sure, Dad. Here—I brought you some groceries." I wasn't sure that the cigarettes, beer, and whiskey qualified as groceries, but that was the word I used.

"You didn't have to do that."

"I know. Just trying to help."

He grunted at that, took two of the bags from me, and went inside. I followed and put the bag with the barbeque on the kitchen table.

The kitchen was messy but not as bad as I'd feared. Apparently he'd make some effort to clean up after my call. The trash can was full, and a large grocery-store bag next to it was also full of trash. A couple of beer cans stood on the table next to an ash tray overflowing with butts, and the sections of the morning paper were scattered around. The place looked like what it was: the home of an elderly single man who didn't give a damn about much anymore.

He put away the things I'd brought him and then got out two plates—

my mother's second-best china—and knives and forks. He asked me what I wanted to drink, and I told him beer, knowing that was what he'd want to have.

As he got two beers from the old white refrigerator, I dug the barbeque and sides out of the Big Poppa's bag. He put a beer in front of me—Budweiser, the only brand he ever drank. I remembered the time I'd brought him some German beer, and he'd sniffed at it, saying he didn't need "designer shit brewed by Nazis." I hadn't bothered to argue with him, but I'd been careful to bring him only Bud ever since.

I opened my beer as he dished himself barbeque, coleslaw, and, of course, beans. He took a roll and then pushed the food toward me. He opened his beer and began eating while I served myself.

He'd never talked much while he was eating, so I didn't try to make conversation. He finished his first plate in a few minutes and got a little more barbeque and beans. When he finished that, he got two more beers from the fridge and handed one to me.

"That was good food, son. Thanks."

"Sure, Dad. Glad you enjoyed it. And you have some leftovers."

"Want to make sure I don't starve, huh?"

"You can't live on beer and whiskey."

"Yeah. Too bad!"

He laughed, and I was glad to hear it because he didn't laugh much anymore. I remembered when he'd laughed a lot. That was when he was much younger, before my sister died and my mom started her long battle with cancer. Afterward it was just the two of us, and he'd long since stopped asking me if I planned to get married and settle down, maybe give him some grandchildren.

He hadn't stopped making fun of me for becoming a lawyer—a "goddamn shark" as he put it—or implying that I wasn't a real man because I hadn't joined the military. But he did those things only when he was really drunk, not just buzzed from some midday beers.

I knew he'd yell at me if I cleared the table and washed the dishes, so I let everything sit. He drank some beer, lit a cigarette, and pushed the pack toward me. "Still smoking?"

"Yes, but I'm trying to quit." I didn't touch the pack. I wanted a cigarette, but for some reason I was reluctant to light one in front of him. Strange way for a man my age to feel.

"What for?"

"My health, I guess. Maybe you should do the same thing."

He snorted. "Hell, no. I don't want live forever."

Or even much longer, I thought. To cover the awkward moment, I drank some beer.

His way of covering it was to change the subject. "You busy these days? Got lots of clients?"

"Fairly busy. Plenty of clients, but they don't all pay."

"Fuck 'em if they won't. Stop working for them."

"It's not that easy sometimes. You always have to be careful about malpractice claims." I knew what I was talking about, having been the subject of two such claims in my career and also having the insurance rates to prove it.

"I never had to worry about that. Another reason I'm glad I'm not a lawyer."

"I don't think you'd like it much." Burning ambition had never been a problem for my father. My ambition wasn't exactly burning, but I did have some even though I didn't have a lot to show for it. Maybe my own problem was the gap between my ambition and what I'd accomplished—or hadn't. And was beginning to seem increasingly unlikely to.

"Do you?"

"What?"

"Like it—being a lawyer?"

His question surprised me, and I wasn't sure how to answer it. Did I like it? I certainly liked it better than driving a tractor or pouring concrete or, the worst, roofing houses—all things I'd done the summers between school years. All things I'd done in good weather and bad and mostly under a blazing sun that made the high humidity feel even worse.

Yes, I liked practicing law better than that. But did I really like it? Was it how I wanted to spend the productive years of my life?

No, probably not. I wanted to be rich, powerful—a wheeler-dealer like Kingman, making barrels of money by sitting around in the Lanchester Yacht and Country Club and talking to other high rollers.

The only trouble was I knew I never would be.

So I was where I was going to stay, where I was meant to stay. What was it the guy in that movie said? *The Hot Spot*, based on a novel by the American writer Charles Williams. Oh, yes: "I've found my level, and I'm living it."

Well, that was me.

I gave my dad a non-answer, saying sure, I liked the law just fine. Then I changed the subject, asking about his friends down at The American Legion hall. They were doing all right, he said, just getting old and useless like him. Then we talked about the weather for a while and finally got onto politics, with my dad cursing both parties and saying all politicians were crooks and ought to be locked up in jail. I didn't disagree, I just listened, and eventually there was nothing left to say.

That was the way all of our conversations ended, and I knew it was time to leave. I went to the bathroom first—he hadn't bothered to clean up in there, and it was as dirty and messy as usual—and then I stepped into his bedroom.

That room was surprisingly neat, as it always was, perhaps something left over from spending many years at sea and having to keep his berthing space tidy. The bed was made, and there were no clothes on the floor. The ashtray needed emptying, but that wasn't surprising.

I stopped, as I always did, to look at the framed pictures on the dresser. The largest was of my mother on their wedding day. She'd been a beautiful bride, slim, impossibly young, and with a smile that managed to be bright and shy at the same time.

I remembered that she'd put her wedding dress away for my sister, but of course Bella never got to wear it. I wondered where that dress was now ... missing, gone, vanished, like so many other things in my parents' lives.

Another picture showed Mom and Dad at the beach a few months after they'd started dating, when they were still in the first bloom of love. Before they knew what the future held.

I wondered if I'd ever love a woman as much as my father had loved my mother. I thought that, given the rocky nature of my relationships with women up to that point, I probably wouldn't.

The third picture was of my sister—my "little sister" as I always thought of her—on the day she graduated from high school. She, too, looked impossibly young, wearing an academic gown and tasseled cap, grinning into the camera, and bearing so much promise of good things to come. But she'd died of a drug overdose less than two years later after following my footsteps to Old Dominion University.

What a tragedy, I thought. I still blamed myself for not seeing the warning signs, not noticing that she was spiraling out of control. Maybe I couldn't have prevented what happened ... but then maybe I could have if I'd paid some attention to her instead of focusing only on myself and my own petty problems.

I opened the top drawer of the dresser, took some money out of my wallet, and added the bills to the thin stack hidden beneath my old baseball glove. Dad had been so proud when I pitched for my high school team—"Lucky Lefty," he called me, and he never missed a game except when he was at sea.

Even given his drinking, my dad must have known I brought him money from time to time. Although he had his Navy pension, he went through money like a lot of sailors and could always use a little extra. But neither of us mentioned it—and leaving him the cash the way I did meant we wouldn't have to.

It suddenly occurred to me that there were things each of us would never tell the other. For my dad it was some of what he'd seen in the Navy—he'd served in combat during the First Gulf War and at a few other times—and probably some of what he'd done then. For me it was some of what I'd seen and done in my professional and personal lives, lesser evils than his perhaps but evils just the same.

Of course I didn't know then of the evil that was to come.

I said goodbye to my dad—neither of us offering to hug or shake hands with the other—got in my car, and drove back to the office.

CHAPTER ELEVEN

I got there a little after two. Kris was at her desk, engrossed in what sounded like, from her end of it, a personal phone call. Probably with her boyfriend of the month. She went through guys pretty fast, and I would have had a hard time keeping score—if I'd bothered to keep score.

She gave me a little wave but kept talking. I went into my office and shut the door. The barbeque and beer had made me sleepy, and I looked longingly at the couch, but I needed to get some work done, so a nap would have to wait.

Kris had left a note on my desk that Jack Greese had returned my call. I picked up the handset and punched in his number.

"Jack Greese, Dominion Investigations."

"Jack, it's Pete Scarcelli."

"Pete! You old shyster. How are you?"

"Pretty good. You?"

"Never better. You still suing widows and orphans?"

"Just for fun. Not much money in it."

"Probably not. Say, we need to meet for a drink. I want to thank you for referring Sam Cunningham to me."

"You're welcome. Were you able to help him with that med-mal case?"

"I think so. He seemed pleased with the results."

I knew Jack wouldn't tell me any more than that, so I didn't ask him. Anyway, whatever he'd dug up on the doctor that Sam's client was suing was none of my business.

"A drink sounds fine, Jack, but right now I have a job for you."

"Sure, Pete. Let me grab a notepad. Okay, shoot."

"I want you to check on Ben Kingman."

There was a long pause. "Ben Kingman."

He said it as a statement, not a question, but I answered him anyway. "Yes. You've probably heard of him."

"Sure. I've even met him—once. At a business function, not in the line of duty." He paused again. "Kingman's a pretty big fish, Pete. Why do you need to check up on him?"

"For his wife. She's thinking of divorcing him, and she asked me to handle it."

"I thought you didn't do much divorce work."

"I don't. Look, do you want the job or don't you?"

"I'm not sure. Kingman. Damn, Pete, he could crush me like a bug."

"What do you mean?"

"A guy like that—money, power, connections. He could fix it so I never work again, at least not at this job. Maybe not at any job around here."

"You're not afraid of him, are you?"

"No, I wouldn't say that, but what's that old saw? 'Discretion is the biggest part of valor'? I just don't want to do something stupid."

That was the first time Jack had ever quoted—misquoted—Shakespeare to me. "Then don't. If you're careful, he won't even know you're digging around."

"Easy for you to say, Pete. You're not the one who'll be doing the digging."

"Okay, okay, I'll find somebody else."

"No, you don't need to do that. I'll take the job. But under the circumstances I'm going to charge you more."

"All right. Justine—Mrs. Kingman—can afford it."

There was another long pause. "Justine, is it? Pete, you sure you know what you're getting into?"

"I'm getting into handling her divorce, that's all."

"Uh huh. Better make sure that's all you handle, boy."

I didn't say anything. After a moment I heard him exhale, almost like a sigh, and say, "What do you want to know about him?"

"Mostly whether he's having an affair. Or affairs. Mrs. Kingman says he is, but I want proof. Also, whether he's hidden any money or other assets from her. I want to make sure she gets her fair share of the marital property."

"Uh huh."

I gave him a moment to jot that down, then added, "I'll get some information through discovery, of course, but I want you to look for the sort of things he won't disclose voluntarily. Things that might give me—her, I mean—an advantage. If he's cheated on his taxes, for example, or screwed someone in a business deal. Things like that."

"Pete, you're a big boy. You damn well know that to get as rich as he has, Kingman's had to cut some corners—probably a lot of them. But that sort of thing is hard to prove."

"I understand. But you're the best, Jack—you can find whatever there is to find."

"Sure, I'm the best. Not that there's much competition around here. But flattery won't get you anywhere—it won't even get you a break on my 'special rates' for this case."

I laughed. "Okay, but it was worth a try. I'll call you the middle of next week to see what you've found."

"That's not much time, Pete."

"It's enough to make a good start."

"Okay, I'll see what I can do. Bye."

After the call I lit a cigarette and thought about what Jack had said. It hadn't occurred to me to be afraid of Kingman, but maybe Jack was right. Kingman had all the things Jack had mentioned, and I doubted that he'd hesitate to use any of them against me if he thought he needed to.

Still, why should a simple divorce get messy? People went through them all the time. And if Kingman really loved Justine—a beautiful, sexy woman—why was he having affairs? And slapping her around? Given the way the prenup supposedly protected him, maybe he'd be glad to get rid of her.

Maybe.

Perhaps I'd learn more about their relationship when I had dinner with Justine. Thinking about seeing her again made it hard to concentrate on other things, but I had a couple of pending matters that wouldn't wait.

One of them was the DUI case I was scheduled to try the following week. My client was a multiple offender, and I didn't see any way I could keep him out of jail. Probably the best I could do was to get him a shorter sentence than Sally wanted the judge to give him, and I wasn't sure I could even do that.

I'd recommended a plea bargain, but my guy was against it. There were some evidentiary problems—chain-of-custody issues—and he wanted to roll the dice in front of the judge. But maybe he'd change his mind if he could be out in months instead of years. I decided to see whether Sally would deal.

CHAPTER TWELVE

I gave Sally a call, dialing from memory. Her assistant answered and asked me to wait. The hold music was the worst kind of super-saccharine stuff—in fact, I'd kidded Sally about it once—but I had no choice except to listen while I waited. Fortunately, she came on the line in less than a minute.

"Hi, Pete. How are you?"

"Fine. And how are you, Ms. Carruthers?"

"Uh-oh. If you're being formal, you must want something."

"I'm simply trying to give our commonwealth's attorney the respect she's due."

She laughed. "Sure you are. I know you, Pete Scarcelli, and I know you want something."

"Well, now that you mention it, we have that trial coming up next week."

"Yeah, and at the end of it your guy is going away for a long time."

"You sound pretty sure of yourself, given how that rookie cop screwed up the evidence." I knew she wouldn't like that criticism of someone on her father's team, but I had to do the best I could for my client.

"Yes, I am sure! This is your client's third offense, he hasn't shown any signs of rehabilitation or even being capable of it, and we need to take him off the street. You know that as well as I do."

I did, but of course I couldn't say so. "Okay, let's grant that he seems to have a problem with the bottle. But he also has a wife and kids whom he needs to support, and he can't do that from inside. Are you going to punish them too?"

"That's not fair, Pete. Your client is the one who'll punish them. And he should have thought about that before he got drunk and tried to drive home from that bar. He easily could have killed someone, himself included. Where would his family be then?"

"Look, I'm not saying he shouldn't do some jail time. The question is how long. You want to throw the book at him."

"Yes, I do. Drunk driving is a serious crime, and your client needs to know that."

"He does know it. He told me so. And he'll know it a lot more after a few months in jail. He's never had to go before, so he doesn't know what it's like."

"So now he gets a chance to find out."

"Okay, but again—how long? I may be able to get him off, and then he won't do any time at all."

"Or you may lose the case, and he goes away for years."

"You want to take that chance?"

"The question is: do you?"

"No, not really. But you've got to give me something to work with. If he's looking at more than a year, then the way he sees it, he's got no reason to plead."

She paused. "The best I can do is two years."

"That won't work, Sally. If that's your best offer, we're going to trial."

"Then what will work?"

"Six months."

She laughed again, but this time it was a harsh, sarcastic sound that I didn't like. "No dice. I always enjoy talking to you, Pete, but I don't see much point in continuing this conversation."

"Wait. I might be able to convince him to go for eight months."

"Try eighteen. And tell him that's a gift—Santa came early this year."

"Ten."

"No. Fourteen months is rock bottom, Pete. I can't go any lower than that."

"Ten, and I think we'll have a deal."

"No deal. Fourteen, or we're done."

"Let me think a minute. Okay, what about twelve months and some community service."

"For how long?"

"Six months."

"Twelve and twelve, and that really is my final offer."

"Twelve and twelve? He might go for that."

"He damn well should. Or he'll go inside for at least three years, probably four."

"I'll talk to him, see what he says."

"You do that. But I have to know by COB tomorrow. Otherwise, we're going to trial."

"I understand. I'll get back to you."

"Fine. Maybe we can make this one go away, save the taxpayers some money."

"I hope so."

"Then I'll expect your call. And, Pete?"

"Yes?"

"It was good to see you last night."

"Thanks. I'll bet your dad wouldn't say the same thing."

"Oh, he just worries about me. You know—since the divorce."

I thought it was more than that with me, but I didn't want to argue with her. "Sure, I understand. Say, what was that about a 'milestone birthday'?"

"Sixty. But he doesn't want anyone to know it."

"Why? Sixty's not old, not these days."

"I know, but he doesn't want people to think he's not up to the job."

"He'll be up to the job when he's ninety. Maybe a hundred."

She laughed again. "I don't think he wants to be chief quite that long. But I'll tell him what you said."

"No, please don't. I don't want your dad to know we were discussing him."

"Why not?"

"He might think it was disrespectful. On my part, I mean."

"Probably not, but, okay, I won't. He has a pretty good sense of humor, but he doesn't show it often."

She was right about that. I didn't think I'd ever seen him smile.

"Well, I know you're busy," I said. "I won't keep you."

"Good to talk to you, Pete." She paused. "Call me again sometime . . . when it isn't all about business."

"Okay." I said it without thinking and then mentally kicked myself. She might expect me to phone her socially, maybe ask her out. "That is, uh, when things aren't so hectic around here."

"Oh. All right then—when you have time."

"I will." I kicked myself again. Why had I said that? Just to be polite? My agreeing meant I probably would have to call her sometime and one thing would lead to another and I'd end up ruining our relationship after all.

After we hung up I sat there for a while, replaying the first part of the conversation. I didn't know whether my client would agree to the plea bargain, but he'd be a fool if he didn't. Judge Morgan had little sympathy for drunk drivers, especially repeat offenders, and he wouldn't hesitate to sentence the guy to three or four years—maybe the maximum of five.

Yes, there was a chance I could get an acquittal, but I wouldn't have bet the farm on it. In fact, I wouldn't have bet more than five dollars. So my client should take the deal, and I hoped he would even though that meant foregoing the considerable fee that trying the case would have earned me.

Then, although I didn't want to, I replayed the second part, the end of it. I thought I'd wait a few days and then maybe call Sally and invite her to lunch. Something casual with no hint of romance—just a friendly lunch between two people in the same profession. Shake hands at the end, imply that I wasn't interested in dating her.

She might be a little disappointed, but it couldn't be much more than that. I knew I was no prize, and Sally could have her pick of the available men around our town of Kilmihil. Not that there were very many, but I could think of one or two who could probably make her happy.

Later it occurred to me that maybe there was another way, that perhaps there could be something between us, something right and strong and good. But that was only later, when I'd already missed the opportunity.

When I'd already gone too far down a long, twisting road that led only to darkness.

CHAPTER THIRTEEN

I shuffled papers for the rest of the afternoon and got a little work done. Kris left at five, and I left half an hour later. I went to the marina, where I touched up my shave, showered, and changed clothes. I had a drink and a cigarette and then another drink.

I was nervous about going to Justine's but didn't know why. I was fully capable of getting through dinner with a woman, even a beautiful, rich woman, and she wasn't going to bite me. At least I didn't think so.

A little after six-thirty I climbed into the Miata and headed for the Kingman place. I drove slowly, partly because I didn't want to be early and partly because . . . I really didn't know why. Maybe it was just that strange nervousness.

I got there just after seven and rang the bell. I waited for a couple of minutes and was just about to ring again when Justine answered the door. She was wearing a sleeveless cotton dress, apple green, that looked cool and comfortable and, as on the day before, a few pieces of jewelry that were simple but elegant.

"Hi." She gave me smile and glanced down at my briefcase. "I see you've bought the tools of your trade."

"Just a couple of documents. Nothing that should take too long."

"Good. Let's have dinner and then we'll take care of business."

"Fine."

I followed her into the dining room, where she had set a place at one end of the long, oval table and another beside it. I wasn't surprised to see a vase of fresh flowers as the centerpiece.

"Since it's just us, I thought we'd fix our plates in the kitchen."

"Sure."

"The salmon needs to cook a few more minutes. If you'll open some wine, we'll have a glass while I finish everything."

"All right."

In the large, gleaming kitchen, which featured a big island with a granite top and copper pots hanging overhead, she opened the enormous stainless-steel refrigerator and handed me a bottle of expensive-looking chardonnay. I got lucky with the corkscrew and managed to open the bottle as though I knew what I was doing. I didn't tell her that screw tops were more my style. Then I realized that I didn't have to—undoubtedly she'd already guessed.

I poured each of us a glass of wine and handed one to her. She gently touched her delicate glass against mine and said, "Better days."

"Cheers." I tasted the wine. Even my uneducated palate could tell it was the best white wine I'd ever had. I'm not a big wine drinker, but I knew I could get used to that chardonnay and probably anything else in their wine cellar—and I was pretty sure they had one. If not an actual cellar, at least a room where they stored more bottles of wine as good as this one.

Pete, I told myself, *you've got a lot to learn about a lot of things. And this dinner is part of your education.*

She had some of the wine—a good bit, actually—and then busied herself at the stove and oven. Everything smelled wonderful, and I let myself enjoy inhaling the aromas, tasting the wine, and watching her work. Perhaps especially watching her work. She seemed completely in control of what she was doing and did it with a brisk efficiency that I—never very efficient myself—admired.

After about ten minutes she said everything was ready. I brought the plates in from the dining room, and we dished up the food in the kitchen. In addition to baked salmon she had saffron rice with almonds, grilled asparagus, and rolls. Each item was simple but elegant, and that seemed to be a theme with her. I made a mental note to try to keep things that way myself. I wasn't very elegant, but, boy, was I simple, so I could do that part all right.

At her request I refilled our wine glasses, and we took the plates and glasses into the dining room. I managed to bring the bottle of wine along, and naturally she had a cut-glass base to set the bottle in. She went back into the kitchen and returned with two small plates of mixed fruit for dessert.

I held her chair for her, and she seemed to like that, thanking me without making a show of it. I sat myself, and we softly clinked the glasses again. Then we ate. Not surprisingly, the food was as good as it looked, and I told her so.

We kept the conversation light, or rather she did, asking me questions about myself, my family, where I'd gone to school, things like that. I told her about my parents and sister and how my sister and mother had died. She said the right things without overdoing it. Then I told her about going to school locally—attending law school at William & Mary after majoring in political science at Old Dominion University.

"Political science? That's an interest of yours? Are you thinking of running for office someday?"

Actually, that had been my plan at one time, but my baggage, mostly with women, seemed to have accumulated to the point where it would be a significant problem. Still, that hadn't stopped Clinton or Trump, so maybe it need not stop me. But I didn't want to get into that with her, so I just gave her a noncommittal answer.

Her questions didn't amount to an inquisition, but looking back I can see that she was bent on getting a good idea of just who I was. I can also see that having such an idea would help her predict what I wanted in life and what I might do to get it.

She was smart, that one. Always very smart. I'm not dumb, but I wasn't in her league. Few people were.

"How did you like W&M?"

"Fine." I was proud of having gone there—it's a good law school and not easy to get into. In fact, I'd been surprised when I was admitted. But all I said was, "I enjoyed law school—not everyone does."

"That's true. Ben didn't."

I tried to remember which one he'd attended but couldn't. "Where did he go?"

"UVA."

Naturally. The University of Virginia's law school is the best in the state and one of the top ten in the country. That fitted with everything else about the man, so I wasn't surprised.

"What's that saying they have at W&M?"

"A saying?"

"Yes, about Thomas Jefferson."

"Oh, that he may have founded UVA, but he attended William & Mary."

She laughed. "Yes, that's it. Well, a little rivalry never hurt."

"No, I guess not. And where did you go to college?"

The question seemed to surprise her. "Uh, SCAD—the Savannah College of Art and Design."

"What was your major?"

"Nothing very useful, I'm afraid. I started in equestrian studies but switched to art."

"Oh, do you still ride?"

"Horses? Not lately. But I would like to ride again."

She gave me a look I couldn't decipher. As I thought about how to reply, she said, "Here, let's finish the wine," and split the remainder between our glasses.

We also finished dinner, including dessert, and then sat for a while, talking about nothing in particular. I asked her a couple of questions about herself, and she gave me short, general answers, so I didn't pursue that line.

There was a large original oil painting on one wall, a view of a broad expanse of water from an old wooden dock. I know little about art, but I liked the painting and thought it was well done.

"That's a fine picture. The Chesapeake Bay?"

"Thank you. Yes, that's the bay. Seen from a dock not far from here."

"Was it done by a local artist?"

"Yes."

There was a signature at the bottom right corner of the painting, but I couldn't read it from where I sat. "Someone I might know?"

"Someone you do know."

Justine didn't say who, so I wondered why she thought I knew the artist. There were several painters in and around Kilmihil, and although I knew one or two of them, I certainly didn't know them all. Then it hit me.

"You did that painting."

"Yes. It's one of the few I like well enough to display."

"I think it's quite good."

"Thanks again. I'm glad you like it too."

"What are you painting now?"

"Oh, nothing. I gave it up—at least for the time being."

"Why? You obviously have talent."

She smiled slightly, seeming pleased with the compliment but not flattered by it. "Not much, but you're kind to say so. This situation with Ben—well, I just don't feel like painting right now. That's all."

"Perhaps after the divorce."

"Yes," she said, drawing the word out and making it almost a question. She looked at me a moment before continuing. 'Yes, perhaps then."

CHAPTER FOURTEEN

She rose then and began collecting the plates and silverware. I offered to help, but she said, "Thanks, but I'll do this. Maybe you can fix us a couple of drinks and take them out on the patio."

"Bourbon?"

"Sure."

I did as she asked, walking through the big house to Kingman's study and over to the bar. The thought struck me that I was in Kingman's house, using his whiskey to make a drink for his wife, and the only reason I was there was that she didn't want to be Mrs. Kingman anymore.

Life is strange, I thought, not for the first time.

I fixed the drinks and carried them outside, where the air had cooled enough to be almost pleasant. The quarter-moon had risen, and it cast a long silver streak across the river, running gently in the windless night. The moon shone in the pool too, where the still water was a black mirror.

There was no sound except the muted hum of the hot-tub pump, and I had to listen closely to hear that. The cover had been on the tub the day before, but now it was off. The lights in the tub weren't on, but there was just enough illumination on the patio to see wisps of vapor rising from the warm water.

I brought one of the glasses to my nose and smelled the familiar scent of vanilla. I wanted to taste the drink but told myself to wait for her. I thought I'd behaved well so far and wanted to keep on doing that. For some reason I wanted Justine to like me even though, despite our being on a first-name basis, our relationship was really business, not friendship.

She came out in a few minutes. I stood and held the chair she took next to mine.

"Thanks," she said in a soft tone that matched the quiet night.

"You're welcome. Thank you for the wonderful dinner."

"Oh, that was just some things I threw together. But it's nice to have a reason to cook. Ben goes to a lot of business dinners—he says—and I don't cook much for just myself."

I handed her a glass of bourbon, and she took a sip. I did the same with mine.

She turned toward me, and I saw moonlight reflected in her eyes. "Do you like to cook?"

"No, I'm not very good at it. I do like to eat though—as you can probably tell."

"I'd say you're in good shape for a guy who works behind a desk. You must go to the gym."

"Some. Not enough to brag about."

"You're modest, aren't you? I mean, you really are."

"I don't know. If I am, it's because I'm like that guy Churchill described—the one he said had a lot to be modest about."

She laughed. "See, that's what I mean. You're smart, and obviously you've read a book or two, but you don't flaunt it. I like that in a man. Too many others are just the opposite."

I didn't know whether she was thinking of Kingman, and she didn't say. She had some more bourbon, and I kept pace. She looked at the sky for a long moment, then looked back at me. "It's a beautiful night, isn't it?"

"Yes, and very peaceful."

"Oh, Ben and I have had some arguments out here, let me tell you. All over the house, in fact. So bad that he sleeps on his boat once in a while."

That made me remember I was supposed to be there for a business dinner. But she didn't seem to want to talk business, and, frankly, neither did I.

"I'm sorry to hear that."

"It happens in marriage—or can happen, I should say. I suppose some marriages are happy. Ours was for a while." She sipped some more bourbon and looked at me. "I think you said you've never been married."

"That's right—I haven't."

"Why not? If you don't mind my asking."

"No special reason. Just never met the right woman, I guess."

"That can happen. But maybe you will someday."

"Maybe."

Then neither of us said anything for a while as we sat there with the big empty night all around us. She finished her drink and looked over at me. "I think I'll have another. What about you?"

"Sure."

She started to get up, but I said, "No, you fixed dinner. This is the least I can do." She didn't answer, and I went back to the bar.

When I came out, she was standing, looking at the pool. I handed a glass to her, and she said, "Thanks," before taking a long swallow of the whiskey. Then she put her glass on the table. "It's such a lovely night. I think I'll go for a swim. Want to join me?"

"Uh, I'm not exactly dressed for it."

"Neither am I. But you don't need a swimsuit here. It's dark, and we don't have any neighbors close by."

I was tempted—very tempted. But even at that point some small part of my brain was still capable of rational thought. "You go ahead. I'll be your lifeguard."

"Okay, suit yourself. Pun intended."

"Good one."

I sat and watched as she had another big drink and then, leaving her glass on the table, ambled down the patio steps and out to the pool. With her back to me, she slid her shoes off and unzipped her dress. It was dark, as she'd said, but my eyes had adjusted to the darkness, and I could see her there as the dress dropped from her, and she stood in bra and panties, the fabric black or maybe dark red.

Blood red, I thought, and then I wondered where that idea had come from. The air was still warm, but something like a shiver went through me. *You're just nervous*, I told myself. *She's a strong-willed woman, clearly in charge of the situation, and you don't know where this is leading.*

She shed the bra, stepped out of the panties, and dropped both on her discarded dress. She went to the side of the pool, struck a diver's pose, and leaped cleanly into the water.

The sound of the splash carried back to me, and after it died I heard smaller splashes as she stroked through the water. It was too dark to see her well, but the sounds she made implied she was a good swimmer. I'd done enough laps in the pool at the Y to know that sound.

I closed my eyes and sipped my drink, trying to enjoy the moment. I hadn't been in that particular situation before, and I thought I probably wouldn't be again.

After a few minutes the swimming sounds stopped. When I opened my eyes, I saw Justine climbing the ladder at the end of the pool closest to the patio. When she reached the top, she paused and slicked her hair back with one hand, then the other. As I'd imaged, she had a good figure—curved but without excess fat, her legs long and lean, her belly flat, and her breasts full but firm. I wondered whether the view was for my benefit or simply incidental. In either case she didn't seem to mind my seeing her nude.

I didn't mind either.

She stepped onto the pool deck and picked up her clothes. Carrying them in front of her—more practicality than modesty I thought—she walked over to me and dropped them in a chair. I was careful to look only at her face.

"That felt great, but now I'm a little cold. I'm going to soak in the tub.

You should join me for that at least."

"I, uh—"

She put her hands on her hips. "Oh, come on. You can't be that prudish—at least I've heard you're not."

What exactly had she heard? I could probably guess, and it didn't suggest I'd be adverse to soaking in a hot tub with a beautiful woman. And I wasn't even though in this case the woman was my client. I didn't know the disciplinary rules of the Virginia State Bar as well as I should have, but I was sure they didn't say anything about hot tubs.

"Okay."

"Good. You get in and I'll fetch us some towels."

I liked her use of "fetch." I've never seen any reason why the use of that word should essentially be restricted to dogs.

I stood and watched her pick up her clothes and go inside. Then I finished my whiskey and got undressed. I padded barefoot to the tub and eased down into it.

The water felt hot at first, but I adjusted to it, and then it felt pleasantly warm. I sank down in the water up to my shoulders and looked up at the stars. They were tiny white lights glued to the vault of the sky, and they seemed to be winking at me. Maybe they knew more than I did. No, certainly they did—I knew just enough to know I didn't know much.

Justine returned with the towels. She dropped them by the side of the tub and got in, sitting close but not touching me. She reached over and pushed a switch and water began jetting from the sides of the tub, forming bubbles that swirled all around us. The jets felt good, and I sank lower in the water.

"That should relax you."

"Oh, do you think I need relaxing?"

"Yes, you seem a little nervous—as though I might bite you."

I looked at her, remembering that I'd had the same thought. "Is there any chance of that?"

She gave me a little mocking smile, her lips slightly parted. "Maybe. We'll see."

Without thinking about it, I scooted closer and leaned over to kiss her. She seemed to be expecting that and put her arms around me. The kiss lasted a long time.

When it finally ended, we looked at each other without speaking. She was breathing faster, and her face was flushed. Maybe her color was just from the warmth of the water, but I didn't think so.

We kissed again, and this time I moved my hands slowly down her bare body. Her breasts felt as good as I'd imagined—even better. As I touched her here and there, her back arched and she shuddered. Then she reached down to touch me.

You can guess what happened next.

CHAPTER FIFTEEN

I'd never made love in a hot tub before, and I discovered that it's not the best place. As with many other things in life, the idea sounded better than the reality proved to be. But it wasn't bad. It's never bad.

Afterward we sat there, touching but not speaking, while the warm water flowed around us. Finally she said, "That was nice."

"'Nice' doesn't do it justice. It was much better than nice."

She snuggled closer to me. "I'm glad you think so. When the woman is older than the man, she always wonders."

"Wonders what?"

"How she compares to someone more his age."

"You don't need to wonder—you come out just fine."

"Good."

She was silent for a while. Then she said, "I suppose we do have to talk about business at some point."

That brought me back to reality and made me think of something I should have thought of before—but then I'd been too distracted to think about anything but Justine. By having sex with a client, I'd broken at least one of the bar rules and maybe more than one. Well, it was a little late to worry about that.

"Only if you want to."

"I don't *want* to, especially not after . . . but I guess I need to."

"Okay."

"When you give me that checklist you mentioned, I'll start doing the things on it."

"Good. What about the prenuptial agreement?"

"I dug that out and made a copy for you. It's on the sideboard in the dining room."

"That's good too. I'll need to review it before we start drafting a property-settlement agreement."

"Ben will probably be very difficult about that—dividing our property, I mean. He thinks of everything we have as his—even me."

"I know the type."

"But you're not that way."

I laughed. "I don't own enough to be possessive about it."

"Or anyone?"

"What do you mean?"

"You've never been so close to someone that you thought she was part of you? That you possessed her in some way?"

"No." I thought for a moment. "Well, just my sailboat. That's the only thing I own that I really love."

"I guess that's why sailors—the men anyway—always call their boats 'she'."

"Maybe. I haven't given it much thought."

"What's the name of your boat?"

"*Law Lass*. I know—kind of silly, isn't it?"

"No, I like it. I'd like to see her. I'll bet she's a pretty thing."

"She has good, clean lines and is well-rigged—at least I think so. Fast in a stiff breeze."

"Maybe you can take me sailing sometime."

"Sure. Kind of hot for it now, but when the weather cools."

"That would be lovely. Thanks, Pete."

She didn't say anything after that, and I wondered what she was thinking. I was thinking that it might feel good to make love to her again, but the first time had gone well, and I didn't want to seem greedy, like some horny teenager.

Plus I wasn't sure how deeply I wanted to be involved with her, at least not while I was handling her divorce. Making love once we could chalk up to chance, simply getting carried away—and *she* had suggested the soak in the hot tub. But if we started on a steady diet of it— that would be something else.

After a couple of minutes she broke the silence. "This is so nice, Pete. Not like with Ben."

I didn't know what to say to that, so I didn't say anything.

"It seems like he's always arguing with me or just telling me what to do. We never have a real conversation and certainly not like this, soaking in the tub or . . . ."

"After making love."

"No. I told you we don't do that anymore. That is, he and I don't. I know he has some women here and there."

"Yes, I have a PI working on that."

"A what?"

"PI—private investigator."

"Oh, anyone I know?"

I wondered why she asked that, but perhaps she was just curious. "A fellow named Jack Greese. I've used him before. He's effective and discreet."

"Greese . . . I don't think I've heard of him. But I'm glad he's discreet—I don't want anything about the divorce getting around."

"I hate to tell you this, but some things will get around. You and your husband are too prominent to avoid all gossip."

"What sort of things?"

"His girlfriends, for starters. And . . . ."

"What?"

"Well, if you have any 'outside interests', that will come out too."

"Outside interests. You mean lovers, don't you?"

"Yes."

"Including you?"

"Not if we keep this between ourselves. Which is what I plan to do."

"So do I. Of course."

I noticed she hadn't said whether she was seeing anyone else, but I decided to let it go for the moment.

"Other things may come out too. For instance, his physical abuse."

"But that might help me, no? Just like the fact that he sees other women."

"It might. But there's that prenup to deal with—we may not be able to get around that from a strictly legal standpoint. But he might bargain with us to keep some things quiet."

"I hope so. I was a fool to sign that agreement." She leaned back to look at me. "A fool in love, I guess."

"That happens. Don't worry—I'll do the best I can for you."

"I'm sure of that. Now let me do my best for you."

She kissed me then, and it was as good as the first time. It was so good we kept on doing it, and after a couple of minutes I forgot my earlier resolution—if that's what it had been. I swung her around until she was sitting on my lap, facing me, and I was inside her.

She did most of the work that time, and she was very good at it. So good I wondered how much practice she'd had, but then I decided I didn't care. I was no angel myself and couldn't expect her to be one.

When her rocking motion took her where she wanted to be, she clung to me and dug her fingers into my shoulders. Her breath coming fast and hard, she let out a series of low moans that grew longer and longer. Toward the end I joined her, paying the usual male price of being there for a much shorter time than she was.

Then it was done, and we sat there motionless in the warm water.

CHAPTER SIXTEEN

After what seemed like a long time she whispered into my ear, "That was wonderful. Thanks."

"Thank *you*."

"No, I mean it. Things were never like that with Ben. It's been a long time since . . . well, thank you for . . . for—"

"The ride?"

She pulled her face back a few inches to look at me. "Yes, the ride."

I thought of making a cowgirl joke but didn't. Instead I pulled her face to mine and kissed her.

After that she slid off my lap and sat very close to me. Neither of us spoke for a while. Then she said, "If would be so nice if we . . . ."

"If we what?"

"Could do this all the time."

"What do you mean?"

"If we . . . that is, if Ben weren't in the picture."

"He won't be after the divorce goes through."

"That's true in a way, but I won't be here. I mean, I won't have this house. He'll keep it just as he'll keep most everything else. Won't he?"

I started to reassure her, but then I thought that would be cruel—she'd have to learn the truth sometime. "Probably. It depends on the prenup, but, yes, probably."

"That doesn't seem fair."

"I know, but that's how the system works. Remember though: you'll still be a relatively wealthy woman."

"I'll have enough to live on but not like this. Not like what I'm used to."

There was nothing to say to that.

"Sometimes I think . . . well, Ben's not a young man. Plus he's overweight, drinks way too much, and doesn't exercise. The doctor has told him to take better care of himself, but Ben doesn't listen. He thinks he knows better than everyone about everything. So . . . ."

"So what?"

"So sometimes I think maybe he'll die of a heart attack."

"Maybe he will. We're all going to die someday."

She looked at me. "That's a cheery thought. And you picked a hell of a time and place to bring it up."

"Just being realistic. Your husband is going to die someday, but that's no reason for not going ahead with the divorce."

"It would be if I knew he was going to die soon."

"Does the doctor think that's likely?"

"No, apparently not. I insisted on going with Ben to his last annual physical, and I asked some direct questions. The doctor said that Ben should make a serious effort to get in better shape but that he's healthy enough for exercise."

"Sounds like he just needs to cut back on some things and start walking every day. What medications is he on?"

"Something for his blood pressure and something else for his prostate. That's it."

"Then I don't think his health should keep you from proceeding with the divorce."

"I told you he hits me sometimes."

That seemed an odd transition. "Yes, you did. There are legal remedies for that, you know."

"Yes, but I don't want people to know about it. If I file a complaint, I know the word will definitely get around, and I can't bear the thought of the other women at the club staring at me and whispering behind my back."

"It may come out during the divorce proceedings anyway."

"You mentioned that, but I hope it won't. Still, that's another reason why . . . ."

"Why what?"

"Well, I hate to say it, but I wish he'd die." She looked at me again. "You're not shocked by that, are you?"

"No. It's a little cold-blooded, but I'm not easily shocked."

"Good. I didn't think you were." She paused. "Things would be so much easier that way."

"Yes, but he's not likely to die anytime soon."

"Not unless . . . ."

"Unless?"

"Unless he has an accident."

I saw it then, why she'd wined and dined me, why she'd gone for that nude swim and then talked me into getting in the hot tub with her. Why she'd made love to me twice—not that I'd resisted even a little bit. Clearly she knew enough—or sensed enough—about me to predict how I'd act each step along the way.

Yes, I saw it then, and I didn't want any part of it. I pulled back and looked at her for a long moment, not saying a word. Then I climbed out of the tub.

She didn't say anything right away. Maybe she thought I was just getting another drink. But when she saw me start to put on my clothes, she said, "Wait! Where are you going?"

"Home."

"But why? Did I say something wrong?"

"You said he might have an accident."

"Yes, but what's wrong with that? He might have one—the way he drinks and stumbles around the house at night. Or out on that boat. He seems to think drunk driving doesn't apply to boats."

I pulled up my pants, shoved my socks in a pocket, and stepped into my shoes. "I don't know or care what he does or what he thinks. All I know is I'm not helping him to have any accidents. And you shouldn't either. The cops will catch you—they always do. Well, almost always."

She stepped out of the tub and came to me, naked and wet. I let her put her arms around my neck and press her bare chest against mine. I was angry with her, but it still felt good. Very good.

"Please don't go. I didn't mean that the way it sounded."

"How the hell did you mean it?"

"I just meant that if something happened to him . . . some random thing . . . well, that would solve a lot of problems. And then maybe . . . ."

"Maybe what?"

"Maybe you and I . . . ."

"Hell, you barely know me. And I barely know you."

She turned her face up to mine and said softly, "After we just made love—twice? I think we know each other pretty well."

She kissed me then, and again it was like the first time. It was always like that first time. That's one thing that never changed with her, never got stale, never ceased to be anything less than wonderful.

Somehow I managed to take her arms down and step back. I grabbed my shirt and put it on as she watched.

"Look, I think it would be better if someone else handled your divorce. I can refer you to another lawyer."

She put on a pout that would have made any teenage girl proud. "I don't want someone else. I want you."

"I don't think that's a good idea."

"But I do."

I sighed. It was getting late, and I didn't want to argue with her. "Let's sleep on it and talk about it in the morning."

"You can sleep here."

I shook my head. "No. Thanks, but no. I'll talk to you tomorrow."

I went inside, found the prenup in the dining room, and shoved it into my briefcase. Then I headed for the front door. She followed me, still beautifully naked as though to remind me of what I was leaving.

   Not that I needed a reminder. I knew. And it wasn't easy to leave her standing there, watching me go. But I did it.

   That was the only smart thing I ever did with her.

CHAPTER SEVENTEEN

I barely slept at all that night. I kept thinking about Justine, how she'd looked and what she'd said. And how we'd made love, of course. Maybe I thought about that first. Anyway, it was all mixed up in my head, which was fuzzy from the drinks. At least I thought it was from the drinks.

About six I finally gave it up and got out of my bunk. I drank a lot of water and then went for a run, about two miles, mentally cursing in the last half-mile at how the cigarettes had cut my wind. I resolved—once more—to stop cold turkey. I didn't think I was easily addicted to things, but I was finding cigarettes a hard habit to break.

Because I didn't have a couple of smokes before I got to the office, I was in a bad mood when I arrived. Reading through the prenup didn't improve my mood any—it said exactly what Justine had told me, and I didn't see any way to break it.

Kris sauntered in half an hour late, wearing a tight denim miniskirt and a sleeveless blouse she'd left half-unbuttoned. The blouse revealed the tattoo on her bicep—some Chinese characters that she'd told me were supposed to mean "happy life" but might have meant "rice noodles" for all Kris or even her tattoo artist knew. Her outfit was too casual—and too revealing—for the office, but I didn't say anything. After all, I'd implicitly encouraged her to wear stuff like that.

She dropped her big purse on her desk and made coffee. Then she brought me a cup, something she did when she wanted a favor. "Happy Friday, boss," she said cheerily, handing me coffee.

"What's so happy about it?"

"Oh, a grouchy bear this morning, huh? What was it she said?"

"Who said?"

"Your lady of the evening. I'm sure you were with someone."

"Why do you say that?"

"Because it's almost always true."

I started to make a sharp retort but then stopped. Kris was right, and there was no need to snap at her about it. Instead I drank some of the coffee. It was good—making coffee was probably what Kris did best around the office.

"Thanks for this."

"No problem. Say, do you mind if I take off early? Ricky wants to take me out on his boat."

Hearing his name made me remember that Ricky was this month's boyfriend. I'd met him once, a tall, skinny guy with a scruffy beard. I think he was an auto mechanic, and he probably made more money than I did.

"How early?"

"Uh, after you get back from lunch? Say, one-thirty?"

That was essentially half a day off, but I didn't feel like pointing that out. "Okay, as long as all of this month's bills are done by then."

"You got it."

She leaned over farther than she needed to and picked up the documents in the "out" tray. I didn't stare, but I couldn't avoid a glimpse of what her blouse barely concealed. I thought Ricky was probably going to have a good time on their boat ride—and Kris would too. Well, there was nothing wrong with that.

I put off calling Justine as long as I could, but as lunchtime approached, I knew I had to do it.

"Hello."

"Hi, this is Pete." I almost added "Scarcelli" but decided that would be stupid after what we'd done the evening before.

"Hi." Her tone warmed considerably. "I wondered if you'd call—the way you took off like a scalded cat last night."

I thought that was an exaggeration but didn't say so. "Thanks again for dinner. I had a good time."

"So did I. Dessert was the best part."

I knew she didn't mean the fruit. Yes, the "dessert" had been great, but her price for it was too high. "Look, the reason I called . . . I really think I need to refer you to someone else."

"Why?"

"Because a lawyer shouldn't get personally involved with a client, especially in a situation like this."

"What difference does it make?"

"It would be harder for me to be objective, to give you my best advice."

"Oh, I'm sure you'll do just fine. You have so far—in several ways."

"Uh, thanks. There's a guy in town, Trey Marston. He's a good lawyer and does more divorce work than I do."

"'Trey'?"

"Yes, he's one of those thirds—William Lee Marston III. His family has been here a long time."

"If he weren't a lawyer—a truck driver, say—he'd be 'Billy Lee'."

"Maybe. But he is a lawyer, graduated at the top of his class at Washington and Lee."

"Any relationship to *the* Lee?"

"Probably." *But that's a disadvantage now,* I thought. "I don't think Trey has ever represented your husband, so he should be able to represent you. Shall I give him a call?"

"No, not today. Let me think about it. I'm pissed that you want to hand me over to someone else."

"It's not that I want to—it's that I need to. And it would be better for you."

"Sure, that's what men always say when they've gotten what they want and are trying to get rid of you."

"Hey, that's not fair. I think that hot-tub thing was your idea."

"You didn't seem to need much convincing."

I didn't say anything for a moment. The conversation seemed to be headed downhill, and I didn't want to argue with her.

"Okay, I won't call him today. Over the weekend you think about what you want to do. We'll talk about it on Monday, but I really think you'd be better off with someone else."

"And do I get a say in this matter?" Her voice became cooler—not frosty but there was definitely a chill in the air.

"Sure. That's why we're talking now."

"Then you think about things too. Maybe over the weekend you'll change your mind."

"I doubt it."

"Well, let's wait and see."

There was no point in continuing the conversation, so I said goodbye and she did too.

After I hung up I had a dissatisfied feeling as though she'd gotten the better of me somehow. But that didn't matter—I was going to turn her over to Trey or someone else and be done with this case. I wasn't going to bill her for the time I'd put in to that point—dinner and "dessert" were payment enough. And I'd tell Jack Greese to report to her new attorney, whomever that turned out to be.

Then I'd be rid of the whole thing.

I picked up the phone again and called my drunk-driving client. I knew he wouldn't like Sally's twelve-and-twelve offer, and he didn't. For fifteen minutes I listened to him vent about how unfair the world was, how he got singled out for punishment that other guys—his drinking buddies, for example—managed to avoid.

I didn't tell him that he was an unrepentant alcoholic and probably always would be, that this was his third conviction and so of course he had to do some time, and that neither I nor anyone else wanted him behind the wheel ever again.

Finally I'd had enough, so I broke in and said, "Look, it's a good deal, the best you're going to get. Can I can tell Ms. Carruthers that you'll accept it?"

"You can tell that bitch to take the fucking deal and shove it up her tight little ass."

I started to count to ten. When I got to six, he said, "You there, Mr. Scarcelli?"

"Yes, I'm here. I'll hang up now, call the commonwealth's attorney, and tell her you want to go to trial. You can start getting ready to spend several years in prison."

That made him pause, but I didn't think he was counting to ten.

"You think it's the best I can do, huh?"

"I know it is, and you're lucky to get it. I have a good relationship with Ms. Carruthers, and I think that helped."

"A 'good relationship,' huh? Does that mean you're getting—"

"You insult her again, and you're on your own. I've fired clients before, and I'm about ready to do it now."

"No, Mr. Scarcelli, don't do that! I'm just mad, you know, about having to do time."

You're mad about getting caught, I said to myself. "Sure, sure. But you'll take the plea bargain?"

I heard him take a deep breath. Then he said, "Yes. I'll take it."

"Good. I'll let the commonwealth's attorney know. I'll call you when they set a date for the sentencing."

CHAPTER EIGHTEEN

After I hung up, I had a powerful desire to wash my hands. I went to the restroom and did that and then told Kris I was going to lunch.

I walked toward the town square, the heat making me take off my sport coat and loosen my tie. By the time I had covered the three blocks, I was sweating and had to wipe my face with my handkerchief.

Welcome to August in the Northern Neck, I thought. It was a slow time for most people but often a busy time for me because of the crazy—no, stupid—things the heat made people do. I'd once had a client who'd carved up his wife and child with a hunting knife. I'd tried to get him off on the grounds of temporary insanity, but the jury hadn't bought it. Not after he'd buried the bodies in his vegetable garden.

The guy was still in prison and would probably die there, either from natural causes or when another prisoner, probably a lifer with nothing to lose, shanked him. And even though I'd been his defense counsel, I knew he was right where he belonged—in a cage with the other wild animals.

Still carrying my coat, I went into the Captain's Café, a small breakfast-and-lunch restaurant on the town square that businesspeople liked. A retired merchant-ship captain and his wife had opened the place in the '50s, and the walls were covered with maritime memorabilia—photos of sailors, nautical charts, ship's chronometers, things like that. The captain and his wife were long since dead, and now the owners were two gay guys from NoVa—Northern Virginia—who'd come down for the supposedly more relaxed lifestyle.

The seat-yourself place was crowded as it normally was at lunchtime. A couple of four-tops were available, but I didn't want to take one just for myself. I hung my coat on the rack near the door and headed for an empty stool at the counter.

I sat and said hello to Marge, who'd been working there as long as I could remember. I ordered without looking at the menu and picked up a copy of *The Kilmihil Chronicle* that someone had left. The paper, circulated throughout two adjoining counties, was short and consisted mostly of advertisements, which is how the publisher could afford to put out a daily edition, but there was always some local news in it too.

I was still reading the front page when a familiar deep voice behind me said, "Mind if I sit here next to you?"

I turned to look at him. "No, Chief, not at all."

"Thanks." He slid onto the stool to my left and adjusted his holstered pistol to be more comfortable.

Marge came back, and the chief also ordered without looking at the menu. She brought both of us ice teas—his sweet, mine unsweet.

I tilted mine and took a long drink, almost draining the glass. The chief had some of his but drank it more slowly.

He lowered his glass and glanced at me. "Hot out there today."

"Yes, sir, it is." I wiped my face with my napkin. Between the air-conditioning and the ice tea, I was beginning to cool down, but I was still sweating some.

"You walk over from your office?"

"Yes, sir, I need the exercise."

"Don't we all? I spend too much time on my butt behind a desk or in a cruiser. Never thought I'd miss the running I did in the Marine Corps, but sometimes I do."

"Yes, sir."

He turned to look at me. "You don't have to 'sir' me, Pete. And you don't have to be afraid of me—I've got nothing against you."

Not as long as I stayed away from his daughter. "Yes . . . Chief. I understand."

"Good."

Marge brought our plates and we dug in. Like most men, we didn't say much as we ate. We talked a little about the weather—hot and humid, no surprise there—and baseball—both of us being Nationals fans. That was about it.

But when we had finished the food and were drinking our third glasses of ice tea, the chief said something that surprised me. "Have you talked to Sally lately?"

"Uh, yes. We discussed a case she's prosecuting—one of mine."

"What's the charge?"

"DUI."

He frowned. "We've got to get the drunks off the road, Pete. You know that."

"Yes, I do. But even drunks deserve a defense."

"I guess so. But they wouldn't do what they do if they'd ever pulled a dead child, mangled and bloody, from a car the way I have."

I knew that many alcoholics, even if they had seen such an awful thing, would drink anyway. But I didn't want to argue with the chief, so I said nothing.

Then he said something else that surprised me. "Sally likes you, Pete.

She's told me so."

I treaded cautiously. "That was nice of her."

"She thinks there's a lot of good in you." He gave me a skeptical look. "I guess I'll have to trust her judgment on that."

I decided to pass it off as a joke and chuckled.

"She even said she thought you'd make a good commonwealth's attorney. Have you ever thought about switching sides?"

I had but didn't say so. Something had kept me from applying, some vague feeling that I wasn't quite good enough to be one of . . . them. One of the good guys, wearing the white hat. Maybe it was a sense that I was just a born ambulance-chaser.

I didn't like that feeling.

"No, Chief, I guess not. I've been too busy with my practice to think about making a change. Plus I think I'm fine where I am."

"Do you, Pete? Really?"

Instead of answering I picked up the menu. "How 'bout some pie? It's good here, especially the apple. Have a slice on me."

"Now, Pete, you know I can't accept a gift from you—even a piece of pie. But thanks for the offer."

He left money on the counter, got up, and adjusted his gun belt. "Good talking to you, Pete. You think about what I said—about Sally's suggestion."

"I will. Thanks, Chief."

He nodded and left. Marge came over with two checks, handed one to me, and scooped up the chief's bills with the other. I could see that he'd tipped her generously, and I made sure to do the same.

"Thanks, Pete. Say, I didn't know you were friends with the chief."

"I didn't either." I took a last drink of tea and headed for the door.

CHAPTER NINETEEN

The next morning, Saturday morning, I decided to go sailing. August isn't a great month for Chesapeake Bay sailing—too hot and humid with too little wind. But that particular day happened to be good for it: bright and clear with some cooler Canadian air and enough breeze to move the boat.

I'd been dating two or three women off and on, very casually, and I considered calling one of them for company but then decided I'd rather single-hand. I thought I'd enjoy having some time to myself on the water.

After a breakfast of coffee and, for once, no cigarettes, I got cleaned up and went out for beer, ice, and a couple of sandwiches. When I got back, I stowed that stuff in the galley, opened the intake valve for water to cool the engine, and disconnected the shore-power cable. Then I took the canvas covers off the helm, winches, and mainsail, hauled in the fenders, and started the engine.

After letting the engine warm up for a few minutes, I cast off the dock lines and headed for the bay. As soon as I cleared the marina I felt more relaxed, as though I'd left my worries behind. I didn't have to think about work or money or anything else except sailing *Law Lass*. And sailing her was always a pleasure, not a chore.

I had a great morning on the water, getting offshore and sailing until noon. I loved the way the boat cut through the water on a perfect heel, her rigging humming in the wind. I loved the way she tacked smoothly, coming about with no fuss and settling into her new course. I loved everything about it, just as I had when I was a child, sailing with my grandfather.

Suddenly I realized that Sally's dad looked a bit like my grandfather. He was now just a little younger than my grandfather had been then, and he had the same manner—direct, even gruff, without being mean. A man to respect but not one to fear.

Unless you'd done something wrong.

When the sun crossed under the spreader, backlighting the shrouds it held away from the mast, I opened a beer and headed for one of my favorite gunkholes. It was a small cove so shallow that most people with keel boats wouldn't enter it, but I knew from experience that from halfway before to halfway after high tide there was enough water for me to ease in and out.

High tide would be about two p.m., so I could stay in the gunkhole for several hours if I wanted. I dropped the sails as I neared the cove and slowly motored in. I cut the engine, dropped the small anchor—the "lunch hook"—and came to rest in the middle of the cove.

After my ears got used to the absence of the engine noise, I could hear the sound of the world. The breeze blowing through the trees, the water lapping on the shore, and finally, after they got used to my being there, the birds calling to each other. I could smell the salty tang of the water and the fresh green scent of the land.

I could also smell the slightly sulfurous odor of the vegetation decaying along the shoreline. It was a natural smell and not unpleasant, but it was a constant reminder that death is part of life.

Well, that was true, but I was alive then, as fully alive as I ever was, and I was going to enjoy the afternoon. I rigged the bimini cover to shade the cockpit. Then I opened another beer and ate one of the sandwiches while sitting in the shade and looking out at the bay. The water was brown near the shoreline but soon brightened to light blue as it deepened and then to royal blue toward the middle of the bay.

It was a beautiful sight, one I'd enjoyed all my life.

The beer and food made me sleepy, and I took a nap, resting my head on a couple of the cockpit cushions. I slept for a little over an hour and woke feeling sluggish.

I got a towel from the head. Then I undressed, climbed down the swim ladder, and lazily paddled around the boat a few times, dunking my head under water before coming back aboard. Drying off in the cockpit, I noticed that the sluggish feeling was gone and I felt alert again.

Too alert, I guess, because I started thinking about Justine. About how she'd looked coming out of her pool. How she'd looked coming toward me. And how she'd looked later in the hot tub.

Thinking about her that way started to give me an erection despite the fact that I'd just come out of the cool water, and I hated the idea that she had that power over me. I hated it, but I didn't think she'd have it for long. I tended to get over a woman quickly, especially once I'd had her.

And I'd certainly had Justine. But as those thoughts swirled through my head, I realized she'd had me too. Otherwise she wouldn't have been on my mind.

Still, I knew that the best antidote for one woman was another, and I had a date that night with a woman I'd gone out with a couple of times before but hadn't yet slept with. Tonight might be the night.

I shook my head to clear Justine out of it and got dressed. Then I started the engine, hauled in the lunch hook, and headed out of the cove.

Once back on the open bay I raised the sails again and steered toward the marina. I sailed for another hour, but the wind wasn't right for sailing all the way back by the time I needed to be there, so eventually I started the engine again and motored for home.

I got back to my slip about five. I fixed a drink and sipped at it while I put the canvas covers back on the mainsail, winches, and helm, flemished all the lines, and reconnected shore power. Then I got some clothes—my casual uniform of khakis, a golf shirt, and loafers—and went to the marina's head to shower and dress.

I still had some time before I needed to leave to pick up my date, so I had another drink while I watched the sun roll down the sky toward the western horizon. It was my favorite time of day: late afternoon, when the world had finished its work and was taking a restful pause before embarking on the evening's pleasures.

Sometimes the pleasures were wicked—they often were with me, I guess. But sleep was an innocent pleasure even if it sometimes brought bad dreams. There were good dreams too, and I figured I was about due for one.

I picked up my date at seven and took her to dinner at the best restaurant in town, Rick's Oyster Reef. The tagline was "Everybody Comes to Rick's," an obvious rip-off from *Casablanca*, but the food was good and the place wasn't too touristy. I'd defended the owner in a slip-and-fall case and gotten him a good result—opposing counsel was even sleazier than I was—so the staff there took good care of me.

Knowing my preference, the hostess gave us a quiet table and we had an excellent dinner with some surprisingly good local wine my date wanted to try. An elementary school teacher, she was in her usual chatty mood and told me what was going on with her students, fellow teachers, and the administrators. Then she got onto her younger sister, how she was a college dropout who was into drugs and bad boys, and how Ellen—that was my date's name—didn't know what to do about it.

I just listened, throwing in a "really?" or "uh huh" once in a while to show that I was following her narrative and also being careful to maintain eye contact. That's a simple technique to make the other person think you're a brilliant conversationalist even when you're not.

Each of us is our favorite subject, and I'm not hypocritical enough to say I'm any different.

After dinner we ordered coffee, and I talked Ellen into sharing a dessert with me. I thought she wanted dessert but was reluctant to order it for herself, at least in front of me. So I went through the dessert menu, calling off each dish until I found the one she seemed to want, and I ordered that. I had a couple of bites, but she ate most of it.

We finished our coffee, and I paid the check. She'd offered to split the cost of our first dinner, but I'd told her I was old-fashioned about such things, and now she seemed content to let me pay. I didn't mind—I was a traditionalist about that aspect of the relationship between a man and a woman. Plus I knew that as a teacher she didn't make a lot.

We walked out into the night, and that Canadian air was still with us, so it was almost cool. I suggested a drink at O'Donnell's, the Irish pub down the street, and she agreed.

The place was crowded, as it always was on Saturday night, but I snagged a vacant stool at the bar and stood next to Ellen. She said she'd have a glass of wine, so I ordered that for her and a double bourbon for myself.

A band was playing on the tiny stage—Irish songs about women and love and drinking—and the music plus the usual noise of a bar made it hard to talk, so we didn't do much of that. Ellen smiled at me and pressed her knee into my thigh. I smiled back and put my hand on her shoulder.

Yes, the date was shaping up very nicely.

We finished our drinks and left the bar. As I drove her home, she got back on the little sister again, how she was really worried about her and afraid something really bad might happen, like having a drug overdose or getting beat up, maybe even killed, by one of the losers she was seeing.

I said sympathetic things but didn't tell her about my own sister. For some reason I didn't want to share that with her—I'd never shared it with anyone except Sally.

I'd told Sally that I felt guilty about not having done something to prevent Bella's death or at least try to prevent it.

"You think you're responsible for her dying?" Sally had asked me.

"In a way."

"But you're not. We're all responsible for our actions but not those of others. Bella was an adult, and she had the right to make her own decisions."

"Even if one of them killed her?" I'd heard the bitterness in my voice.

Sally must have heard it too. She'd put her hand and mine and said softly, "Yes, even then."

It took a long time, but eventually I realized that Sally had been right: one person can't save another from self-destruction. You can offer support, sure, but ultimately we all make our own decisions and have to live with the consequences, whatever they may be.

I considered telling Ellen that, but I didn't know her all that well—not nearly as well as Sally knew me. So I didn't think she'd appreciate my giving her advice about something so personal.

When we got to Ellen's house, I thought she'd invite me in, and I also thought one thing would lead to another and she'd be making breakfast for me the next morning. But she didn't invite me in. She said her sister was staying with her for a few days, trying to "get herself together," so she needed to focus on Gloria—that was the sister's name—for the time being.

I was gracious about it—at least I think I was. Ellen tried to make up for it by kissing me goodnight for several minutes, but that actually made things worse, at least for me.

Realizing that the longer I lingered, the more frustrated I'd be, I finally said, "I guess I better go."

"Okay. Thanks for understanding about Gloria."

"Sure."

"And thanks for a lovely evening."

"You too."

I think Ellen may have hoped I'd say something about taking her out again or at least calling her, but I didn't. I wasn't trying to be rude, I just didn't know whether I wanted another date with her.

Driving back to the boat I felt something like relief that I wasn't still with her. At first I couldn't figure out why, but then it hit me: she wasn't Justine. She wasn't the one I really wanted.

Scenes from the dinner at Justine's and what happened afterward began flashing through my head. That movie kept running as I pulled into the marina and parked near my slip. It didn't shut off until the cool night air hit me as I walked along the pier and boarded my boat. But I knew it would be a long, dark time before sunrise and I wouldn't get much sleep.

It was, and I didn't.

CHAPTER TWENTY

I slept late the next morning and woke up so grumpy I was almost angry. I told myself it was because I hadn't been able to spend the night with Ellen, but even I didn't believe that. I was still thinking about Justine.

I decided to do something to take my mind off her. The boat needed some work—boats always need work—so after a breakfast of coffee and a granola bar I got to it.

I broke out the bucket and hose, a couple of scrub brushes, and detergent and washed the outside of the boat from the top of the cabin to the waterline. When I'd finished, I put that gear away and cleaned the inside, putting things where they belonged, wiping down the galley, and rubbing all the woodwork with teak oil. That all took about two hours, but at the end of it *Law Lass* gleamed.

I checked the time and saw that I could still make it to Saint Stephen's if I wanted to go. My parents—my mother anyway—had raised me as a Baptist, but as an adult I'd drifted away to the Episcopal Church. That was partly because the Episcopalians didn't talk much about hellfire and brimstone and partly because they didn't frown on drinking the way some Baptists did even though I'd run into Baptists at the liquor store more than once.

Part of me did want to go to church that morning, but a bigger part thought that because I hadn't been in so long, the building might fall in on me. More seriously, I thought that it had been so long since I talked to God, He might not talk to me. That was foolish, I knew, but it was how I felt.

So I compromised by saying a simple prayer of thanks for the beauty of the natural world, the world I could see all around me, and got out my toolkit. I spent another hour replacing a couple of worn fittings for the running rigging and then tightening and adjusting a few things that needed it.

By then it was almost noon, and I was hot and sweaty and getting hungry. I showered and shaved, got dressed, and drove to The Barge for lunch, buying a copy of *The Washington Post* along the way. I don't know whether I was hoping to run into Sally, but I didn't see her, so it was a moot point.

I didn't run into Justine either, but she was on my mind. I was thinking about what I'd tell her in the morning—that she needed to call Trey

Marston or someone else to handle her divorce and leave me out of it. Maybe when she was single we could see each other.

Then I told myself that idea was another foolish thought. A woman with her wealth and connections—and older to boot—wouldn't want to get emotionally involved with me. The sex had been merely that—recreational sex or, to use the vulgar term, "sport fucking." She'd probably done it because she was frustrated that Kingman hadn't touched her in a while except to slap her around. I'd just been a man on the scene with a hard dick, and that was all she really wanted.

I ate inside, in the cool of the air-conditioning, and lingered over lunch, watching the other patrons come and go. I knew a few of them and exchanged hellos. One man, an insurance salesman, oozed over to me and wanted to chat, but the waitress saved me by swooping in after a couple of minutes and directing him to his own table. She gave me a wink, and I nodded, thinking that my history there of tipping well was paying dividends.

After I'd finished eating and the waitress had taken the plates away, I took another twenty minutes to read the newspaper front to back while I drank two more glasses of ice tea. The news was much the same as it always is: war, terrorism, poverty, foolish government policies, starlets ostensibly regretting the sex videos that had made them famous only for being famous, and sports.

The sports page was the only part of the paper that didn't routinely make you disgusted with human nature.

By the time I'd gone through the paper, it was almost two o'clock and the sky was beginning to cloud over. The weather was still hot but had turned sultry, and I thought it would probably rain later in the afternoon.

I didn't feel like going back to the boat, so I went to a movie. We were lucky we had an art house in our little town, a place that showed classic and foreign films in a small theater made over for that purpose. The afternoon's feature was *Murder, My Sweet*, with Dick Powell as Marlowe and Claire Trevor as Helen Grayle. It's a great Hollywood noir, and although I'd seen it several times, I decided to see it again.

The movie held up as well as I'd remembered, Marlowe cracking wise as he did his detecting, Helen femme-fataling all over the place, and the rest of the cast playing their roles effectively. There were only eight or ten other people in the theater, and I made sure to tell the manager when I left how much I'd enjoyed the picture and how much I appreciated the theater's showing it.

By the time I came out, experiencing that always-odd transition from a dark movie house to the light of day, the sky was completely cloudy, even dark in the west, and I felt the first few drops of rain.

It was too early for dinner, so I went back to O'Donnell's and had a drink while I read a novel on my phone. The drink was good and so was the novel, so I had another drink and kept reading. When I'd finished the second drink and three chapters of the novel, I was ready for dinner.

I thought about having pub grub where I was, but then I decided to have a decent dinner before the work week began, so I went back to the Reef. (I guess you can tell I'm a creature of habit. Some of them bad.)

The same hostess welcomed me back and gave me a fairly good table, not sticking me by the kitchen door as they often do when you dine alone. I got a drink and looked over the menu, wanting to order something different from what I'd had the night before. I chose the grilled trout almondine with rice and vegetables and asked for a cup of crab bisque to start.

Not having brought anything to read, I was people-watching while I ate the soup, and that's why I saw them come in. Kingman and Justine. Both of them were dressed casually but tastefully in well-tailored, expensive-looking clothes. Several heads turned to watch as the hostess led them to a reserved table, one of the best in the house.

They stopped at a couple of tables along the way to greet people they knew. Kingman didn't look in my direction. Justine did but gave no sign of knowing me or even seeing me. That made me angry for some reason although I could understand why she did it.

The waiter brought my main course and took away the soup. I got another drink and sipped it as I ate the trout, which was very good, cooked enough to be done but not so much as to be dry.

While I had my dinner I glanced at the Kingmans from time to time. They didn't say much to each other. He had several drinks of brown liquor, and she sipped white wine. I couldn't tell exactly what they ordered, but it appeared as though he got steak and she got some sort of seafood.

I finished before they did and thought about leaving, but something made me stay. Perhaps I just wanted to observe them some more. I skipped dessert but got coffee and drank it slowly, still glancing at them occasionally and seeing that they still weren't saying much.

Well, maybe they'd been married long enough that they'd largely run out of things to say. I'd heard that could happen. One more reason I wasn't married, I guess.

I finished my coffee and paid the check as their dessert arrived. His was some sort of pie, and hers was a small dish of fruit.

I told myself I was wasting time and mental energy cataloging what these people were eating and drinking. What difference did it make to me? Then I realized that for some reason I simply wanted to know more about Justine. I also realized that to know her better, I had to know more about her husband.

But it was all academic, merely a matter of curiosity. I was pretty sure that in the morning I was going to turn Justine and her case over to another lawyer. *Or,* I thought, *at least her case.*

That last part bothered me, but I couldn't help thinking it.

I started to leave by a route through the tables that wouldn't take me close to theirs, but two waiters blocked it by bringing out a large tray of dishes for a party of eight and a folding table to support the tray. I didn't want to stand there foolishly while the waiters distributed the food, so I took the other route, the one that required me to walk past the Kingman's table.

At first Kingman didn't seem to notice me, and I thought I might be able to slip out of the restaurant without having to speak to him. But he looked up as I neared their table and gave me a wolfish smile.

"Well, well . . . Scarcelli, isn't it?"

I had to stop. To keep going would have been rude, not to mention strange.

So I stopped. Looked at him. Forced myself to smile back. "Yes, Mr. Kingman, how are you?"

"Fine. And I hope you are. Ambulance-chasing must pay pretty well if you can afford to eat here."

It was hard, but I kept the smile on my face. "I'm doing all right." I glanced at Justine then, and she was looking at me with no hint of recognition.

Kingman saw her looking, and that prompted him to remember his manners. "Justine, this is Pete Scarcelli, a local lawyer. Mr. Scarcelli, my wife Justine."

"How do you do, Mrs. Kingman?"

"I'm fine, Mr. Scarcelli. I think we've met before."

That sent a chill through me, and I wondered what she was up to. Was she going to give everything away by playing games in front of her husband? He was many things but a fool was not one of them. Justine had said she could sense when Kingman was having an affair. Maybe Kingman could do the same thing with her.

But Justine didn't add anything, and that gave me a chance to say, 'Oh, yes, I think it was last Christmas at Mr. Kingman's open house."

"That's right. Now I remember."

I thought she might add something but was grateful she didn't.

Kingman did though. "I remember too. I didn't realize that having an open house at my office would be an invitation for every lying politician, every used-car salesman, and every shyster lawyer within thirty miles to come and scarf down free food and booze."

Maybe the liquor had gotten to him. He spoke loudly enough for people around us to hear, and most of them stopped eating to listen. Several looked at us, and I knew some of them.

Kingman didn't seem to care. He gave me another intimidating smile. "But that's what it turned out to be. Right, Pete?"

I didn't answer. I just looked at him, thinking about how I'd like to punch his face so hard he wouldn't be able to smile again for a long time.

After a few seconds he said again, ever louder than before, "Right, Pete?"

I didn't want him to draw any more attention to us than he already had, so I said quietly, "If you say so, Mr. Kingman."

"I do say so." He glanced around at the people staring at him and lowered his voice somewhat. "Yes, I do say so."

The hostess had noticed the scene. She came over to the Kingmans' table, looked at him, then her, then me. "Is everything all right, Mr. Kingman?"

"Hell, yes, everything's fine, Barbara. I was just talking to my friend here—Pete, Pete Scarcelli. You know him, don't you?"

She looked at me, clearly embarrassed. "Yes, Mr. Kingman, I know him."

"Good. Because if you're ever hurt in an accident—or even just think you may have been hurt—ol' Pete here is the lawyer for you. Why, he'll be at your bedside before you know it. The ambulance driver will probably give you his card."

He paused, apparently savoring the moment. "Ol' Pete is such a shyster, I'll bet he hands out his cards to every ambulance driver around."

Barbara looked at me, her eyes pleading. "That's fine, Mr. Kingman. But I believe Mr. Scarcelli was just leaving, weren't you, sir?"

"Yes, just leaving."

She held up an arm and gestured toward the door. "After you, sir. And thanks for coming in."

"Yes, Mr. Pete, sir." Kingman's voice dripped with sarcasm. "Thanks for coming in."

I had taken two steps toward the door, but I stopped and turned to look back at him. Then I looked at Justine, whose eyes kept flicking from her husband to me and back again. She had a sort of excited look on her face.

I forced myself to remain calm. "It's good to see you, Mr. Kingman. You too, Mrs. Kingman. Have a pleasant evening."

I think he expected me to lash out in some way, and I wanted to—I wanted to as much as I've ever wanted to do anything in my life. But I didn't, and that was one of the hardest things I've ever done.

Kingman seemed to sense what was going on inside me. He didn't say anything. He just gave me that smile again as I turned and headed for the door.

I didn't look back to see if he—or Justine—watched me leave. I didn't care. Because in taking those few steps I'd decided I would represent Justine. I'd represent her to the best of my ability and take that son of a bitch for every dime I could.

CHAPTER TWENTY-ONE

I called Justine on her mobile at ten o'clock the next morning. I'd forced myself to wait until then to give Kingman plenty of time to leave for the office. I used my own mobile to make the call and closed my office door so Kris wouldn't overhear my end of the conversation.

I wasn't sure why I was taking all those precautions, but something told me to do it. Something I didn't want to examine too closely.

She answered on the third ring. "Hello." Her voice was soft and cool and gave no hint of recognition even though her phone display must have told her who was calling.

"It's me. I'm going to represent you in the divorce."

"Oh, you are, are you? What if I've changed my mind and want someone else?"

"You can't get anyone else who'll fight as hard for you." *Not after last evening*, I thought.

"Can I get someone else who'll fight better?"

"Maybe. Maybe not. Do you want someone else?"

She paused. "No, I don't. I never have. That was your idea."

"And it was a stupid one, a mistake. I won't make another like that."

"No, don't . . . please." She paused again. "Now, when and where can we meet and talk about this?"

"You can come to my office."

"No, I want to be alone with you. Without that girl of yours around."

"She takes a lunch hour. You could come then."

"Don't you understand? I don't want us to be interrupted."

I got it then and mentally smacked myself for not getting it sooner. "What about your place?" I knew that was risky, but I wanted to see her so badly I didn't care about the chance of being caught.

"No good. The maid is here today, and Ben might find out if I send her home this early. Plus he could pop in anytime—he does that once in a while, always with some excuse. I think he does it to check on me."

And with good reason, I thought. I could've asked her to meet me at the boat, but the mid-day weather was too warm for that and there was too great a possibility that someone would see her there. A well-known married woman coming aboard my boat without her husband was bound to cause talk in our tight little community.

So I did the sensible if tacky thing—I asked her to meet me at the

Riverside Inn. It wasn't on the river and it wasn't much of an inn—just a cut above sleazy. But it wasn't one of the chain motels I used when the weather was too hot or cold for the boat to be comfortable. I wasn't sure she'd agree, but she did.

"I'll be there at noon," she said. "Call me when you have the room number."

"Okay."

After I hung up it occurred to me that there was no guarantee the motel would have a room available. But I decided to chance it. If the place was full, I could always call Justine and arrange to meet somewhere else.

I stopped by the liquor store and then drove to the Riverside, where I got lucky on two counts. The motel had a vacancy—probably several, from the looks of the parking lot—and I didn't know the clerk who checked me in. I had a story ready about how it would be too hot to sleep on the boat that night, but I didn't have to use it. The clerk, an elderly, grizzled man, looked as though he'd heard every conceivable reason a man needed a motel room in the middle of the day and didn't believe any of them. None except the real reason, the one nobody ever gave.

After I let myself into the second-floor room, I called Justine to give her the room number. She said she'd be there in twenty minutes.

Then I found the plastic ice bucket and filled it from the machine near the stairwell. I fixed a drink, opened the window curtains a tad, and sat in the room's one chair, looking out over the parking lot to the trees on the far side.

I sat there and tried to switch my brain off, tried not to think about anything. It didn't work. I kept thinking about Justine and why I thought she wanted to see me alone.

I didn't think it was to discuss her case. Well, not just that.

I'd finished my drink and was about to make another when Justine arrived. She had on large sunglasses and was wearing a short, dark-blue dress of some stretchy material that flattered her curves—not they needed much flattering. She gave me a smile as warm as the weather and kissed me on the lips.

"Hmm, a bourbon-flavored man. My favorite kind!" She laughed, a little harshly I thought, and tossed her purse on the desk. "And meeting him in a motel, something I haven't done in ages."

"You said you wanted to see me alone, so I thought—hey, what's that?"

She'd taken off the sunglasses, revealing a black eye. She folded the glasses and laid them on the desk, then looked at me steadily.

"What happened?"

"I ran into a door. Isn't that what women usually say in these circumstances?"

"He hit you."

"Yes. I told you that he's done it before—several times. He was drunk last night—he was well on the way when you saw us in the restaurant—and when we got home and I said he shouldn't have been so nasty to you, he hit me. Just once, and then I locked myself in my bedroom. I heard him stumbling around the house for a while, and eventually I saw a light on his boat, so I knew he'd gone there to sleep."

"Did you see him this morning?"

"No, I stayed in my room until he left for the office. Then I had the pleasure of waiting for you to call and say you wouldn't help me."

"I changed my mind about that."

"Good. I'm glad you did. Now let's not talk for a while."

She came into my arms and kissed me again, and we didn't talk for a while. We undressed each other, clumsily because we were in a hurry, and got into bed.

It was better than in the hot tub. Although the mattress was lumpy and the springs creaked, the bed was more comfortable and we knew each other better—we knew more about what the other wanted and how to give it.

It was much better, and afterward we lay there, getting our breath back and letting the sweat dry.

When I started to feel chilly, I got up and fixed each of us a drink and then got back into bed, pulling the sheet over us.

"Thanks," she said, sipping her drink. "For this and . . . that."

I knew what she meant by "that." "You're welcome, but I should thank you."

"Why? I enjoyed it as much as you did."

"Good."

Justine had more of her drink and then slid out of bed. She went into the bathroom, leaving the door open. After a minute I heard the toilet flush and then water running in the sink.

She came out, wiping her hands on a towel. She went over to the desk and dropped the towel on the chair. Then she pulled her cigarettes out of her purse and lit one.

I don't know what it is exactly, but there's something very erotic about a nude woman smoking, especially a beautiful nude woman.

After taking a couple of puffs, she held up the pack. "Want one?"

"No, thanks, I'm trying to quit."

She drew on the cigarette again and blew a plume of smoke. "Aren't we all?"

The room was non-smoking, so there wasn't an ashtray. She unwrapped another of those crappy plastic glasses they give you and tapped her ash into that.

Then she sat on the towel and smoked moodily, neither of us saying anything else for a while. She was watching me, and I was watching her, staring at her black eye.

Finally Justine crushed out her cigarette and got back into bed. She lay on her side, looking at me.

"I'm glad you decided to help me with the divorce after all."

"Just doing my job."

"Yes, but you don't have to do everything a client wants you to do. Like . . . well, what we talked about."

I didn't let her dance around it. "Kingman's having an accident you mean?"

"Yes. I realize it's a lot to ask, but you can see why I've thought about it." She touched her black eye, winching as she did it.

"Thinking about it is one thing. Doing it is another. I don't mind your thinking about it, but you shouldn't do it."

"I won't—I mean, I can't do it alone."

"I told you I won't help with that."

"Yes, I know you did. But I know something else too—something that might change your mind."

"What?" I couldn't imagine anything that would persuade me to help her kill Kingman. I was sorry he beat her, but I wasn't going to murder him for it.

"You had a sister, didn't you? A younger sister, Annabella, who died of a drug overdose while she was a student at ODU?"

"Yes, about ten years ago. But how the hell do you know that?"

"Oh, I did a little checking before I approached you about handling my divorce. I wanted to know who I might be dealing with."

I already knew Justine well enough not to be surprised that she'd investigated me—or had someone do it. She'd implied she didn't know Jack Greese, but maybe she hadn't been candid about that or maybe she'd used someone else. Regardless, I couldn't imagine why she'd brought up Bella's death.

"My sister died when she was a sophomore." I wanted to stop there, but I forced myself to continue. "From heroin. She'd fallen in with a bad crowd and, I guess, succumbed to peer pressure."

"That can be a dangerous age."

I laughed, and it sounded bitter even to me. "It damn sure was for her."

She studied me for a moment. "Sounds like you blame yourself for her death."

"I blame myself for not seeing the signs, not looking out for her better."

"You don't know—you can't know—whether you could have gotten her to leave drugs alone."

"No, but she was my little sister. I could have tried. I owed her that."

"I think you owe yourself forgiveness. Especially since there's something you do about it now."

I couldn't keep the skepticism out of my voice. "What? Only Jesus could raise the dead, and I sure ain't him."

"Ah, but in this instance you do have the power of life and death."

"What the hell are you talking about?"

"Where do you think that heroin came from?"

"I don't know—a drug dealer, I guess."

"Right. But who bankrolled the dealer to begin with? And then who laundered the money the dealer made?"

I started to say I had no idea, but then I remembered something Sally had said. Something about Kingman having done some money-laundering at some point in the past.

"Kingman?"

CHAPTER TWENTY-TWO

She nodded. "Give the man a cigar. Kingman did both of those things, so you could say that he killed your sister—indirectly, of course, but he was still behind it. Besides, that dealer, Javon Davis, has been dead for years. Somebody shot him—probably some other dealer although he was never caught."

"How do you know this Javon Davis was the dealer who sold the heroin that killed Bella?"

"Because he worked the area around ODU then, and dealers don't like rivals in their territory. The police think Davis was killed by somebody who wanted to take over that area."

I thought about what she'd said. If it was true, maybe there was something I could do to avenge my sister. Bella and all the other people who'd died or had their lives ruined by the poison Kingman had underwritten. *If* it was true. . . .

"Do you have proof of any of this?"

She smiled. "I thought you'd ask that. Yes, I do have proof."

Justine slid out of bed and went over the desk. She pulled a small manila envelope from her purse. Then she came back, sat on the edge of the bed, and opened the envelope.

"Here's a news clipping about Davis's death."

I scanned the short article, and it confirmed much of what Justine had said. There was a photo of Davis, a mugshot from one of what the article described as his "numerous arrests."

I gave the clipping back to Justine. "Okay, maybe he sold the dope that killed my sister, but there's nothing in here about Kingman."

"Of course not—Ben's too smart to let himself be connected with a drug dealer. But look at this."

She pulled a photo from the envelope and handed it to me. The grainy picture, apparently taken from a considerable distance, showed Kingman at the wheel of a parked car with Davis beside him on the front seat. Kingman looked angry, and Davis looked sullen, so I supposed Kingman had been reaming him out for something. I didn't know what it had been, but I could imagine how Davis felt.

Maybe Kingman was lucky that someone killed Davis before Davis came after Kingman.

I turned the photo over and saw that a date and time were written on the back. The date fit with what Justine had told me. "Who took this picture?"

I thought she'd name a PI, maybe Jack Greese himself, but she said, "I did," sounding rather proud about it.

"You did?"

"Yes, I followed him and took the picture without his knowing it. Ben had been going and coming at odd hours, and I thought he was having an affair. This was early in our marriage, when I thought that perhaps he would be faithful to me. Of course, I quickly learned that he wouldn't. But at least this one time he wasn't sneaking out to see another woman."

"What made you keep this? At that time you'd never heard of me or my sister."

"No, but I knew it gave me leverage against him—leverage I could use if I ever needed to."

And that fit with what I knew about Justine. "This proves that Kingman knew Davis, but that's all it proves. It's not proof that Kingman was backing him."

"My God, Pete, how much proof do you need? If Kingman wasn't doing business with Davis, why was he sitting in a car with him? And Davis was into only one thing—dealing drugs."

She shook her head, clearly frustrated. Then she snatched the photo out of my hand, shoved it and the clipping into the envelope, and went back across the room. She tossed the envelope onto the desk and lit another cigarette, her movements a little jerky. She didn't look at me as she smoked.

I thought about what she'd told me. It made sense. It also explained why Justine had come to me—if having her wasn't enough motivation for me to help kill her husband, maybe avenging the death of my sister would be.

And as I remembered Bella, how full of life she'd been, how full of promise for the future, I realized that ending Kingman's life would be justice for his ending her life and probably the lives of other people, maybe several of them.

That made up my mind for me.

And as soon as it was made up, I felt myself relax. I mean, I was already physically relaxed from our lovemaking, but I felt my mind relax, let go of the tension I hadn't known I'd been carrying around inside of me since Justine came to my office.

I'd made the hard decision, so then I could start considering how to implement it. And if I knew Justine as well as I thought I was beginning to, she'd already had some thoughts along that line.

After a couple of minutes she crushed out the cigarette, got back into bed, and pulled the covers up. She lay on her back, staring at the ceiling. "So I guess we're back to dealing with the divorce aren't we?"

"If you like. But a divorce is going to be a moot point after . . . ."

She raised herself on an elbow to look at me, the sheet slipping down to reveal her lovely breasts, each tipped with a perfect pink rose. "After what?"

"After his accident."

I knew she'd heard me, but she must have wanted to make sure of my meaning. "His accident?"

"Yes, you won't need a divorce after that. He'll be dead."

She smiled. It was a happy smile, but there was something else in it too, something that might have been satisfaction mixed with triumph. And behind all that there was one thing more, something I sensed more than saw—a hint of darkness.

We looked into each other's eyes, and she leaned over to kiss me. I tasted her cigarettes and, behind that, the bourbon. The kiss was still great though, and I made it last a long time.

As we were kissing, she reached down to touch me, moving her hand on me slowly and firmly, and I wanted that to last a while too. When I reacted to what she was doing, she straddled me, guided me into her, and began rocking, slowly at first and then faster, bracing herself with her arms.

I looked at her again, but her eyes were closed, and she seemed lost in some private dream. I closed my eyes too and surrendered to the dark.

CHAPTER TWENTY-THREE

"What do you want for . . ."

"Helping you to kill him?"

She'd been cradled in my arm, her head on my shoulder, but now she pulled back a little. "Yes, since you put it so bluntly. For that. What's your price?"

I paused. I hadn't thought about the money angle. I'd decided to represent her after all as a way to get back at Kingman, to punish him for how he'd treated me. Plus it would be a way to show the town that I could take on a power player like Kingman and win.

The black eye had solidified that decision although it hadn't been enough to persuade me to . . . do the other thing. No, only learning about Kingman's involvement with my sister's death had done that.

I knew it was a bad decision, one I'd probably regret it, but I didn't care. I wanted Kingman dead, partly for Justine and partly for myself but mostly for Bella.

I turned toward her. "I don't know. I wasn't going to do it for that."

"That's one of the things I love about you, Pete. You're not all about money like so many people I know."

"Oh, I like a dollar bill as well as the next guy. I just hadn't thought about doing this for money."

"Well, start thinking about it. How does a million dollars sound?"

A million sounded good—fine, in fact. But then I remembered how much Kingman had, and a million didn't sound so great after all. "How about two million?"

"All right, two. Not having to live with *him* will be well worth it."

She agreed so readily that for a moment I wondered if she really planned to pay me. But she'd have to, wouldn't she? After all, we'd be in this thing together. Each of us would always have something on the other. She couldn't afford not to pay me. The logistics might be tricky—each of us would have to avoid attracting attention to the flow of money—but we could work that out later.

When I didn't say anything, she asked, "What else do you want?"

I thought I knew what she was getting at, but I didn't want to guess and be wrong. "What do you mean?"

"Isn't there something else? Me, for instance?"

"Sure. That goes without saying."

"You don't have to marry me, Pete. I know there's a difference in our ages, and you don't seem like the marrying kind. But I like being with you and not just for this." She gestured down the bed. "Although this is nice. Very, very nice."

I was relieved that she wasn't going to pressure me into marrying her. I liked her a lot, but I honestly couldn't say I loved her. I'd never really loved any woman other than my mother and sister although in the heat of passion I'd told a few I did. And always regretted it later.

"I agree." That could mean one or more of several things, and I left it to her to figure out what.

I thought about getting up, but she beat me to it. Then I couldn't take my eyes off her—not that I wanted to—as she gathered her scattered clothes from the floor and put them on the chair.

Watching her move about the room, I asked, "So how are we going to do it?"

She stepped into her skimpy panties and shimmied them up over her hips. "I don't know. I thought that perhaps you'd have an idea."

"No, I don't. Not yet anyway. I'll have to think about it." I sat up in bed and reached for my glass. The ice had melted, leaving heavily watered whiskey, but I was thirsty, and the cool liquid felt good in my mouth.

I swallowed and put the glass down. "The key thing is to make it look like an accident . . . a plausible accident. Chief Carruthers is no fool, and he'll be suspicious of anything that smacks of foul play."

She smiled slightly. "I don't think I've ever heard anyone say 'foul play' before—not unless it was in a movie."

"This isn't funny, Justine! And it's damn sure not a movie."

Anger flared in her face, and she turned away from me to put on her bra. "Look, I'm sorry. But we have to take this seriously."

Hooking her bra with her back to me, she said, "I know. I'm the one with a black eye, so you can be quite certain I'm taking it seriously."

"I don't want either of us—more probably both of us—to end up in jail."

"Neither do I." She picked up her dress and slid it over her head. The she turned to look at me again, zipping the dress behind her. "So we'll just have to be very careful."

"Right."

She slipped into her shoes and came over to stand beside the bed. "When will I see you again?"

"Soon. Just give me some time to think about the best way . . . ."

"To do it."

"Yes, to do it."

"All right. Call me."

"I will."

She leaned down to kiss me but didn't linger over it. Then she shoved the envelope and her cigarettes into her purse, put on her sunglasses, and was gone.

I lay there for a few minutes, thinking. I'd probably made a huge mistake, telling her that I'd help her commit murder. But Kingman deserved it, I told myself. He deserved it because of Bella.

Of course the brutal way he treated Justine and the insulting way he treated me made it easier. I wasn't especially thin-skinned, but I could tolerate only so much, and Kingman had crossed that line, crossed far beyond it.

And Justine had just promised me two million more reasons to do what I was going to do. So the die was cast.

I got out of bed and gathered my own clothes. As I dressed, I thought of various ways I might kill him. Ways *we* might kill him, I told myself firmly. Justine would have to play a part, a key part. I'd make sure she was in it just as much as I was.

Just as guilty.

I picked up my keys and the half-empty bottle of bourbon and opened the door to leave.

The day was still sunny and hot, but a little breeze had sprung up and blew in my face. I felt a chill, but I knew it wasn't from the breeze.

I felt the chill all the way back to the office.

CHAPTER TWENTY-FOUR

I spent the afternoon preparing documents for Justine's divorce. I didn't need them for a divorce that wouldn't happen, but I wanted them as evidence that I'd been preparing for the divorce—that is, not preparing for something else. I'd meant what I said about Chief Carruthers being smart.

So was his daughter, whose job involved prosecuting criminals. Folks accused of murder, for example.

Kris buzzed me about four o'clock. "Mrs. Kingman is on line one."

"Okay, thanks." I picked up the phone. "Hello, this is Peter Scarcelli."

"So formal! Is that for the benefit of the girl?"

I glanced out the door to make sure Kris had hung up. "Yes, that's right."

"Why don't you just close your door?"

"Well, in cases like yours it's not that simple."

She paused. "What? Oh, you mean you don't want her to be suspicious."

"No, we wouldn't want that to happen." *Especially now*, I added to myself. I glanced out the door again. Was it my imagination or did Kris seemed to be listening while she pretended to be focused on her work?

"I guess not. But I need to talk to you. I've thought of a way to do it."

She didn't have to tell me what *it* was.

"Good. I'm glad to hear that you're considering options."

"When can I tell you about it?"

"Getting a divorce is a big decision, so I think you need to consider it very carefully. Give yourself time to really think things through."

"You want me to call you later, is that it?"

"Exactly. It's not something you can decide in five minutes or even five hours."

She paused again. "Call after five, right?"

"Yes, that sounds like a good approach. Thanks for calling, and I'll be in touch."

We said goodbye and I hung up. Because I normally wouldn't have looked at Kris, I was careful not to look at her then. I thought I felt her looking at me, but I told myself I was just being foolish. I hadn't done anything that should make her wonder about Justine and me.

At least I didn't think I had.

Kris came into my office half an hour later and asked me if I needed anything else. I knew that was her code for "I want to leave now," so I said that I didn't need anything and that she could leave.

"Thanks," she said, less bubbly than usual. I'd noticed she was wearing what was for her a conservative outfit: a blouse that was only moderately low cut, a skirt hemmed just above the knee, and shoes that didn't look painful to walk in.

"Everything okay?"

"Yeah, I guess."

"How's Ricky?"

That popped the cork. "He's a dick! Just like all men, I guess, at least when it comes to how they treat women."

She didn't make an exception for me, but then she knew me pretty well, so there was no reason she should. "I'm sorry to hear that. I thought the two of you were getting along great."

"We were until he decided to fuck another girl." She paused, took a deep breath. "Look, I'm sorry about my language—I'm just upset."

"Sure, I understand. And you know my old man is a retired Navy chief, so it's not like I never heard anyone cuss before."

"Thanks, boss. I guess I just needed to vent."

"We all do once in a while. Why don't you call it a day? Go do something to take your mind off him?"

"I will. Monday night is pretty dead, but later in the week I'll go bar-hopping with a couple of my girlfriends and maybe meet some guys. After all, the best cure for losing one man is to find another!"

She smiled, and I could see that she felt better. I didn't think it would take her long to get over Ricky.

I envied her for that. I wanted to be able to get over something. I wanted to badly, but I knew that I wouldn't, at least not anytime soon.

Kris left right after that, and I was alone. If I'd had any cigarettes, I probably would have smoked one. But I'd stopped carrying them, so all I had was the desire with no way to satisfy it.

I sat there in my stuffy, not-quite-shabby office and took a hard look at myself. I didn't much like what I saw. I hadn't liked it for quite a while.

As the minutes dragged by, I developed a nagging suspicion that I was being a fool over a woman. I'd acted that way before, so I knew what it felt like.

I debated phoning Justine to call the whole thing off. Maybe my instinct to refer her to another lawyer had been correct after all. Although it would be awkward, I could tell her I'd changed my mind—again—about representing her.

She'd be pissed, but that was too bad. Sitting there, surrounded by dusty, dispassionate law books and without Justine's face and body to distract me, I realized that killing Kingman wouldn't bring Bella back. There was no reason, or at least not enough reason, for me to risk ruining my life for her.

I was reaching for the phone when I heard the front door open. I got up to see who it was, and there was Justine, closing the door behind her.

I said nothing.

To cope with the summer heat, she was wearing light khaki pants and a loose teal top. When she turned to look at me, she smiled.

"Hi, Pete. I saw the girl leave, so I figured you'd be alone."

"Yes, I'm alone."

"Good. I thought it would be better if we talked in person instead of over the phone. Especially since I was calling from the club."

"What?"

"From the club—I was having drinks with some friends. I think you'd like them. Maybe, uh, afterward you can join—"

"You called me from the *club*?"

"Don't worry—I went into the coat room and closed the door. No one overheard me."

That reassured me a little but not much.

"And when you said to call after five, I just decided to come here and talk to you in person."

"I see."

When I didn't add anything, she said, "Maybe we could sit down to talk."

I finally remembered my manners. "Oh, yes, sorry. Please come into my office."

I stood aside and let her enter and take one of the guest chairs. As I pushed the ashtray toward her, I said, "I'd offer you some coffee, but Kris emptied out the pot before she left."

"Oh, that's all right. It's too late in the day for coffee. But I'm guessing you have some bourbon around."

She'd guessed right. I dug the office bottle and a couple of glasses from the bottom drawer and poured each of us a double shot. She didn't ask for ice or water, so I let that go.

"Here's to us." She raised her glass.

I didn't really want to, but I did likewise. "Cheers."

She noticed that I didn't echo her toast. "Not having second thoughts, are you?"

"Well, actually—"

"Because I've thought of a foolproof way."

Nothing is foolproof, I thought. But I was curious to know what she thought might be, so I said, "Okay, tell me."

"A fire on his boat."

CHAPTER TWENTY-FIVE

"Fire . . . ."

"Yes. I told you he gets mad, almost always when he's drunk, and goes there to sleep. He smokes cigars out there too. Sometimes he falls asleep with one in his hand. He's probably lucky the boat hasn't caught on fire before now."

I don't know why—perhaps it was indecision or simply weakness on my part—but I thought about that. Fire is the greatest danger on a boat, not sinking. If the boat is sinking, you can find something to keep you afloat. But if the boat is on fire, there's nowhere to run, especially if you get trapped below. Eventually the fire finds you, and it's a horrible way to die.

Burned to death so close to water.

"So, what do you think?" She was looking at me expectantly.

Maybe she had something. If I took the boat out on the bay, if it burned and sank there with no one else aboard, it would be hard to prove foul play. And I could simply swim ashore, using a life jacket just to be on the safe side. Yes, it could work.

"It's not a bad idea. It fits his habits. But does he take the boat out at night?"

"Yes. Not often, but he has a few times."

"Alone?"

"He says he goes out alone. I don't know for certain. After I go to bed he might have some woman sneak out there to join him. It wouldn't be hard. But I know he's having affairs, so I haven't bothered to try to catch him with a woman—or women—on his boat."

"Okay, then your idea fits that too."

"I'm glad you like it."

I gave her a harsh look. "I didn't say I like it—I just think it might work. That is, if we were actually going to do it."

"What do you mean *if*? I thought we agreed on that."

"We did, but I've done some more thinking since then."

"You have?"

She arched her eyebrows, and I could tell she knew what was coming. "Yes. I don't think we should go through with it."

"And why not?"

"Because we could get caught and spend the rest of our lives in prison. Not to mention that we'd be killing a man."

"Look at this!" She touched her bruised face. "And what about your sister? Don't think he deserves killing?"

"Maybe. But why should we be the ones to decide that?"

She laughed scornfully. "Don't tell me you're getting religion! Not after what we've done together."

"Adultery is one thing. Murder is something else."

"Don't you have the balls for it?"

I knew she was trying to bait me, so I let her remark hang in the air and took a sip of my drink. She waited, perhaps wondering if she'd gone too far.

After a long moment I said, "Yes, I can do it. That's not the issue. The issue is whether we *should* do it."

She didn't say anything. She just looked at me, seeming to study my face. Then she stood and walked around the desk.

She put her hand to my face. "Yes, we should. We should do it—together. I know you don't care about the money, not really. But I think you care about me. And afterward . . . we could be together. If that's what you want."

I thought about that too. Yes, she was older but not by much. And she was certainly a skilled and passionate lover. It would take a man a long time to grow tired of having sex with her.

Then there was that big, beautiful house on the water. The kind of house I had always wanted but never thought I could have. The deck, the hot tub, the pool. And the dock—*Law Lass* would look perfect tied to that dock.

And then there was the money. Justine had said I didn't care about it, but I did. Maybe not enough to kill just for that, but it was certainly another entry on that side of the ledger. A big one.

I thought how it would be to spend long, lazy afternoons with Justine on the deck, in the pool, on the boat. And how it would be to soak in the hot tub after dinner with the moon and stars shining overhead.

That was a lifestyle I could get used to. Hell, I wouldn't even have to practice law if I didn't want to. Or I could be a deal maker like Kingman. Let my money make more money.

It sounded pretty good. No—it sounded great. And why shouldn't Kingman give it to me, to us? He didn't deserve the life he had. Maybe I didn't either, but I thought I was more worthy of it than he was.

I've said that Justine was smart, and another proof of it was that she kept quiet and let me think. She could probably imagine the wheels turning in my head.

"That's an attractive offer."

She patted my cheek. "I hoped you'd think so."

"But I don't think your plan will work—it's too unpredictable. How can you know in advance when he'll sleep on the boat? And we couldn't take a chance on his waking up. We'd have to . . . do it at the dock while he's still asleep. That means an autopsy would show he'd been murdered."

"The fire won't leave anything for an autopsy."

"We can't know that for certain. And if we do it, we can't risk being caught."

"But there's some risk in anything. We've already taken a risk by making love."

She was right about that. But they don't throw you in prison for screwing another man's wife. Kingman would be furious if he found out about us, but there wouldn't be much he could do about it. Not if he didn't want the word to get around that his wife slept with other men.

"Okay, but there's still the unpredictability. How can you know he's going to be on the boat on any given night?"

"Because I'll pick a fight with him. That's not hard to do. And I'll put something in his drink to make him sleep. That way you won't have to worry about him waking up."

"But would he take a sleeping pill before taking the boat out at night? An autopsy might show that he had."

"He could do it if he'd been drinking." She leaned down to kiss me, and I let her. "Don't you think you're over-analyzing this? It's not going to be that complicated."

"It'll be damn complicated if we get caught. You just think about that."

"And you just think about this."

She kissed me again and reached down to touch me. I thought about moving her hand, but I hesitated a moment too long and then stopped thinking altogether. Before long we were on the couch I used for afternoon naps when things were slow.

That day I used it for something else. And, looking back, she used me.

But it felt good at the time.

CHAPTER TWENTY-SIX

We decided that we'd carry out our plan the coming Friday night. Kingman was supposed to be in town then, and there was no reason to think he wouldn't be home that evening, whether early or late.

Each of us had a few things to do before then. She had to buy some over-the-counter sleeping pills—the same brand she'd bought previously—take out a couple to put in his drink, and throw away a few more. Then, just in case there'd be enough left of the boat to search, she had to put the half-empty bottle of pills on board.

She also had to make sure there'd be plenty of his brand of bourbon in the house and on the boat and that the boat's fuel gauge showed the tank was sufficiently full for the trip he supposedly would have taken—the one I was actually going to take.

And she had to make sure he'd be home that evening. Not necessarily all of it but enough of it that they could fight and he'd stumble out to the boat. Or pass out in the house, in which case she and I would have to carry him to the boat. He was a big man, but I thought we could manage it.

We'd have to manage it.

And I also had things to do. I had to check weather, wind, and tide to make sure all three were favorable for us to carry out our plan. I had to examine a nautical chart to find a place deep enough for the boat to sink but close enough to land that I could swim ashore without too much trouble.

And then there was the fire itself. I needed a simple way to set the boat on fire so that it would burn but not explode, at least not right away. After all, I had to jump off and get far enough from the boat not to be caught in my own trap.

What was that line from Shakespeare? Oh, yes: "Hoist with his own petard." I wasn't sure what a petard was, but I didn't want to find out the hard way.

I went to the grocery store and bought some things for my dad and myself. I made sure to get a small plastic bottle of shampoo, the kind that has a nozzle in a twist-off cap. I'd bought that kind of shampoo before and doing it again wouldn't be unusual. Wouldn't even be remembered.

Filling the bottle after I dumped the shampoo would be trickier. I thought first of using gasoline, but *Law Lass* had an inboard diesel, so someone might remember if I bought a gasoline can. I could siphon some diesel from her tank, but it's hard to get diesel to burn in the open air—too high a flash point.

Then I got an idea. For a while I'd wanted a kerosene lamp for my boat, and here was a perfect excuse to buy one.

Leaving my mobile on the boat so that there'd be no GPS record of my trip, I drove to Doverton, right on the bay about twenty miles south of Kilmihil, and went to the big-box Seven Seas ship chandlery. There was a small local chandlery in Kilmihil, but I'd shopped there often, so they knew my face and name. I'd been to the Seven Seas store too but only once in the last couple of years.

I found what a wanted: a small kerosene lamp with a brass base and fittings and an enclosed glass chimney, the kind that makes a warm, pleasant glow in the cabin. And if I had a kerosene lamp, I needed some kerosene to fill it, didn't I? I got one of the quart cans of kerosene they'd shelved near the lamps and then picked up a few other things so that the lamp and kerosene wouldn't stand out too much when I paid for the goods.

The bored young man at the checkout station barely looked at me as he scanned and bagged my purchases. I paid with cash and was on my way.

Justine called me a couple of times that week. She was careful to phone when Kris took her lunch hour, and I was careful to keep the calls fairly short. During the second call she started to get into some sexy stuff, telling me that she was sitting there naked and touching herself while thinking of me, but I cut that off.

"Not now. It won't do either of us any good, especially this week."

"Oh, I think it'll do me a lot of good. You too if you'd just relax a little and enjoy yourself—if you know what I mean."

"Yes, I know, and all I need is for Kris to walk in and catch me at that."

"Close your door, silly."

"No. Look, Justine. We've got to be careful. I mean all the way careful, about everything."

"We are being careful. We haven't seen each other at all, and we barely talk on the phone."

"That's right." I made a mental note to get both of us burner mobiles that I would destroy after this thing was over. "And that's why we need to hang up now. Understand?"

"Oh, all right. I just wanted you to know how much I miss you. Miss being with you."

"Thanks. We'll have plenty of time for that . . . afterward. Okay?"

"Okay."

I could tell she was annoyed, but I didn't care. I was going to do this thing my way or not at all.

We talked for another minute or two, and she said things still looked good for Friday night. She'd made all of her preparations, and I'd made mine. The only thing left was to go through with it.

Sure, I told myself. That was all—just go through with it.

Then we got off the phone, and I listened to the silence for a while. I wanted it to tell me something, but it didn't. After a couple of minutes I thought I could hear my heart beating. In the silence it sounded loud.

But not as loud as the phone when it rang. I wondered if Justine was calling again, maybe to tell me how mad she was or maybe to try that phone-sex thing again. I hoped it wasn't her at all.

"Peter Scarcelli."

"Hi, Pete. It's Sally."

"Oh, hi. How are you?"

"Fine. A better question is how are *you*?"

"What do you mean?"

"I mean I haven't seen you or heard from you in a while, and I wanted to make sure you're okay."

"Never better. Just busy."

"I imagine that's a good thing for a lawyer in private practice. Plus maybe it will keep you out of trouble."

She laughed, so I laughed too. *Trouble?* I was practically dancing with trouble, getting closer to the edge of disaster all the time. If I fell over—a distinct possibility—it was a long way down.

"I hope you're not too busy to meet me for lunch soon."

"No, we can do that."

"How about the day after tomorrow? Friday's always a good day to meet someone for lunch."

"Uh . . . ." Not this particular Friday. I knew I'd be too keyed up to be good company, and Sally might sense that something was wrong. "I'd like to, but that day won't work for me."

She waited, but I didn't add anything.

"Then how about next week?"

"Maybe. I need to check my calendar and get back to you."

"Okay." She paused again. "You sure you're all right, Pete? Something on your mind?"

"Nothing in particular. Just busy, like I said."

"Uh-huh. Yeah, that's what you said. Well, I would like to see you, Pete. So call me if you want to get together."

"I will."

"Good. You do that. Have a good weekend."

"You too, Sally. I hope you have some time to ride Rusty."

"Yes, that would be fun. And relaxing. I think horses are easier to deal with than people. You always know where you stand with a horse."

I knew what she was implying, but I let it go. I liked Sally and didn't want to argue with her. But she'd caught me at a bad time.

No, the worst possible time, I amended.

"I'll call you next week, promise."

"Okay."

She said it as though she didn't believe me, and I couldn't blame her. Then I told myself that I should call her . . . afterward. I should make a point of doing everything I would usually do.

I thought—maybe "hoped" is a better word—that in another week, after this thing was behind me, I'd be back to my usual self.

I'd never been so wrong.

CHAPTER TWENTY-SEVEN

I tried hard to act normal that week, and I think I succeeded—mostly. The only unusual thing I did was to make another quick trip to Doverton, where I bought two burner phones with prepaid SIM cards at a convenience store. Again I left my regular mobile on the boat and paid with cash.

I used one of the burners to call Justine's mobile and tell her that someone had left something for her on the top of my right front tire. When I left the office that day, the phone and the scrap of paper with my burner number were gone from the Miata.

Kris seemed to know something was up, but she didn't say anything, just gave me odd looks once in a while. After a couple of days of that I dropped a remark that I was "worried about my dad" and didn't elaborate, hoping she'd think that was the reason for my distraction.

Part of acting normal was sticking to my usual routine, so I forced myself to go to lunch at my usual places even though I didn't want to run into anyone I knew well. So naturally I ran into Justine that Wednesday.

I got to the Captain's Café about one-thirty, timing my arrival so that most of the lunch crowd would have left. And most of them had, but Justine was at a table in a corner, sitting across from a dark-haired woman angled away from me. In front of each woman was a half-finished salad and an almost empty glass of white wine.

Turning around and leaving would have looked suspicious, so I didn't do it. Besides, I didn't think she saw me come in. I took a table as far away from hers as I could and sat facing a window, hoping that would stave off an encounter.

It didn't. I was nervous, so I ordered my "guilty pleasure" lunch: fried catfish with hushpuppies, coleslaw, and black-eyed peas. (I think fried catfish, not fried chicken, should be the signature dish of the South. But I'm probably in the minority on that.) The food came in a few minutes, and I was about halfway through it when I sensed someone standing next to me. I didn't think it was the waitress.

It wasn't. I looked up, saw Justine, and got to my feet. She gave me a smile and said softly, "Hi, Pete. I saw you and thought it would look odd if I didn't come over to say hello."

I kept my voice as low as hers. "Sure, sure, I understand. It's good to see you. I hate that we can't be together right now."

She briefly touched my arm. "Soon, darling, soon."

I glanced toward the table where Justine had been sitting but didn't see her companion. I assumed she'd gone to the ladies' room.

"Is everything ready?"

"Yes, on my end. What about on yours?"

"The same. And we're still on the same schedule?"

"Yes, Friday night. Nothing's changed."

"Good." I thought I should add something, but I didn't like discussing murder, however veiled the conversation, in a public place. And talking about the weather seemed inane under the circumstances. So I remained silent, trying to think of something to say.

Justine studied me as the seconds ticked by. "You seem tense."

"Of course I am!" I didn't raise my voice much, but it was enough to cause the waitress to glance at me. I gave her a tight smile, and she went back to what she'd been doing. "Aren't you?" I asked in a near whisper.

"Yes, a bit. But don't worry—I know what I'm doing."

That seemed like a strange comment. I was wondering what she meant and was about to ask her when her friend came out of the ladies' room and walked toward us.

"Shh, she's coming."

Justine knew whom I meant. She quickly rearranged her face into a more placid look and asked about my father. I started to give her a plain-vanilla answer, but her friend's arrival kept me from having to do it.

Justine turned to smile at her and then gestured at me. "Maya, this is Peter Scarcelli, a lawyer here in town. Pete, Maya Martínez is a very good friend of mine—we've known each other for years. She's thinking of moving here from Richmond."

"Hello, Peter." The woman, who spoke with a faint Spanish accent, had a dark tan, dark eyes, and full, ruby-red lips. She was lovely if not as breathtaking as Justine—but then, of course, few women were.

She held out her hand, and I shook it. Her grip was firm, stronger than the handshake of most women.

"Hi. My friends call me 'Pete'."

She flashed a bright smile that contrasted nicely with her deep tan. "I like that. Mine call me 'M&M' sometimes just as a joke."

"M&M—like the candy?"

"Exactly." She was still holding my hand, and I gently removed it from hers.

If we'd been alone, I would have made some quip, maybe asking her if she was as sweet as her nickname, but I wasn't going to risk that in front of Justine.

So I played it safe. "If you do decide to move here to the River Realm, I'm sure you'll like it."

"I think I would. Everyone seems so friendly—even the lawyers."

I laughed, hoping it sounded reasonably natural. "I'm glad you think so. Not everyone does."

"Probably just the people you have beaten in court."

"If only that were true."

She didn't say anything—she seemed to be waiting for me to continue, so I cast about for some innocuous remark. "I'm glad our little town appeals to you."

"It is not so little, and small towns can be very pleasant."

"I suppose, but there's not much to do in the evenings." I knew I was babbling but couldn't stop for some reason. And Justine was no help—she just stood there, listening. Maybe she was waiting to see whether I was smart enough to extricate myself from the situation.

"Oh, I am not sure about that." She gave me a long, slow look. "I can usually think of something."

I felt that look down to the bottom of my pockets—no, right in my crotch, and I knew that was what she intended. There was a sort of heat coming from her—a radiation that was more direct if not necessarily more powerful than Justine's subtle, catlike emanation of sex.

I thought Maya Martínez would be wearing in the long run, but she'd certainly make for a jazzy weekend. I started to imagine her on *Law Lass*, browning her bare tan lines as we lay anchored in my favorite cove.

Probably sensing what I was thinking, Justine snapped me out of it. "And I know just what," she said, giving Maya one of those woman-to-woman looks men will never understand.

Then she turned back to me. "We've got to run now, Pete. See you later."

I wished she hadn't made that last remark, but I didn't say anything to underscore it. "Sure. Goodbye."

They said goodbye and left, and I watched them go. Maya was a couple of inches shorter than Justine but had a figure as good, maybe even a little better. More voluptuous, anyway, with broad shoulders tapering to a narrow waist that flared into the lyre of her hips. My imagination was right: she'd be something to see in a bathing suit—or out of one.

I knew I shouldn't be thinking such thoughts about my lover's friend, but I told myself I was a guy and couldn't help it. So many guys tell themselves things like that, and it usually ends badly for them.

And they—we—never see it coming.

CHAPTER TWENTY-EIGHT

On Friday I was wound as tightly as I'd known I would be. I think Kris sensed something—a few times I caught her looking at me in what I thought was a strange way. I told myself that I was just being paranoid, but I couldn't get myself to believe it.

I got nothing done all morning. Oh, I shuffled papers in my office and even had a few phone calls although none with Justine, whom I hadn't talked to since the day before. But I wasn't doing anything productive, just watching the minutes drag by more slowly than condemned men marching to the death chamber.

Kris went to lunch but I didn't. My guts were so knotted up that I knew I couldn't eat anything. Or at least not keep it down.

When Kris came back, I told her to take the rest of the afternoon off. She gave me a puzzled look.

"You sure, boss? I have some things to do—bills and such."

"It'll wait 'til Monday. Go on—enjoy yourself."

"Okay, if you're sure."

I'd known I wouldn't have to coax her. But I was surprised when she added, "You should do the same thing. You look tired, sort of distracted. Is everything okay?"

"Sure. But I guess I am a little tired—it's been a long week."

"Aren't they all? But that's why God made weekends!" She gave me a wink.

"Right. Well, like I said, go enjoy yours."

"You too, Pete."

She turned and went out, knowing, I'm sure, that I'd watch her walk away in that miniskirt that barely covered her round bottom. As I was doing what she'd known I'd do, it occurred to me that if Kris could see through me so easily, no doubt other people could too.

That chief of police, for instance.

After she left, the office was quiet again. I sat there for a long time, not moving, just going over the plan in my mind.

When Kingman got home, whether before dinner or after, she'd serve him a doctored drink and then pick a fight with him. She'd make sure there was a lot of yelling and even some things thrown. If he didn't head for the boat then, she'd say enough nasty things to drive him out there. She'd have doctored the booze on the boat too, so he'd certainly be passed out when I showed up at midnight.

She wouldn't be there. She needed an alibi, so she'd check into a motel, a better one than where we'd met a few days ago. Later she could claim that Kingman had gotten violent—there'd be some broken things to prove that—and she'd been too afraid of him to spend the night at their house.

Probably only the desk clerk would see her, but that would be enough. The best alibis are those good enough to serve the purpose but not so good they look planned. To help the alibi along, she wouldn't take any luggage with her—nothing but her purse.

At first she'd said she'd call to let me know everything was on track. But I didn't want to risk a record of that call, even on burner phones, so I'd told her to call only if something had gone wrong. That way I'd go through with it only if I didn't hear from her.

I forced myself to stay in the office until six, and I made a couple of calls between five and six to prove I'd been there that late. Then I closed up, took off my tie, and drove to a semi-seedy bar on the waterfront. I wanted to be seen in public but not by anyone I knew well.

A former Navy chief who'd served with my father owned the place. He'd named it "The Chief's Club" and given it a nautical theme—lots of Navy photos and memorabilia on the walls. The "club" was dark and almost dingy, but the beer was cold, the burgers were tasty, and there was good liquor for people who wanted it.

There were several empty tables at that hour, and I took one. A tattooed and buzz-cut waitress took my order—draft beer and a medium-rare cheeseburger—and then I looked around the place. As I'd thought, I didn't recognize anyone.

The owner, Larry Robinson, spotted me from behind the bar, said something to the other bartender, and came over to my table. I rose to shake hands.

"Hi, Pete, how are you?"

"Fine, Chief. You?"

"Can't complain. If I did, who'd listen?"

I laughed even though I'd heard that joke many times. I was tense but didn't want him to remember my being that way.

"How's your dad?"

"He's fine. Well, maybe not fine but doing all right. His health is still pretty good, but I think he needs to get out more."

Robinson frowned. "Sorry to hear that. He's always welcome here. Hell, tell him that the next time he comes in, his tab's on me."

"I'll do that."

The waitress brought my beer and set it on the table. I thanked her, and Robinson said, "Let's sit for a minute, Pete."

Each of us took a chair, and I had a sip of my beer while Robinson looked at me contemplatively.

"You know, Pete, I think you're a good guy. But—and don't take this the wrong way—you're not getting any younger. Why don't you find yourself a nice girl and settle down?"

I laughed again but not quite so much. Who was he to be giving me advice about getting married? He'd been divorced twice, and I happened to know his current, much-younger girlfriend was cheating on him. I knew because she'd done it with me one weekend when he was out of town.

"I mean it, Pete. A good woman could steady you, give you direction in life."

I bristled. "What makes you think I don't have direction?"

"What are you doing in here by yourself on a Friday night? Not that I don't appreciate your business. But you're missing out. You know what that country song says—the wife and kids, that's the good stuff."

I wondered if my father thought my mother and sister and I had been the 'good stuff'. Maybe he did. I hoped so.

"Sure, sure. But I still have time for all that."

Robinson smiled. "You think you do, son, but time goes by faster than you realize. Everything after thirty-five is just a blur."

"If you're right, Chief, I'm about to find out."

"Damn straight I'm right. Just ask your old man—he'll tell you. I remember when he and I were your age and thought we had the world by the tail." He glanced around the bar, which was beginning to fill up with people who worked with their hands for a living. Auto mechanics, construction workers, and plumbers. Dog groomers, grocery-store cashiers, and hair stylists. People who, I had to admit, were more important in everyday life than I was.

"Yep, that's what we thought," Robinson continued. "But now we're just at the tail end."

He turned back at me. "And you'll be at the tail end too someday. Best to be there with a woman who loves you and some kids to be proud of."

"I'll keep that in mind."

I didn't say it sarcastically, but he gave me a sharp look. "Yeah, sure, who cares what an old man thinks? What the hell do I know? But I can tell you this, lad. I know what I'd be doing tonight if I were you."

"What's that?"

"Taking some good-looking woman to dinner. Maggie Henderson, for example, that real-estate lady. She's easy on the eyes and likes to laugh."

He was right—Maggie was attractive and did have a good sense of humor. But somehow my charm was lost on her. I'd flirted with her a couple of times and gotten nowhere. Maybe she was too smart to get involved with me.

"Not my type, Chief. We all have our types."

"Okay, then what about Sally Carruthers? She's single now, but she won't be for long. No, sir. And both of you being lawyers—you'd make a good pair."

I started to say something—I'm not sure what—but stopped when the waitress appeared with my burger. She put in front of me and asked if I wanted anything else.

"No, thanks." I pulled the plate a little closer toward me and looked at Robinson. "I think I have everything I need right now."

She nodded and left. Robinson looked at me for another moment, then shook his head slightly.

"Enjoy your dinner, Pete. It's good to see you. And remember what I said to tell your father."

"I will. Thanks, Chief."

He went back to the bar and I got back to the burger. I ate slowly, thinking about what Robinson had said. He was probably right. What was it my dad had told me in one of his rare philosophical moments? "Some things you learn only by living a long time."

I pulled the burner out of my pocket. Justine hadn't called or texted to call things off. I found myself wishing she had.

But, no, she hadn't. I guess I could have called it off on my own, but it seemed too late for that.

Too late for a lot of things.

CHAPTER TWENTY-NINE

After I finished eating, I lingered over another beer as long as I thought I could without being obvious about it. Two women came in and sat at the bar drinking colorful mixed drinks and laughing a lot, relaxing at the end of the work week.

After they'd been there about half an hour, one of them looked at me and smiled, but I didn't smile back. After a few seconds the woman turned back to her companion, looking pissed.

Sorry, lady, I thought. *Not tonight. Tonight I have something else on my mind.*

When I finally finished the second beer, I paid the check and left. I drove to my boat, opened it to the night air, and changed into black chinos and a black golf shirt. Then I set my phone alarm and lay down to sleep for a couple of hours. I wanted to be rested for what I had to do that night.

But sleep wouldn't come. I told myself that it was because the cabin was hot and stuffy. It was, but that wasn't why I couldn't sleep. I kept picturing myself splashing that kerosene around and, when the bottle was empty, striking a match.

Would he scream? Maybe, but I hoped not. At least not until I was well away from his boat.

After a long while I gave up and got up. I put on boat shoes, drove to the nearest convenience store, and bought a pack of cigarettes. Then I went back to the boat.

I fixed a drink and sat in the cockpit. I lit a cigarette—my first in several days—and was surprised that it tasted like straw. I thought I'd wanted to smoke, but I really didn't. I ground out the cigarette and pushed the pack away, disgusted with myself for even buying it.

I checked the phone again. Nothing.

I sipped the drink slowly, making it last as I had with the beer earlier. The rising moon, now almost half full, rolled a pale-gold ribbon across the calm, black water. The night was still and quiet with only the usual bird and insect sounds. As the forecast had predicted earlier in the week, it was a good night for doing what I planned to do.

I'd half-hoped for rain, but God wasn't going to save me that way. Apparently not in any way.

I finished the drink and thought about having another but decided not to. One more might partially relax the steel spring coiled inside me, but it might also dull my senses, and I needed to be sharp for the night's work. So I rinsed the plastic cup—glass can be dangerous on a boat—and put it away. Then I got what I'd need for the night's "work." A pocket flashlight, matches, and, just in case, my bosun's knife, which I slid into a leather case clipped to my belt.

There was one more thing: the little squeeze bottle that was now full of kerosene.

I thought about taking my pistol, the Glock 19 I kept on the boat for personal protection. My dad had given the gun to me as a birthday present, saying that any son of his should know how to defend himself. I'd never had to use the weapon that way, but I felt safer with it on board. As I considered the idea, I took the Glock out of the drawer and hefted it, the black shape solid in my hand.

But then I remembered how well sound carries across open water, and I decided to go with just the knife as backup. I knew that if I had to kill Kingman with something other than fire, it would be harder to stab him than shoot him. But mentally and emotionally I had passed the point of no return, and I was determined to see the thing through.

So I put the pistol back in the drawer. Then I thought about using shoe polish to blacken my face, but I knew it would look too suspicious if someone saw me. And besides, I didn't need to camouflage myself from Kingman—he wasn't going to see me. At least he wasn't supposed to.

I hoped Justine was right about that. She and I had to be right about that and a lot of other things.

I stuffed my "tools" into my pockets and closed and locked the boat. I walked out to the car and drove about half an hour to get to the cove on the bay I'd carefully selected on a chart and then scouted a few days before. This cove was deeper than my favorite gunkhole, so it was used more and had a dirt road leading down to the water. Before I turned onto the road, I made sure I didn't see any headlights behind me or in front of me.

When I got close to the shoreline, I parked in among some cedar trees and killed my lights and engine. A big cedar that stood off by itself was dead, its limbs almost bare, so I could use the tree as a maker. I checked the burner one last time, and there was still no message from Justine.

So it was a go.

I put the phone on the passenger seat and took a deep breath. I knew I needed to get going, but for some reason I just sat there, letting the night, with all its familiar sounds and smells, close in around me. After a couple of minutes I noticed that even though I wasn't hot, my hands were sweaty.

Finally I wiped my hands on my trousers and forced myself to get out of the car.

The forecast didn't call for rain, but forecasts can be wrong, so I put the top up on the car. If it did rain, I didn't want to explain why I'd left an open convertible out in the weather.

I locked the car and considered what to do with the key. I didn't want to take it with me and risk losing it when I . . . did what I was going to do. In the darkness it might fall out when I pulled other things from my pocket, or it might come out while I was swimming. Without that key I'd be a thousand times more likely to get caught. So I carefully scooped out a shallow hole behind the right rear tire and buried the key in it.

Then I started walking. I had a ways to go, about three miles. I stepped along the side of the narrow two-lane blacktop, being careful to keep a good watch for cars fore and aft. A couple of times I saw headlights coming toward me, so I ducked into the trees. Dressed in black, I was hard to see, and neither of those cars slowed down or gave any sign of having spotted me.

But another almost caught me. At a tight curve the shoulders were narrow with a deep ditch on both sides. To avoid slipping into the ditch, I had to walk on the edge of the pavement.

As I approached the midway point of the curve, I heard a car coming toward me. I didn't see any lights but jumped into the ditch anyway and ducked down as low as I could.

Seconds later the car skidded around the curve, and I heard crazy laughter coming from its open windows.

Goddamn drunks, I thought. *Probably teenagers if they're stupid enough to drive without lights.*

Then I remembered doing exactly the same thing when I was that age. Maybe even doing it coming around this curve.

Suddenly that seemed like a long time ago. In a different world—a simpler, less dangerous world.

We hadn't had rain in a few days, so the ditch was dry except at the very bottom. I got some mud on my shoes but none on my clothes. I climbed out of the ditch, brushed myself off, and resumed walking.

The night was dark out there in the country, the glow from the moon, well above the horizon, giving me just enough light. The moon washed out the dimmer stars, but the ones I could see glittered like diamonds in the clear, cloudless sky, looking distant and cold and hard. The nocturnal scents and sounds were still with me but seemed subdued as I moved through them.

It took me about an hour to walk to the Kingmans' house. By the time I got there, I was sweating despite the light golf shirt. I mopped my face with my handkerchief and then started up the long driveway, being careful to step quietly on the grass next to the drive and not crunch the oyster shells on it.

Not that it should have made any difference. It was almost midnight, and Kingman was supposed to be sound asleep by now. In a drugged sleep.

One from which he'd never awake.

The house was dark except for dim lights on in what I thought were the kitchen and Kingman's den and two floodlights shining over the big garage. There was no movement anywhere, and the house had that hushed look empty houses often have.

So maybe it was empty just as Justine had said it would be. Still, I wasn't taking any chances. Instead of walking straight up to the house, I skirted the edge of the big lawn, as carefully groomed as a golf course, and moved slowly, stopping every minute or so to look and listen for movement.

Nothing.

Before I'd been to Kingman's house the first time, I'd have figured he would have a dog, a big one, maybe a Golden Retriever or a Lab, but he didn't. Not having to deal with a dog, whether by poison or some noisier way, made things a lot simpler.

So did the fact that Justine had promised to switch off the security cameras. I hoped she'd remembered to do so.

I went along the edge of the lawn until I could see Kingman's big boat moored at the dock. In the moonlight *Loophole* was a pale ghost, bone-white and absolutely still. The river spread out beyond the boat, black except for the gold streak of moonlight and flat except for a few ripples the light breeze stirred up offshore.

It was a beautiful scene, one I would have really enjoyed if I hadn't been there to kill a man.

But I was.

The boat didn't show any lights, and I thought that was odd, given the lights in the house. Apparently Kingman had been so drunk and drugged that he hadn't turned the house lights off when he staggered out the boat but not so incapacitated that he left lights—or at least a light—burning on the boat.

I had my flashlight, so I didn't think much about the darkened boat. I should have, but I didn't. I should have thought about a lot of things then, but I guess the time for thinking was past.

I pulled the flashlight from my pocket but didn't turn it on. Then I walked slowly past that end of the house. After I turned the corner I saw the deck and the covered hot tub.

How long had it been since I'd made love to Justine there? Only a week? It seemed much longer.

As I came even with the shallow end of the pool, I remembered how she'd looked coming out of the water. There was a reason that Italian guy had painted Venus standing on the seashell. Of course, Venus had been coy, covering part of herself with her hands.

My Justine wasn't coy. Not a bit of it. She was more like Eve, proudly naked as she offered the apple. And I'd eaten some of it.

I kept walking toward the boat.

CHAPTER THIRTY

I've already described how I went aboard *Loophole* and took her down the river and into the bay. How I saw the sleeping figure in the double berth, splashed the kerosene around, and lit it. How I put on a life jacket, stepped off the boat, and swam for the shore.

I can still see how the boat looked behind me, its interior a mass of flame with those tongues of yellow and red licking up from the main hatch. How the fire threw off a cloud of thick, black smoke darker than the night sky. And I can still hear the popping and crackling of the fire and the loud *smash* when that window blew.

But the main thing I remember is the awful scream. That scream of pure terror. The surprisingly high-pitched scream that made me think of the damned, screaming in hell.

Now I know—I know all too well—why that thought came to me. And still comes to me. Even if I put my hands over my ears, I can still hear that scream.

Sometimes I scream along with it.

□ □ □

I was tired when I finally reached shore. Part of that was physical—it had been a long swim even with the life jacket—but part was mental. Relief, I guess you could call it, at having the thing behind me.

Literally as well as figuratively. I turned to look at the boat, which had burned almost to the waterline. The fire was much smaller then but still easy to see out there on the water.

And I could see something else—another boat. A small skiff, a boat to fish from. Someone who lived nearby, probably in a house on the water, must have spotted the fire and going out to investigate. Now that someone would probably call the chief's office, and they'd come out to investigate too.

I didn't think they'd find any evidence of me—I'd been careful not to leave any evidence for them to find. The plastic bottle would have melted in the heat, and the matches would have burned up. The deputies might find traces of the kerosene, but that was doubtful and in any case wouldn't point to me.

No, I wasn't too worried about that. Even if Chief Carruthers called in forensic specialists from Virginia's Bureau of Criminal Investigation, I didn't think they'd link me to the murder.

The cops would sweat Justine some, but I'd told her to play the grieving widow and just say she didn't know why Kingman had taken his boat out at night or why it caught on fire. If they kept pressing her, she was to act highly offended and refuse to answer any more questions.

That's where most criminals go wrong, of course—I mean the ones who get arrested, and that's the vast majority of them eventually. If they were smart enough to clam up and not answer questions, a lot of them would go free.

Also, Justine hadn't killed her husband, at least not directly, so the police couldn't prove she had. Some people were bound to suspect her, and there'd be some ugly talk, but it would all come to nothing. After a few months people with nothing better to do would find something else to gossip about.

That's what I was thinking as I stood and walked through the shallow water to the shore, mud sucking at my boat shoes. I stepped onto some rocks and dipped my shoes back in the water, trying to wash off the mud. I might have gotten some of it off, but a lot of the gummy black mud still stuck to them.

I went over to the car, dug up the key, and wiped it on my trousers. I untied the life jacket, opened the trunk, and tossed the jacket into it.

I got in the car and checked the time on my burner phone: 3:47 a.m. The whole thing had taken longer than I'd planned but not too much longer. I'd still be back at my boat well before daylight.

I called Justine, but she didn't answer. I figured she'd probably fallen asleep while waiting for me to get in touch.

So I drove home, being careful to stay just under the speed limit and obey all the stop signs. The last thing I needed was to get pulled over by some bored cop who had nothing else to do at that time of night.

I didn't get back to the marina until well after four, but the sky was still dark, and no one seemed to be up and about. I parked the car in my usual spot, closed the door as softly as I could, and crept almost soundlessly onto my boat.

I undressed and crawled into my bunk. I was keyed up from . . . what I'd done and didn't think I'd be able to sleep. But I closed my eyes, and the next thing I knew, my regular mobile was ringing.

I reached for it groggily. "Hello?"

"Pete, it's Jack Greese."

I started to chew him out for calling me so early, but then I checked the time and saw that it was almost ten a.m. "Hi, Jack. What's up?"

Suddenly I realized that I'd never called him to get his report on Kingman. Even though I wasn't going to need the report for Justine's supposed divorce, calling Jack would have been part of my normal pattern, and I should have done it. But I'd been so busy and distracted that calling him had just slipped my mind. That mistake made me wonder what else I might have missed.

"I guess you've heard the news?"

And I could guess what he was talking about, but of course I didn't want him to know that. "What news?"

"About Kingman's boat. That big power job, *Loophole*."

"No, what about her?"

"She burned and sank last night. Out on the bay. They sent a diver down this morning, and he found a body."

"Oh, that's awful." I tried to sound sincere and maybe I did.

"Yeah. I got this straight from a friend on the force. What they can't figure is why she took the boat out alone."

She? I froze. Time seemed to stand still. There was no sound at all, not even of my breathing.

"Pete? You still there?"

"Uh, yes. I'm here. Did you say 'she'?"

"Yeah, Mrs. Kingman. Justine. Your client."

A big black wave swept up and slapped me hard. My eyes felt hot, my throat tight. After a long pause I managed to choke out, "They're sure it was her?"

"Oh, yeah. She was badly burned but still recognizable. The water put the fire out as the boat sank. She probably died of asphyxiation or maybe drowned. It comes to the same thing: she's dead."

I didn't speak for several seconds. I felt wetness on my cheeks, and I wiped my burning eyes with my fingers. Justine . . . gone.

Gone forever.

I hadn't been in love with her, but I had been . . . what? Obsessed with her? Yes, I supposed so. Obsessed with possessing something—several things—I'd never thought I'd have.

And now it looked as though I wouldn't have them after all.

Underneath the intense sadness I felt stunned. Now I understood why that scream had seemed high-pitched—it was Justine screaming, not Kingman.

But why was she on the boat instead of him? It couldn't be suicide. She wasn't the type. She could kill someone else but not herself. And it wasn't to frame me. She had no reason to do that, and if she'd had a reason, she was smart enough to do it in a way that wouldn't kill her.

No, it had to be Kingman. He must have found out what she was planning. But how? I didn't know. Maybe I could find out, but that didn't matter at the moment.

What mattered now was that he had found out and had decided to pull a switch on her. On me too, I realized. He'd probably arranged an alibi just as she had. Now he could point the finger at me and be completely in the clear. I couldn't prove he'd drugged Justine and put her on the boat.

"Pete, you okay?"

And if Kingman or I was charged—probably, to top it all off, by Sally Carruthers—who would a jury believe? Kingman, a rich, powerful man who'd hire a crack defense lawyer, or me, a well-known ambulance chaser who'd probably end up with a public defender?

And what about motive? Kingman would stress that Justine had been a beautiful, desirable, and rich woman and that I had a reputation for chasing woman—including married ones.

"Yes. I'm just . . . well, I'm just surprised. That's all."

"Sure, I understand. It's a shock, all right. Look, I know there won't be any divorce now, but I uncovered some interesting stuff about Kingman. About Mrs. Kingman too—from before they were married. I'm going to have to charge you for my time anyway, so maybe you'd like to have the information."

I started to say no, that it no longer mattered. But then I realized that there might be something I could use against Kingman, something to give me a hold over him the way he now had one on me.

"I guess so." I tried to sound normal. "I can just stick it in the file."

"All right. I'll stop by your office on Monday."

I thought fast. I didn't know what, if anything, Kingman was going to do to me or about me, but he might move quickly. So I should too.

"I've got to go in this afternoon, so maybe you could meet me then."

"You working on weekends these days?"

"When I need to. Don't you?"

He laughed. "Sure, that's the best time to catch philandering husbands. Some wives too."

"Okay, come at two o'clock. How's that?"

"Fine. See you then."

After he hung up, I lay there for a long time, thinking. How had Kingman known what Justine and I were planning? Surely she hadn't let it slip. And I hadn't told anyone about our plan. I was dumb enough to agree to help her carry it out but not dumb enough to talk about it.

Then I looked at my mobile. Kingman hadn't had access to mine, but maybe he'd found a way to tap hers. Or to put some sort of listening device in her purse.

Or maybe he'd beaten it out of her. He was capable of that. Justine was no coward, but everyone has a breaking point. He could have hurt her enough to make her tell him.

Regardless of how he'd done it, he'd found out somehow and decided to let me do what perhaps he wanted to do. Kill Justine.

My eyes felt as though I had sand under the lids. I closed my eyes and rubbed them, and my hand came away wet. I gave into it then, letting the tears flow and sobbing. I cursed out loud, damning Kingman for what he'd driven her to. Damning myself and what I'd done. The horrible thing I could never undo.

It took a couple of minutes to get it all out. Gradually I stopped shaking and cursing. When I finally calmed down, I thought about how Kingman's face had looked when he taunted me in the restaurant. That made me punch the bulkhead so hard I thought I might have broken my hand. But the pain helped.

It helped me focus on what I was going to do to him.

CHAPTER THIRTY-ONE

I shaved, showered, and got dressed in casual clothes. Then I had lunch at the Captain's Café. I thought about going somewhere else—I certainly didn't want to run into Chief Carruthers—but I decided that keeping to my usual routine would be best.

I got lucky: the chief wasn't there. But Sally was, standing near the register and apparently waiting for a to-go order. There was nothing I could do but go over to say hello.

"Hi, Sally."

"Hello, Pete. How are you?"

"Good. You?"

"Fine." She paused. "I guess you heard about Justine Kingman."

I swallowed hard. "Yes, I did."

"What a tragic thing! I can't imagine how it happened."

"Uh, probably just some sort of accident."

"Maybe." She looked at me closely. "Accidents do happen. Or it could be . . . something else."

She didn't say what. She didn't have to—I knew what she was thinking. I just hoped she wasn't thinking about it in connection with me.

"Well, the police may be able to figure it out."

"Probably. Dad's working on it now. He's called in some people from Richmond."

I knew she meant the Bureau of Criminal Investigation. "That makes sense. They're the experts with this sort of thing."

"We'll see what they come up with. Right now I'm getting them some lunch."

"That's nice of you."

"Thanks. Actually I'm just being practical. If I didn't get them something, Dad probably wouldn't stop for lunch. He'd work straight through, and all the others would feel they had to do the same thing."

"I guess you know your dad pretty well."

"I know I need to take care of him sometimes. Lord knows he doesn't take care of himself. He's been married to his job since . . . ."

She didn't have to finish. I knew she was thinking about her mother. I'd met Mrs. Carruthers once and knew she'd been a fine woman, well thought of in the community. She'd died the same way my mother had—from cancer although of a different type.

I didn't intrude on her thoughts, but after a moment she said, "You know, that's another thing we have in common—besides being lawyers. Both of us with just our fathers now."

"Yes, I suppose so." I didn't add that my father wasn't much like hers—she knew that as well as I did.

She paused, then rushed ahead. "Look, Pete, why don't you come over for dinner tonight? I'll make something special."

When I didn't answer right away she must have thought I wondered if her father would be there. "Something for just the two of us."

I didn't know what to say. I wasn't in the mood for company—I wasn't in the mood for anything but hiding in a hole somewhere. But I didn't have a good excuse for not accepting Sally's invitation, and maybe having dinner with the chief's daughter would suggest I didn't have anything to hide. Murder, for instance.

"Uh, okay, if it's not too much trouble."

She smiled. "No trouble at all. I like to cook. Maybe you can bring some white wine."

"Sure. What time?"

"Oh, six-thirty?"

"Fine."

"Know where I live?"

I did. I'd even driven by her place a few times, telling myself I was just taking a shortcut through the neighborhood but always giving her house, a large, newish ranch with an inviting porch and carefully tended flower beds, a long look.

"No."

"It's not hard to find." She was writing the address on a paper napkin when the cashier brought out her order in a big, white bag.

She handed the napkin to me and gave her credit card to the cashier. I read the address as though I didn't know what it was.

I folded the napkin and put it in my pocket as she was adding a tip and signing the receipt. She tucked away her card, thanked the cashier, and picked up the bag.

Then she turned back to me and smiled again. "So, see you tonight."

"Okay."

I knew I should have come up with something better than that, but I just couldn't. I felt numb and could barely think. I wondered whether I'd be able to get through dinner without Sally's figuring out that something was wrong. Well, I'd just have to find a way to do it.

She left then, and I took a table and ordered lunch. I ate mechanically without even tasting the food.

I got to the office about 1:30. Without Kris there, bustling about, the place looked bleak, even a little worn. I'd been off cigarettes long enough to taste the stale air, and I switched on a fan in my office.

Then I sat behind my desk and looked blankly at the guest chair where Justine had sat that first time she came to my office. Looking so fetching in that little white tennis dress with a sheen of sweat on her lovely face. That's the main image I've kept of her—not how she looked emerging from the pool or soaking in the hot tub or even lying beneath me in the motel bed.

No, I usually think of her—and I think of her often—in that white dress. Not virginal, not like a bride, but shinning in white as though untouched by the dark ugliness of this world.

Not even what Jack told me about her changed that image for me.

He got there right at two. When I heard the door open, I called out, "In here, Jack."

I heard his heavy tread cross the floor and then his bulk filled the doorway to my office. Normally he would have given me a grin, but he held back, probably in deference to Justine's death.

"Hi, Pete."

"Hello, Jack. Thanks for coming in on Saturday."

"That's okay. I've got something to do later. I usually do on Saturday night."

He didn't need to elaborate. He did a lot of divorce work—"spousal surveillance" as PIs and the lawyers who hire them call it. Sad, dirty business, squinting through a camera to snap adulterous couples having sex. A necessary business sometimes, but something I'd managed to stay away from almost entirely.

Not that most of my accident-faking clients were much better. But at least they were cheating insurance companies, not their spouses.

Jack was wearing dark trousers and a dark short-sleeve shirt, and it struck me that he was dressed almost exactly as I'd been the night before. *Maybe,* I thought, *I shouldn't be too quick to think I'm somehow better than he is.*

He had two file folders in one of his big hands, neither folder fat nor thin. I stood, and he came into the office and put the folders on my desk. Then we shook hands and he sat in one of the guest chairs.

"Drink? Bourbon?"

"Maybe a short one. I'll probably be up late."

"I suppose you are most Saturdays." I got out the bottle and two glasses and splashed some whiskey into each glass.

"Yeah, if business is good. And it is good right now—probably this hot weather. Makes folks frisky."

I tried without success not to flash on an image of Justine in the hot tub. "I guess so. Ice? Water?"

"Neat is fine."

"Okay." I handed him a glass and took the other with me behind the desk.

He waited until I was back in my chair, then raised his glass. "Here's to luck."

That seemed an odd toast, but I didn't point it out. I could use all the luck I could get. "Okay, to luck."

He drank, and I did the same. The bourbon tasted good even neat, and I was glad I'd suggested a drink. I'd never forget about the night before, but the drink might help me push it to the back of my mind and think about what I needed to do next.

I had another taste and put down my glass. "So, what did you find?"

Jack swallowed more bourbon and smacked his lips. "Some great stuff. Surprised even me, and I'm hard to surprise."

I was getting impatient, but I wanted to keep Jack cooperative, so I forced myself to smile. "I'll bet you are . . . the things you must've seen."

"Man, like you wouldn't believe. There was this one case—"

"I'd love to hear all about it, Jack, but some other time. When you don't have to work later, and we can really enjoy the bourbon."

He looked a bit disappointed, so I added quickly, "Besides, I want to see what you dug up. Sounds interesting."

"Oh, yeah, it is." He put down his glass and picked up one of the folders.

CHAPTER THIRTY-TWO

"First, Kingman." He opened the folder and started thumbing through it. "He's dirtier than I thought. Lots of sharp business deals, some borderline illegal, a few definitely illegal."

"But he's never been charged with anything?"

"No. Apparently commonwealth's attorneys have investigated him from time to time, and a source told me that the FBI looked him over once. But he's been too slick—or maybe just too lucky—to get caught actually breaking the law."

That information didn't really surprise me. It just confirmed what I'd thought about Kingman. "He'll be caught eventually and probably do some jail time."

"Maybe. Unless he can hire some crafty lawyer like you and get out of it."

"He's not likely to hire me." I let it go at that. "Did you find anything to indicate he'd been involved in drug dealing—not selling himself but bankrolling a dealer?"

Jack frowned. "No. Apparently the FBI thought he might be engaged in money-laundering, but none of my sources said anything about drugs. Why do you ask?"

"Oh, just a rumor I heard."

That Jack, who was a damn good investigator, hadn't found anything to corroborate Justine's story about Kingman and Davis didn't mean the story wasn't true, but it did make me wonder. If Kingman hadn't played a role in Bella's death, that meant . . . something I didn't like to think about.

I decided not to worry about that right now—I had plenty of other things to worry about. Such as keeping myself out of prison. "What else did you find?"

"He likes to play high-stakes poker in house-run games. Commercial, land-based poker is illegal here, of course, but no one is likely to prosecute it."

No, no one was. Gambling on cards was a Virginia tradition as old as betting on horses, and a prosecutor would just look foolish trying to make a case against it.

"But somebody might want to prosecute this other thing."

"What?"

"Kingman likes hookers. He likes to screw them and then beat them up. He pays a lot more for the second part than the first."

"Where? Not around here."

"No. Northern Virginia and Washington, D.C."

"You sure about this?"

Jack looked hurt. "Of course I'm sure. I wouldn't tell you otherwise." He flicked through the documents in the folder, pulled out an eight-by-ten photo, and handed it to me. The photo showed a young, light-skinned African American woman. She would have been attractive but for the black eye, cut lip, and purplish bruises on her face.

I looked at Jack. "He did this?"

"Yep, about a week ago. She probably looked worse then. But she's in the life, so presumably she knows what's she doing. She charged me a hundred dollars just to take the photo."

"You've got her contact information?"

"Yeah. Why?"

"In case I need her to testify against him."

"For what? There won't be any divorce now."

"No, but you never know what else might come up. Just the threat of her testifying or otherwise exposing him could be useful."

"Could get her killed too."

"You think he'd do that?"

"Yeah, I do. That's the part I didn't get to yet. He had a guy iced—so I was told."

"By whom?"

"By a guy who said he knew the guy who did it. My contact said it was a few years ago. Somebody was standing in the way of a deal Kingman wanted to do and wouldn't take money to get out of the way. So Kingman got him out of the way—permanently. Cost him ten thousand, but that was less than he'd offered the man to let the deal go forward, so he came out ahead."

"He took a big risk."

"Maybe not so big. He used a professional, not some amateur who'd have screwed it up. His guy made it look like a hunting accident. Apparently no one suspected it was anything else."

I felt a chill. I remembered that incident. To put up an office building, Kingman had wanted to buy some residential lots and tear down the houses on them. Old houses but none historically important. He'd offered the owners fair, even generous prices, but one owner wouldn't sell. He was a man in his sixties, a widower, and his family had lived in the house for generations.

To echo Jack's words, the man hadn't wanted to move, so Kingman moved him. Moved him into the cemetery after a supposed hunter no one ever identified put a rifle round in the center of the man's blaze-orange vest. Not knowing what else to do, the authorities had called it accidental death caused by a person unknown and had closed the file.

The man's only child, a son, had sold the property to Kingman then, and he'd been able to put up the office building he wanted. It was a well-designed, expensive-looking building—I'd been in it a few times—but I never knew it cost a man's life.

"Anything else on him?"

"One minor thing—he likes to bug people."

"Bother them?" I was confused for a moment, but then I got it. "Oh, you mean with electronic bugs. Listen in on them."

"Yeah. He worked in an electronics store when he was a teenager and picked up the habit then. Apparently he's gotten pretty good at it—and that's coming from someone who knows how to do it himself."

I'd wondered that morning whether Kingman might have bugged Justine or hacked her phone, and Jack's comment confirmed my suspicion. That was probably how he'd discovered our scheme. Then it occurred to me that maybe Kingman had bugged me too.

"Jack, has Kingman bugged this office?"

He raised he eyebrows. "Your office? Why would he do that?"

"Because he's an asshole. And hates me."

"Hates you? Why?"

"Let's just say he has his reasons. Can you see if he's planted anything here?"

"Okay, if you want me to."

First Jack checked my desk phone, my computer, keyboard, and monitor, and everything else on the desk. Next he checked the two lamps on the credenza and looked behind the pictures hanging on the wall. Finally he got on his hands and knees, grunting, and crawled around the office, looking at the electrical outlets and the undersides of the furniture.

The whole thing took several minutes. Then he stood and dusted off his trousers. "I don't see anything, Pete. That doesn't mean there can't be a bug or even a camera here, but if there is one, it's well hidden. I'd have to bring in a sweeping device to be certain. Want me to do that next week?"

I thought about that. If Kingman had eavesdropped on Justine some way, he wouldn't have needed to bug my office. And there was no evidence he'd done it anyway, so I was probably all right in that regard.

"I'll let you know. Thanks. Now what did you learn about Justine?"

I thought Jack paused when I referred to her simply by her first name, but he didn't say anything about it. He put down Kingman's file and picked up the other one.

"There wasn't as much to find on her, but I turned up a couple of things."

I was getting impatient again. "Such as?"

"She says she has a degree in art, but she never graduated from college. Apparently she was a big party girl and flunked out."

That didn't surprise me. Justine had been smart and talented, but she hadn't seemed like the type to apply herself to anything other than getting what she wanted.

"A couple of years later she spent six months in prison."

That did surprise me. It was hard to imagine Justine, with her elegant look and aristocratic air, wearing prison clothes and walking the yard with rough women off the streets.

"For what?"

"Passing bad checks. She'd go to a strange town, open a bank account with fake IDs, and buy stuff, jewelry and luggage mostly, that she'd pawn in some other town. She got away with it for a while, but finally the law caught up with her."

That was a side of her I'd never seen. But I guess I should have imagined it possible if she was willing to kill her husband, abuse or no. Or more precisely, talk me into helping her kill her husband.

When I didn't say anything, Jack asked, "Does that surprise you?"

"Yes. I wouldn't have guessed that about her."

"Nobody would. She turned herself into someone else when she came here and then married Kingman."

"I suppose so." I wondered whether I would have stayed away from Justine if I'd met her in her former life. Maybe. But maybe not. She was like candy—not good for you but hard to resist.

"There's more."

I waited.

"She was married once before, in her late twenties. Like Kingman, the guy was quite a few years older than she was."

"And?"

"He died. The cops thought—still think—she killed him."

CHAPTER THIRTY-THREE

"Killed him? How?"
"They think she shot him but made it look like suicide."
"His prints on the gun?"
"Yeah, just his."
"Gunpowder residue?"
"A little. Not as much as you'd expect but some. The cops think she rubbed her hand on his afterward."
"Did he leave a note?"
"No. They don't always, you know. His friends said he'd been depressed, most likely because he and Justine were having problems, but that doesn't mean much. Lots of depressed people don't kill themselves."
"Did she have an alibi?"
"Yeah. A friend of hers said she'd been at the friend's place. That was kinda weak, but nobody could prove anything different."

I thought about what Jack had told me. Could Justine really have done that? Sure, she'd plotted to kill Kingman, but he'd given her good reason. Hadn't he?

Or—and the idea froze me—had Justine given herself that black eye? I'd heard of a few cases where women had supposedly done that or something similar. Hardly anyone believed a man who said his woman had marked herself up to make him look bad. And of course hardly any women would do it.

But maybe a few would. And maybe Justine had been one of those few.

Then I thought of something else. I don't know where the idea came from, and it seemed crazy, but maybe I was acting on instinct.

"Jack, who was her friend?"
"Her friend? You mean the one who alibied her?"
"Yes, that one."
"Let me see." He paged through his notes. "I think it's in here somewhere." He paged some more. "Yeah, here it is—some Hispanic chick. Maya Martínez."

I got even colder then. As cold as I've ever been in my life.

When I didn't say anything, Jack looked at me. "Does that name ring a bell?"

I quickly debated whether to tell Jack. I didn't want him to know more about Justine and me than he needed to. On the other hand, he might have some more information that would be useful to me.

"Yes. In fact, I met her. Earlier this week—she was with Justine."

"She was here? In town?"

"Yes. Probably still is. She said she was thinking of moving here." Jack paused. "Quite a coincidence, isn't it? Her being here right when Justine is killed?"

I started to speak, then stopped. "What do you mean 'killed'?"

"Just what I said. 'Murdered,' if you want to be exact."

"You don't think it was an accident?"

Jack snorted. "Hell, no. That boat was Kingman's toy, not hers. Oh, she went out on it some but always with him. Never by herself."

"How do you know?"

"My guy on the force told me. They've already established that. It wasn't hard to do." I didn't want to ask the question, but I had to. "So what do they think?"

"Right now they don't know what to think. If Kingman didn't have a solid alibi, they'd probably think he did it, but four solid citizens swear he was with them in an all-night poker game in Tappahannock."

Justine had said he was going to be home that night, and he probably had been—early in the evening. After he'd drugged Justine and put her on the boat, it would have taken him less than an hour to drive to Tappahannock.

"Maybe he had it done."

"Maybe. That does happen from time to time. But what about motive? Why would he have wanted to kill her?"

I couldn't think of a reason. With that prenup a divorce wouldn't have cost him all that much, so if he wanted her out of the way, divorce would have been a much simpler and safer way to go.

"I don't know. But then who does know what goes on inside a marriage—I mean, other than the people in it?"

"Amen, brother. I've seen enough cheatin' hearts to learn that lesson five times over."

"So, like I said: maybe he had it done."

"The police will look into that possibility, but I'm pretty sure they'll find something else."

Again, I had to ask. "Such as?"

"A lover—her lover. Some guy who was having an affair with her and got really mad about something she did. Or maybe wouldn't do—such as divorcing Kingman. He must've gotten so mad he decided to end her . . . and then did it."

I thought about that. I'd been her lover, but I didn't think anyone could prove it. And I certainly hadn't planned to kill her—that was on Kingman. So maybe I was safe. Kingman couldn't expose me without exposing himself.

Suddenly I felt a lot better. But that lasted only until Jack said, "What do you think about that theory, Pete?"

"Uh, well, maybe. Who knows?"

He gave me a look of skepticism mixed with . . . what? Pity, I guess you could call it. "Someone knows. And that someone better hope no one else finds out."

CHAPTER THIRTY-FOUR

That was all the information Jack had, so I thanked him and he left. After the door closed behind him, I sat there for a long time, thinking some more. I fixed myself another drink and sipped it slowly, watching the shadows move even more slowly across the floor.

When I'd finished the drink, I rinsed out the glasses and put them and the bottle away. Then I locked the office door behind me and walked to my car.

I went to the boat and put on nicer clothes—khakis, a golf shirt, and loafers. "Country club casual" for my dinner with Sally.

Then I bought some supplies for my dad and a bottle of good wine. I drove out to my dad's trailer and "visited with him," as we say in the South, for about an hour. He was just the same as the last time I'd seen him—unshaven, red-eyed, and a little hungover.

"Have you had anything to eat today, Dad?"

"What? Oh, yeah. I had something out of a can."

"That's it?"

"I don't need to eat much. I don't do anything but sit around here."

"I'll be happy to take you to lunch or dinner sometime. It would do you good to get out and see folks. Larry Robinson even said he'd pick up your tab at his place."

"Yeah, but I'd have to get cleaned up. Shave and such. Too much trouble." He looked at me closely. "You're dressed up for a Saturday. Going somewhere?"

"Uh, dinner with Sally Carruthers. You know, the police chief's daughter."

"Don't know her, but I do know the chief. I've had a couple of run-ins with him over the years."

I'd heard about them, mostly from Dad. Several speeding stops back when he drove more. One potential reckless driving charge he'd bargained down to simple speeding. Fortunately, no DUIs.

"Where you taking her?"

I didn't want to say, but there was no good way to avoid it. "She invited me to her house."

He laughed. "Then I'd say she don't know what she's getting into. But I have a good idea what you want to get into."

I'd never been comfortable talking that way with my father, and I wasn't now. He must have noticed the look on my face. "Oh, come on, boy, don't be so prissy. There's nothing wrong with fu . . . uh, making love to a woman if she wants it."

"We're just friends, Dad."

"Sure, it always starts like that. Your mom and me were friends before we started dating and then got married. And where would you be if we hadn't?"

There was no way to answer a hypothetical like that. So I just said, "I know, Dad," and left it at that.

And I did leave soon after, putting some money in the drawer as I always did. He seemed to think he'd offended me—he hadn't—so he said, "Thanks for stopping by, Pete. I'm always glad to see you."

"It's no trouble. Somebody's got to take care of a crazy old sailor like you."

He smiled. "That's right—somebody does. Looks like you've got the job."

He reached out to shake, something he seldom did with me, and I took his rough, brown hand. His grip was like iron, so firm it almost hurt although I knew he didn't want it to.

He looked into my eyes. "I'm proud of you, Pete. I want you to know that."

I was surprised, almost shocked. He'd never told me that before. I'd always thought he was disappointed that I hadn't joined the military, especially given that after college I could have gone in as an officer. Not that the grizzled old chief had much use for officers—he didn't. But I know he would have been proud to have me be one.

"Thanks, Dad. I appreciate your telling me that."

He flushed beneath his farmer's tan and pulled his hand back. "Just don't get a swelled head about it and make me wish I hadn't." He grinned to take some of the sting out. "Now you better go if you don't want to keep your lady waiting."

There was still plenty of time—it was only about five-thirty—but to me a suggestion from my father was the same as an order. I almost said, "Yes, sir." What I actually said was, "Yes, I probably should. Well, goodbye, Dad. See you again soon."

"Bye, son."

As I got in my car, I saw him still standing there, watching me go. I waved at him, and he moved his hand in reply, making a short, tight arc.

Then I drove away.

CHAPTER THIRTY-FIVE

I didn't want to arrive at Sally's early, so I stopped to put gas in the car. To kill time, I washed the front and rear windows and even the side windows, making a thorough job of it. Then I checked the oil and saw that I was half a quart low. I had a bottle of motor oil in the trunk and would have gotten it out, but another car had just pulled in behind me, and the expression on the pimply face of the teenage attendant said he wanted me the hell out of there.

To kill the little extra time left, I took a long route to the house and got there at 6:35. I parked in the two-car driveway, grabbed the bottle of wine, and went up the low steps to the porch. The polished oak door had a bright brass knocker that matched the equally bright brass kick plate. But there was a bell next to the door, so I pressed that, and Sally opened the door right away.

"Hi, Pete."

Her smile was dazzling, so I smiled back. "Hi."

"I hope you didn't have any trouble finding me."

That seemed an odd way to put it, but I just said, "No, it wasn't hard."

"Good. So please come in."

She stepped back and I went inside. She was wearing a short summery dress, light yellow with blue trim that matched the blue of her eyes—blue like her father's but as warm as his were cold. Her dark-blonde hair was pulled back into a ponytail—I'd rarely seen it down like that—and her scent, subtle but noticeable, was that of a spring garden.

"You look very nice, Sally."

"Thanks. I like getting out of those dark suits when I can."

"One of the downsides of our profession, I guess."

"Perhaps our penance for having chosen it."

I'd never heard her say something that philosophical, and I didn't know how to respond. I dodged by holding out the bottle of wine. "Here. I bought you this. Sorry it isn't chilled."

She took the bottle. "That's no problem—half an hour in the freezer will do it. Anyway, I thought you might like a cocktail before dinner."

"That sounds great."

She led the way to the dining room, where bottles, glasses, and an ice bucket sat on a sideboard. She gestured toward them. "Please help yourself."

"All right. May I fix you something?"

"I'll have whatever you're having."

"Bourbon with a little water okay?"

"Sure. That's what I drink with my dad when he's here."

While I made the drinks, she carried the wine into the kitchen, from which wonderful odors were emanating. Then I took the drinks in there and handed one to her.

"Cheers," I said, clinking her glass.

We drank, and a thought struck me. "You know, I think that's only the second time I've seen you drink. The first was the bar association's holiday party last year, and then you had only one, as I recall."

"Oh, so you're counting my drinks, are you?"

"No, it's just unusual to see you do it. I know you and your father are careful about not drinking in public."

"We have to be. There's always someone watching and waiting for us to slip up."

"Like Caesar's wife, huh?"

"Pardon me?"

"Julius Caesar said his wife must be above suspicion. He used that as an excuse to divorce her."

I shouldn't have referred to divorce—the memory was still raw for her. Sally put down her drink and turned to the stove, where three of the four burners held pans.

To cover my faux pas, I said, "Everything smells great. What are you cooking?"

"Oh, nothing too complicated. Sautéed shrimp and scallops with angel-hair pasta. Green peas with pearl onions. And I made a salad."

"It sounds complicated. Of course, anything that doesn't come in a can is complicated to me."

She smiled at the joke. "I like to cook, and it's nice to have someone to cook for."

"Well, a home-cooked meal will be a real treat for me. I haven't had one in . . . ." I started to say 'years,' but then I remembered that dinner at Justine's place. It was just last week but already seemed like years ago. "Quite a while," I finished lamely.

"Then I hope you enjoy this one."

"I'm sure I will. Can I help you do anything?"

"Just keep me company while I finish up."

"That I can do." I had some more of my drink. I wanted to ask if she knew any more about Justine's death or the investigation into it, but I knew she wouldn't tell me anything she shouldn't, and in any case that topic wouldn't make for good dinner conversation. I cast about for some safe subject.

"How's Rusty? Have you been riding lately?"

"No, not in a week. Just too busy. But I've promised myself to take him out tomorrow. He needs it, and so do I."

"Good."

That pretty much exhausted my store of safe conversation, so I fell silent, watching her cook. Sally seemed comfortable with silence for a couple of minutes, stirring and tasting things and adding bits of spice here and there. As she did, I tried to cover by taking long, thoughtful sips of my drink, trying to give the impression that I was savoring the whisky while I was really just standing there numb, wondering if I'd made a mistake by accepting her invitation.

The good smells got even better. She slowed her movements and looked over at me. "Everything is just about ready. Want to open the wine?"

"Sure."

She took the wine from the freezer. When she handed the bottle and a corkscrew to me, she looked into my eyes. "Is everything okay, Pete?"

"What? Uh, yes, everything's fine."

"You're very quiet."

I tried to make a joke of it. "They say there's a first time for everything."

She smiled. "Okay, but you seem a little nervous. You needn't be—no matter what some of your clients may have told you, I don't bite."

I forced myself to smile in return. "I'll try to remember that." Then I busied myself with opening the wine while she put the food onto plates.

When she was finished, she carried the plates into the dining room, and I followed with the wine bottle. "Here, Pete, you sit at the end of the table."

That surprised me a little but gave me the chance to say something. "Don't you know that the person who sits there always gets stuck with the check?"

Sally laughed. "Maybe most of the time but not tonight."

She put her plate in front of a chair next to mine, and I held the chair for her as she sat. "Thanks. It's nice to see there are a few gentlemen left."

"Who says I'm a gentleman?" I took my seat and unfolded the napkin that matched the place mats.

Apparently she took the question seriously. "I do. And other people I know."

"Probably not everyone you know."

"Well . . . ." She hesitated before adding, "You do have something of a reputation with the ladies."

"Like I'm some sort of player, huh?"

She put her napkin in her lap. "I guess so."

"That's an exaggeration. I've dated different women, sure, but this is a small town and people like to gossip. You know how it is."

"Do I ever."

"I hope you don't pay any attention to that kind of talk."

"As little as possible."

"Good."

I poured some wine for each of us, and we began eating. The food was excellent, and I told her so. Sally thanked me without making a big thing of it—not saying that preparing the meal had been "nothing at all" or asking something like "do you really think so?" I liked that, and I wondered how her ex could have been stupid enough to lose a woman like her.

Then I realized I was in no position to call someone else stupid. Not considering the fix I was in—one I had no idea how to get out of.

CHAPTER THIRTY-SIX

I knew I wouldn't be able to talk much over dinner, so I tried to cover by asking Sally questions about her job. She answered the first few, keeping her remarks general, not revealing any confidential information, and not complaining. In fact, she had an air of ironic detachment from her job, something that surprised me because I knew she took her work seriously.

Then she said, "So—finally—we were able to dispose of that case. But let's talk about something else, okay? I like to leave work at work and not let it interfere with my personal life. Don't you?"

"Sure, when I can. Clients can be rather demanding at times."

"Oh, I know. I just have one client, but it's pretty big—the Commonwealth of Virginia."

I was able to chuckle at that one, and she smiled.

"Plus," she continued, "mobile phones don't make it any easier to get away from the job once in a while."

"I know. That's why I left mine in the car."

"Good. And I turned mine off so we wouldn't be disturbed."

I switched to family then, asking about her father.

"Dad's fine, just working too much as usual. This Justine Kingman thing won't help any."

I tried harder than I ever had at any poker game to keep my face blank.

"I try to make sure he eats right and takes a day off once in a while, but it isn't easy. He's stubborn . . . like someone else I know."

She looked at me then, waiting. I couldn't pretend I didn't know whom she meant. "You think I'm stubborn?"

"Only about as much as a mule. Not that I've known many mules."

"What makes you say that—the part about my being stubborn?"

"Oh, lots of things. The way you negotiate plea bargains for one thing. You always seem to get more from me than I thought I was prepared to give."

"Just trying to do my job."

"I know." She hesitated. "And then . . . well, you never asked me out, so finally I had to do the asking." She waited again, perhaps wondering if she'd said more than she should have.

"I'm glad you did. I've just been so busy lately that I haven't had much time for a social life."

"Uh huh." She didn't seem to believe my rather feeble excuse, but she didn't pursue the subject. Instead she talked about books she'd read lately, movies she'd seen. That was safer ground, and I did a little better in carrying my part of the conversation.

She was still talking more than I was, so I finished my food first. Then I poured both of us more wine and sipped it while she took her last few bites.

"That was really good," I said again. "I didn't know you were such a great cook."

"Hardly great, but I'm glad you think so. I like to cook, and I like to see people enjoy the food."

"Since you did all the cooking, let me clean up."

"Thanks, but you're my guest. I'll get to it later. Why don't we go into the living room and finish the wine? Or would you like some coffee?"

"No coffee for me, thanks." I knew I'd have a hard enough time sleeping as it was.

"All right. If you'll take the wine, I'll go get dessert."

I took the bottle and glasses into the living room and put them on the coffee table in front of the sofa that faced a big bay window. The sky had turned purple with twilight, and there were only two table lamps on, so the room was evening-dark.

I picked up my glass and sipped some wine as I walked around room looking at the pictures on the walls.

Sally had a couple of original oils by a local artist whose work I recognized. The paintings showed views of the bay—one in sunshine and one in rain. Both were well executed, I thought, but for some reason I liked the rainy-day picture better. Maybe it just matched my mood that evening.

An antique cabinet held some china but also three framed photographs. One showed Sally and Rusty, her standing next to his head and holding his bridle. She had a happy smile on her face. Another showed Sally and her father sitting in the stands at some sports event—a UVA football game judging from the autumn-weight clothes people had on and the prevalence of orange and blue.

The third photo was a studio portrait of a couple with a small child. The man was Sally's father about thirty years younger, and the woman must have been Mrs. Carruthers although I'd largely forgotten what she looked like. Sally seldom spoke of her. Once or twice Sally had alluded to her mother's long, slow death, and I could tell that the pain was still there, so of course I never mentioned her.

The child was Sally. She wore a short white dress that looked meant for church and was in keeping with her father's dark-blue suit and her mother's lighter blue dress with white trim. All three of them were smiling happily, but Sally's smile had something mischievous in it too, something that suggested she wasn't quite the little angel the photographer wanted her to be.

Well, angels were probably boring, I thought, although I'd never met one. And it didn't look as though I was going to—in this life or the next.

Sally brought in the dessert on a tray—two dishes of peach cobbler with vanilla ice cream. They looked delicious.

"How did you know?"

"You told me once. You said your favorite dessert was your grandmother's peach cobbler. She used to make it for you when you were a kid and spent your summers with them in Norfolk."

"You remembered that?" I didn't remember the conversation myself, but we must have had it. All the details were correct.

"Sure." Sally set the tray on the coffee table and looked up at me. "Why wouldn't I?"

"It seems so trivial."

"I just thought it was worth remembering, so I did. Here, let's sit down and relax."

She sat on the sofa and patted the cushion next to her, then watched as I sat in an armchair near the far end of the sofa. "Hmm, I told you I don't bite."

"This chair just looked so comfortable—and it is."

"Uh-huh." She handed me one of the desserts, having to scoot toward me to do it.

"Thanks. You really went to too much trouble."

She picked up her wine glass and took a long drink from it. "I hadn't thought so. But you're welcome. I'm glad you enjoyed it."

I sensed from her manner, not to mention her "didn't think so" remark, that the spell, or whatever you want to call it, was broken. The evening hadn't turned out as she'd hoped, and she was disappointed.

I was sorry I had disappointed her. Sitting there in that comfortable, tastefully decorated living room after a delicious dinner prepared by a smart, attractive, and desirable woman, I realized what I'd given up. I'd let my lust for Justine, my love of money, and my dream of being a big man in a little town blind me to something far more valuable—being happy with a woman I could love, one who could love me as I was.

And now it was too late. I'd done something so wrong, so evil, that I could never forgive myself. I could learn to live with the guilt, I supposed, but

I wasn't going to risk ruining Sally's life by making myself part of it. I liked her too much for that.

A sort of heaviness settled over the room, like the air before a thunderstorm, and we ate the dessert almost without speaking. Sally had some more wine, but I left my glass alone.

After I'd eaten about half of the cobbler and ice cream, I put my dish on the tray. "Thanks, Sally. That was great, just like everything else. I don't deserve to be spoiled like this."

She put down her dish and looked at me. "Why do you say that?"

The question caught me off guard. "Pardon me?"

"Why do you say you don't deserve a good dinner? It's almost like you think you don't deserve to be here, with me."

"Well, I, uh—"

"It's a damn good thing we don't get what we really deserve—that would be awful. People aren't angels—trust me, I know—and all of us have some sins to hide. I'm sure yours are no worse than the average person's. Mine, for instance."

I looked back at Sally, her face a little flushed, her eyes wide. "It's hard to believe you have anything to hide."

"As I said, all of us do."

She stood then and came over to me. Without speaking she reached down and took my hands in hers. She pulled me toward her, and I stood. When I came out of the chair, I was very close to her, so close I could feel the heat from her skin.

She looked into my eyes for a long moment. Then she kissed me, and I realized I'd never been kissed by a woman before. Not really—not the way Sally kissed me. She put her whole heart and soul into it, kissing me as though she wanted to fuse the two of us together.

I'd enjoyed kissing Justine—enjoyed it a lot—but Sally took the act to an entirely different level.

I tried to kiss her back the way she was kissing me, but it was no good. It was too late for that—at least it was too late for me. Maybe Sally could find someone worthy of her. I hoped so.

When the kiss ended, Sally pulled her head back and looked at me. "This isn't going to work, is it?"

I didn't insult her intelligence by pretending I didn't know what she was talking about. "No. I'm sorry."

"Is there someone else?"

If she'd asked me that the day before, I would have had a hard time answering. But that Saturday night the answer was clear. "No, there isn't."

She sighed. "Well, I guess it's me then."

"Yes, it is you—you deserve someone better, someone who can really make you happy."

"And you can't? Why don't you let me be the judge of that?"

"Because I like you too much to hurt you. And I seem to end up hurting every woman I get involved with. I don't want that to happen to you."

For a long moment she didn't say anything. The room got so quiet I heard a clock ticking. And I heard her breathing—long and slow as if she was trying to calm herself.

Then she said, "All right. I can't change how you feel—or how I feel. But now that you know how I feel, give it some thought. And if you change your mind . . . at least now you know where I live."

"Thanks, Sally. You've always been a good friend to me, and I hope you'll still be one."

"Sure, Pete. I'm still your friend."

She managed a weak smile then and followed me to the front door. With my hand on the knob, I turned to look at her. "Thanks again for dinner—it really was wonderful."

"You're welcome. I'm glad you like my cooking."

She left a lot unsaid with that remark, but I knew the best thing I could do was leave, so that's what I did. She closed the door behind me, and I went down the steps.

When I reached the walkway, I thought I heard sobbing from behind the door. But it was a thick, heavy door, and I couldn't be sure.

CHAPTER THIRTY-SEVEN

I wanted to go to a bar and get drunk. Very drunk. So drunk that I'd forget how Sally's face looked when she said, "Well, I guess it's me then." But I knew there wasn't enough liquor in the world for that.

So I went to the boat. By the time I got there, night had fallen, and the world was black except for the stars and a few lights here and there.

I changed into shorts and a T-shirt, fixed a drink, and sat in the cockpit, cursing myself for being so stupid. Stupid enough to get involved with Justine and agree to her crazy scheme that had backfired so badly. Stupid enough to put myself in a position where I couldn't have Sally, a woman who could make me happy. One kiss had shown me that.

Then I wondered whether I was as stupid as Kingman thought I was. No, I thought, nobody could be that stupid. And Kingman had underestimated me. He didn't know what I was capable of. I hadn't known myself until the last couple of days.

But now Kingman and I would find out together.

As I was sitting there, thinking my deep thoughts and, frankly, feeling sorry for myself, I heard someone walking down the wooden pier toward my boat. A woman, judging from the quick steps and heel taps.

I waited, and she came into view. Maya Martínez. She was reading the boat names as she came down the pier, and she stopped when she came to *Law Lass*.

She looked up from the name on the transom to where I sat in the cockpit. "Mr. Scarcelli, is that you?"

"Yes, it's me. 'Pete,' remember? Are you looking for me?"

"Yes, I am. May I come aboard?"

"Sure." I put down my drink and went over to her. She was wearing a short white skirt and a blouse that looked flame-red in the dim light. I glanced at her shoes—some sort of open-toed platform things not meant for boats.

"You may want to slip off those shoes—I don't want you to fall."

"All right." She slid her small feet out of the shoes and lost a couple of inches in the process.

"Hand me your purse and then cross over."

"No, I will keep it." She slid the strap over her head so that it crossed her chest and held out her hand.

I took it and held tightly as she stepped from the pier and over the gunwale onto a cockpit cushion. The skirt hiked up to the top of her thigh, but for once I acted like a gentleman and didn't look. Although I got the impression she wouldn't have minded if I had.

She sat on the cushion and looked up at me. "I am glad I was able to catch you here, especially on a Saturday night."

The Spanish accent seemed stronger than when we'd met. Her eyes were red, and she looked as if she'd been crying. It wasn't hard to guess why. "How did you find me—the boat, I mean?"

"You were right: this *is* a small town. Everyone seems to know everything about everyone else."

Not quite everything, I thought. "Is there something I can do for you?"

"Yes. You can tell me about Justine."

I paused, sensing danger. "Uh, what about her?"

"About—say, is that a drink?" She gestured toward my cup.

"It was. I'm about due for another. Would you like one?"

"Yes, please." She lifted the purse strap over her head and set the purse next to her. "If you don't mind."

"Not at all." I went below, fixed her a drink, and refilled mine. When I came back on deck with a cup in each hand, she was pointing a gun at me.

Judging from the other guns I'd seen when I took my Glock to the target range, her shiny little pistol was a semiautomatic, maybe a .32. If she fired it—and she couldn't miss at such short range—the pistol wouldn't make much noise but certainly would make a hole in me. The first bullet might not kill me, but the second probably would. And Señora Martínez looked both comfortable and confident with that gun.

I stood still, trying not to appear scared. After a long moment I said, "I guess you can hold the drink with your other hand."

She smiled at that, a little grimly. "Yes, amigo, I can. But you sit down first so you're not tempted to try some tricky move."

"I don't think I know any tricky moves."

"Then do not try to learn one now."

I sat, put one drink beside me, and sipped from the other. "Would you like me to hand you yours?"

"No, not yet. Let us talk first."

"Okay. What about?" I was pretty sure I knew, but it was a natural question.

"I think you know. About Justine—how she died."

"She drowned." Actually, she had probably burned to death before going into the water, but with that gun pointed at me, I didn't want to say so.

"Yes, she drowned. But why?"

"She was out on a boat, and it caught fire."

She shook her head, making her hair sway. "You know that is only part of it. You are not stupid, and do not treat me as if I am. She was on the boat, but she was not supposed to be."

A chill ran through me. If this woman knew that, she must have learned it from Justine. I was sure Kingman hadn't told her. No, it had to have been Justine—who'd promised me not to tell anyone.

"What makes you say that?"

"Because I know what you and Justine planned to do. Why did you change your mind?"

I could see that acting innocent wasn't going to work. "I didn't."

"I told you I am not stupid. It is clear what happened. Did Kingman offer to pay you? I do not know him well, but I know him enough to imagine what he is capable of."

"You don't have all the facts. An important one is that I didn't know Justine was on the boat. I just knew someone was, and I assumed that it was Kingman. It was supposed to be him."

"Do you really expect me to believe you could not tell Justine from him?"

"Not lying in a berth and covered with a blanket in a pitch-black boat."

"Pendejo! You should have checked." She raised the pistol, and if there'd been enough light, I probably would have seen her finger tighten on the trigger.

"I wish I had, but I can't undo what happened."

She paused. "No, none of us can do that. But I can do something about what happened."

Starting with me, I thought. "You said you knew Kingman was supposed to be on the boat. How did you know that?"

"Justine told me. We are—were—very close, like sisters. She told me about you and what you were planning—the two of you."

I didn't say anything. Now at least two people knew about the plot—Kingman and Maya. And how many more people had either of them told? I had no idea.

"It did not surprise me. She had hated him for some time. And who could blame her? The way he beat her and was cruel in other ways. Sometimes . . . sometimes a man's words hurt more than his fists."

"Sounds like you know what you're talking about."

"Oh, I do. I know all too well."

"I'm sorry."

She gestured dismissively with the gun. "That does not matter now. What matters is how to avenge Justine's death."

From someone else "avenge" might have sounded funny or at least odd. But coming from this woman, with her white-hot anger barely under control, the word seeming fitting.

"I can help you."

"I do not need your help."

"Yes, you do. Unless you plan to charge in and shoot Kingman and have the police pick you up an hour later."

"I do not care about the police."

"You will if they catch you. Let's figure out a way to get Kingman without getting caught ourselves."

"You seem to assume I am going to let you live."

With her gun aimed at me, I hadn't assumed that at all. But I sensed an opening, and I took it.

"You can worry about me later. Right now the thing is to make Kingman pay for what he did to Justine."

She seemed to think about that. Then she lowered the gun but didn't put it away.

"All right. I am listening."

CHAPTER THIRTY-EIGHT

We talked for over an hour, coming up with various ideas about how to kill Kingman and discarding them one by one. After a while Maya did put the gun away and accepted her drink—but only after having me taste it first.

"You're not very trusting, are you?"

"No, I am not. If you had lived my life, you would not be trusting either."

I wanted to ask her about her life, but I knew that wasn't the time, so I didn't do it. What I did do was suggest a way to get at Kingman that I thought might work.

She didn't like the idea at first, and I certainly didn't blame her. But I pointed out how we'd be using one of Kingman's weaknesses against him, and she saw the logic of that. I also pointed out that if the plan worked as intended, no suspicion would fall on either of us. She liked that aspect too.

"So, are you in?"

She tilted her cup and had the last of her drink. "Yes. I have no better idea, and yours may work. It will not be the first time I have done something like that."

"Good. Now would you like another drink?"

"No, thank you. I am tired and want to sleep." She looked at me. "You should sleep too after . . . ."

She didn't have to finish the thought. Black visions from the night before kept running through my head like a horror movie that had no ending. I hoped that sleep would banish them, but I didn't think that was going to happen.

She fished in her purse, pulled out a card, and handed it to me. There was just enough light for me to make out her name and telephone number. There was nothing else on the card.

"That's my mobile number. Don't call unless you need to."

"All right."

Maya stood and I steadied her as she stepped up onto the pier. She slipped into her shoes as I came up after her. I walked her to her car, a little sports job that looked fast even standing still. I would have predicted that she'd drive something like that, but I'd have gotten the color wrong. It wasn't the bright red I would have guessed but rather as black as the night.

Or as black as her hair, cut to brush her rather broad shoulders. As black as a raven's wing, I thought, and then wondered what had made me think of that.

I also thought about kissing her, but I didn't think she wanted me to, and the memory of Sally's kiss was too fresh. I knew it would be a while, maybe a long while, before I could enjoy kissing someone else.

So I just held the car door as she gracefully tucked herself inside, inevitably showing a lot of leg in the process and not seeming to care whether I looked. I looked all right but was careful not to stare.

Then she drove away, and I watched the red taillights until they vanished.

☐ ☐ ☐

Because the medical examiner said he couldn't release Justine's remains before Wednesday, her funeral was scheduled for Thursday. I spent the interminable interval sleepwalking through the days, trying to appear as normal as possible.

Kris knew something was wrong, but after a few failed attempts to draw it out of me, she gave up and kept her distance, talking to me only when necessary. I ran into Sally a couple of times, and she was polite but distant with a look of hurt in her eyes. I didn't know what to say to her, so I said almost nothing.

I didn't run into Maya and I didn't call her. We'd decided to put our plan in motion after the funeral, so there was no need for us to speak until then.

Chief Carruthers and a state cop came to see me Wednesday afternoon. I went out to shake hands and invited them into my office.

The state cop was a tall, slim African American man in a well-cut poplin suit, snow-white shirt, and a beautiful gold-and-blue tie. He looked like a Brooks Brothers model. He showed me his badge from the Virginia Bureau of Criminal Investigation and said he was Senior Special Agent Reginald Baxter.

The chief also showed me his badge, a gesture that seemed silly to me until I realized he wanted to go by the book in front of the BCI man.

They sat and looked at me the way cops always do, as though they knew all of my secrets. They didn't, of course, but they wanted me to think they did, and I had to fight against that feeling.

Baxter must have been an expert with murder investigations, because, after he pulled out a small notebook and a gold pen, he did most of the talking.

"Did you know Justine Kingman, Mr. Scarcelli?"

"Yes. Not socially, not really, but she asked me to handle her divorce."

"Did she say why she chose you to be her lawyer?"

"I think it was because her husband had used most of the other lawyers in town at one time or another, and they were conflicted out."

He made a note. "How far along were you with the divorce?"

"Not far. We'd met a couple of times to discuss her options and what she needed to do to prepare for a divorce proceeding, but that was about it."

"Did her husband know that she wanted a divorce?"

"I'm not sure. I don't think so."

"Do you know Mr. Kingman?"

"Just from seeing him around town. He's a prominent businessman in Kilmihil."

"But you've never done any legal work for him?"

"No, as I said, that's probably why Mrs. Kingman asked me to represent her."

He made some more notes. "Did Mrs. Kingman like boating?"

"I have no idea. We never discussed it."

"Do you know why she might have taken their boat out alone on Friday night?"

I knew why she'd been on the boat, but I also knew better than to speculate and draw more questions about what had happened, questions that I wouldn't want to answer. "No."

He looked at me then, and so did Chief Carruthers, both of them waiting for me to add something. I didn't say anything, and the silence stretched out uncomfortably—which is undoubtedly what they wanted.

"You don't know why she might have done it?"

"No, I don't. Mr. Kingman might, of course. I suppose you could ask him that question."

"We already have," Baxter said, his impassive but slightly cruel expression not changing at all.

"Look, Pete," the chief said, "if you know anything at all about this business, you should tell us. Things will go a lot better for you if you do."

I looked straight at him and tried not to let my eyes widen the way liars' do. "I would, Chief, if I knew anything more than what I've told you."

He studied me a moment. "Okay, Pete, I hear you. But I'm sure you agree it seems damn odd that she'd take that boat out alone late at night—or anytime, for that matter. Apparently, the boat was more his than hers, and she never went out on it by herself."

They were silent again, watching me, and I thought I had to say something. It would have seemed unnatural not to. "Well, people can do strange things when they're under stress, and there's nothing more stressful than going through a divorce. Not much anyway."

"That's true," the chief said, and I wondered if he was thinking about Sally's divorce. Based on what I'd heard—and not from Sally—it had been a tough one.

"So you think that was the reason?" Baxter asked. "Stress caused by the pending divorce?"

"I said I don't know. Maybe it was stress. Maybe she just decided to go for a boat ride. I don't know."

"You seem a bit defensive, Mr. Scarcelli." Baxter's expression didn't change, but his eyes bored into me.

"No, I'm just . . . affected by Mrs. Kingman's death. That's all. It's horrible for anyone to die the way she did."

"Yes, it is." The chief shook his head. "A terrible way to go. Not that there are many good ones."

There was a long silence then. I'd thought about offering them coffee earlier, but now I was glad I hadn't, because I wanted them out of my office as soon as possible. But I couldn't ask them to leave—that would have made them dig all the harder.

Baxter looked over his notes and made one or two more. Then he looked at Chief Carruthers, who shrugged slightly and turned back to me.

"Do you have anything to add, Pete?"

"No, sir. I've told you all I know—I realize it wasn't much."

"Okay, if that's all you know, then that's all you know. We'll keep talking to folks and see if we can't get to the bottom of this thing."

"Yes, sir."

Baxter put his pen and notebook away. Then they rose, and I did likewise. Neither of them offered to shake hands again, and I didn't either.

I walked them to the front door. Kris, typing away at her computer, pretended to be oblivious to their presence.

I said goodbye and watched as they got into the chief's car. As the car pulled away I closed the door and started back toward my office.

"What did they want?" Kris blurted out the question as though she knew she was overstepping to ask it but couldn't help herself.

"They're investigating the death of Justine Kingman."

"Oh. Yes, that was terrible, wasn't it?"

"Of course."

"Surely they don't think you had anything to do with it?"

"They're just talking to anyone who knew her and might be able to shed some light on what happened. Why she went out on their boat that night."

"I've wondered about that myself. Do you have any idea?"

I turned toward the coffee pot. "No, I don't."

I got some coffee and went back to my office. I closed the door and felt myself shaking as if from cold.

But it was a hot August day. Hotter than hell, as the saying goes.

CHAPTER THIRTY-NINE

When Kris went to lunch on Thursday, I changed into the dark-blue suit I kept with my three other suits and some dress shirts and ties in an antique armoire in a corner of my office. I'd had a sandwich delivered, and I ate it while sitting at my desk and staring into space, trying not to think.

I'd been trying that all week and having very little success. Almost none, in fact. And I hadn't been able to sleep much. I kept having bad dreams filled with fire and water and screams—the screams of a woman. The dreams woke me, and I found myself lying in the berth, covered in sweat.

I wished I'd never met Justine or at least that she hadn't asked me to help her with anything, not her divorce or . . . the other. But of course it was too late for that. Too late for anything except what Maya and I planned to do to Kingman.

What we planned to do that weekend. After Justine's funeral, which I'd been dreading but felt I had to attend.

And apparently a lot of other people thought they needed to attend. The funeral was held at "my" church: Saint Stephen's, a semi-Gothic red-brick building that was the largest Episcopal church in town.

When I got there, the place was packed. I'd thought it would be, and I'd told myself I needed to get there early to be assured of finding a seat.

But something held me back—fear, I guess, of Kingman or God or both—and I didn't arrive until right before the service started. I looked around, didn't see an empty seat anywhere, and started to leave. But Sally saw me and, after seeming to hesitate the barest moment, waved me over.

She was sitting near the back with her father, both of them in black suits. Most women have at least one black suit, but most men don't, and I was surprised to see the chief in one. Then I realized that, as a prominent government official in our town, he probably had to go to a lot of funerals.

As I approached, she tapped her father's arm and pointed my way. He nodded at me and slid a few inches down the pew. Sally also slid down, and there was just enough room for me to squeeze in next to her at the end of the pew.

"Thanks," I said, careful to keep my voice low.

"You're welcome." She said it a bit primly, which wasn't like her but told me she hadn't gotten over the way our dinner ended. I was sorry she felt that way, but there was nothing I could do about it.

I leaned forward and turned my head slightly. "Hello, Chief."

"Hello, Pete."

He didn't add anything, so I didn't try to have a conversation. We couldn't have anyway, because the service started then.

The funeral was simple and fairly short. Kingman didn't speak, and there didn't seem to be any other family present. The only layperson who spoke was a woman who'd volunteered with Justine at the local arts center. She said some nice things about Justine, especially what a fine artist Justine had been, but, although somber, she clearly wasn't overcome with grief.

I remembered seeing Justine's painting of the bay as viewed from an old wooden dock, and as I thought of that, I had to wipe my eyes. When I lowered my hand, I felt Sally looking at me strangely.

There were some hymns, including my favorite, "The King of Love My Shepherd Is," which we sang to the lilting Irish melody "St. Columba." I don't sing well, but Sally does, and hearing her pure, clear voice carrying the beautiful tune made my eyes wet again.

The rector spoke after we sang that one. He kept his homily general, saying the usual things about life and death and "dust to dust." He referred directly to Justine only a few times, indicating that he hadn't known her well. Still, he was a professional and did a good job of offering comfort to the grieving.

Except me. I was grieving, but I wasn't comforted. Of course there was no way anyone could comfort me, not after that horrible night on the boat. The only thing that might offer me some comfort would be seeing Kingman's eyes right before Maya and I killed him.

The funeral ended soon after that. After thanking the congregation for coming, the rector invited everyone to a reception at the country club.

Because Sally and her dad and I were sitting toward the back of the church, we were among the first to walk outside. The air was warm and humid but the sky had clouded over, so the afternoon wasn't blazing hot.

Chief Carruthers said he had to get back to the office. He gave Sally a peck on the cheek, shook hands with me, and left, his face inscrutable as always.

I asked Sally if she was going to attend the reception.

"No, I don't think so. I didn't know Mrs. Kingman well, and I don't really know Mr. Kingman either." She paused, looked away, then looked back at me. "Are you going?"

I hadn't planned to, but Sally's question made me wonder if it would seem strange if I didn't go. As I was trying to decide what would be the right answer, Maya walked up to us. Despite the cloudy sky, she was wearing dark glasses.

"Hello, Pete." She took the glasses off, and I saw that her eyes were red and the tissue around them was swollen.

"Hello. Maya, this is Sally Carruthers. Sally, Maya Martínez. Justine Kingman introduced us a few days ago."

The two women said the usual polite things and looked each other over the way women do when meeting for the first time. Maya was wearing a black dress that was just a bit too short, too tight, and too low-cut for a funeral, and I saw Sally's eyes narrow as she took inventory.

"So, you were a friend of Justine's?"

"Yes, a good friend. We had known each other many years and were very close."

"I'm sorry for your loss."

"Thank you." She attempted a smile but didn't quite make it. "I will miss her very much."

Sally has good taste and proved it then by not adding anything to what she'd said. In the ensuring silence I felt I should say something, so I ventured, "She was lucky to have such a good friend."

"Thanks. As I said, we had known each other for a long time—practically my whole life,"

"Oh, you were childhood friends?" Sally asked.

"Yes. I am a few years younger than she is—or was—but we were both children when we met."

"Then you were almost sisters."

Maya gave her a probing look. "Yes, we were that close." She paused, glancing from Sally to me. "And you two—have you known each other long?"

The question seemed odd, but perhaps Maya wondered if I'd been two-timing Justine with Sally. I hadn't been around Maya much, but I'd already learned how direct she could be. Pointing that gun at me, for example.

Sally paused, and when I didn't say anything, she spoke. "For several years. Right, Pete?"

"Four years, I think. We met through work. We're both lawyers."

"Oh, I see. Then you are sort of brother-in-law and sister-in-law."

I think she meant it as a joke, a pun, but Sally didn't laugh, and I noticed she still had that narrow-eyed expression. "No, it's not like that at all. Is it, Pete?"

I thought of the kiss she'd given me—the one I knew I'd never forget. "No, not like that."

"I see. Interesting." Maya drew the word out like a cat purring.

Sally looked at her a moment longer, then turned to me. "Well, I've got to get going, Pete."

"Do you need a ride somewhere—back to the office maybe?"

"That's where I'm headed, but I have my car. Dad and I drove separately."

"Okay."

"Actually, Pete, if you do not mind, I could use a ride." Maya's expression was blandly innocent. "I have a car too, but I do not know how to get to the reception."

"You could get directions on your phone," Sally said. "It's not hard."

"Maybe not for you, but I am not good at things like that."

"Oh, I'm sure you're good at . . . other things." Without waiting for an answer, she kissed me on the cheek, gave Maya a final glance, and walked away.

When Sally was out of earshot, Maya said, "She is attractive—at least outwardly. Is she your girlfriend?"

The question implied I'd been cheating on Justine or helping her only for money—maybe money and sex—but I was in no mood to argue about either possibility.

"No, just a good friend. As Sally said, we've known each other for several years. Plus, being in the same profession, we have a lot in common."

"I think she is interested in you—romantically, I mean."

Maya had hit the mark, but I tried to pretend she hadn't. "Oh, I don't think so. She could do a lot better than me."

"Perhaps, but a woman can tell about these things."

Although that "perhaps" could have been insulting, she didn't say it in a snarky way, and I could tell she'd simply sized me up and come to a logical conclusion. Sally could do better than to choose me, and both Maya and I knew it.

"Maybe so, but it's a moot point because I'm not interested in Sally—not like that."

She studied me for a moment. "All right. If you say so. Now, can you please take me to the reception?"

That answered the question of whether I was going myself. "Sure. Let's go."

As we walked toward the parking lot, Maya put her dark glasses on and took my arm in hers. She walked very close to me all the way to the car.

CHAPTER FORTY

The reception at the country club was almost as crowded as the church had been. I had to park at the far end of the lot but at least found the shade of a massive old oak tree. Then we crunched over the bed of crushed oyster shells to the flagstone walkway that led to the front door.

Food was laid out on tables in one room, and there was an open bar in another. Neither Maya nor I wanted anything to eat, so I got her the glass of white wine she requested and got a bourbon for myself.

I knew several people there and said hello as they came by, introducing Maya as a long-time friend of Justine's. They reacted as you'd expect, the men more cordial than the women, who studied Maya the way Sally had and probably drew the same conclusions.

Trying to be subtle about it, I glanced around the room a few times, looking for Kingman. I didn't see him but knew he had to be around somewhere. Finally, as the crowd began to thin, I could see through a double doorway into the next room, and there he was.

The room was the club's library. Books, many of them beautifully bound, filled the built-in shelves and covered the large table in the middle of the room. A big picture window took up much of the far wall, and although I couldn't see through the window because of the people standing in front of it, I could imagine the lovely view of the emerald-green lawn sloping down to the water glinting like silver in the bright sun.

Kingman stood in front of an enormous stone fireplace, a semicircle of people around him. Behind and above him hung an oil portrait of the man who'd had the original house built—Brigadier General Rufus Belmont Wallingham, Confederate States of America.

Trey Marston, the lawyer I'd recommended to Justine, was a Civil War buff and had told me about Wallingham. Trey said "R.B." was a young cavalry officer in the Army of Northern Virginia who worked his way up through the ranks and got promoted to brigadier a few months before the war ended. Called "General" for the rest of his life, he became wealthy speculating in real estate and, despite outliving two wives, was randy enough in his sixties to bed a married woman three decades younger than he was.

Unfortunately for the general and the woman, her husband caught them in the act. But fortunately for them, they were in the general's house, so the husband was an intruder and R.B. thought he was justified in shooting the man, an act he accomplished without even leaving his bed. Some of the local citizens thought that putting not one but three pistol bullets into the husband's chest was perhaps taking self-defense a bit too far, but the husband had been armed with a shotgun and was not well liked around town, so the general wasn't prosecuted.

The general married the young woman and had two children with her, ending up with a total of nine, several of whom had descendants living in Kilmihil. The general's eldest son wasn't good with money—like me in that respect, or vice versa—and eventually had to sell the house and the land around it to a group of prominent citizens who, in 1896, got together to establish a country club.

And here it was. And there Kingman was, standing beneath the portrait of old R.B. in Confederate dress gray, the general's dark eyes peering out of his stern face and seeming to disapprove of what he saw in each succeeding generation. I had heard that a few of the club's members had proposed taking down the portrait and replacing it with something less likely to offend people who objected to anything related to the Confederacy, but so far they hadn't prevailed. Still, they probably would someday. The world changes, and only a fool refuses to acknowledge that fact.

I couldn't help but think of how appropriate it was for Kingman to be standing where he was. He probably had more in common with the general than anyone else in the room—hell, anyone else in town.

I was about to tell Maya that Kingman was in the library, but she was already staring at him. And he was staring back. As I turned toward him, his gaze shifted to me, and his dark-gray eyes, already cold, hardened into balls of ice and sent a chill into me even at that distance.

"We must go talk to him," Maya said, touching my arm.

"No, we don't. I have nothing to say to him, and he has nothing to say that I want to hear."

"But I have something to tell him."

"Write him a letter."

Maya gave me a scornful look. "Are you a coward? Justine said you are not, but perhaps she was wrong."

"Don't bait me. I simply have nothing to say to him."

"Not even that you know what he did? We should let him know that we know—put some fear into him."

"Why? Then he'll just be watching for us to do something."

She made a dismissive gesture. "Ah, you know nothing of revenge. You may not be a coward, but you must be—what is the word?—naive."

"Maybe I am. But I still have nothing to say to him."

"Then suit yourself."

She walked toward the library, and I watched her take three steps before I started after her. I knew I was crazy to talk to Kingman, but I couldn't help myself. Maybe it was Maya's example. Maybe I thought I owed it to Justine. Or maybe I was just filled with anger at Kingman and all he stood for.

Whatever the reason I caught up with Maya and walked with her through the door and toward Kingman. The crowd had thinned further, and only four or five people still stood around him. Maya hung back a little, giving them time to say their goodbyes.

I knew some of them, including the last person to linger, an attractive, fortyish woman who'd divorced her husband a year earlier. Dressed much as Maya was, she stood close to Kingman, looking up at him with a sympathetic expression that needed only a little encouragement to turn into a smile. I bet she could already imagine herself married to him and living in his big house, redecorating it to get rid of any vestige of Justine.

Well, good luck, sister, I thought. *He's not going to be around to marry anyone.*

The woman glanced at us and realized we were waiting for her to leave. Her mask slipped, making her annoyance plain, but she realized it would be rude not to give us a chance to express condolences to Kingman. So, taking one of his hands in both of hers, she said something to him so softly we couldn't hear it and then turned to go.

Kingman watched her walk away in her tight, black dress and then looked at us, hard, as we stepped over to him.

"Hello, Maya." He didn't smile when he said it. "It's been a while."

"Yes, Ben, it has."

He didn't seem to know what else to say to her, so he turned to me. "Scarcelli, you bastard, what the hell do you mean by coming here?" He kept his voice down, but there was anger in it and maybe some surprise that we'd been brave enough—or stupid enough—to show our faces at the reception.

As I thought about which of several obscene insults to give him, Maya spoke first. "I have something to tell you." Her voice, low and thick with emotion, reminded me of a snake's hiss.

He shifted his angry glare from me to her. "What?"

"We know what you did to Justine."

"I didn't do anything to her."

"Yes, you did. You put her on that boat."

"The hell I did. I was with several people that evening and didn't go home that night. The police have talked to them and are satisfied that I had nothing to do with Justine's death."

"You drugged her and put her on that boat. That's the only way it could have happened."

"I did nothing of the kind. She must have taken the boat out by herself."

"She would not have done that."

"Well, if she didn't, I can think of someone who knows something about boats and could have taken it out."

He looked back at me with those hard, cold eyes. "Someone who knows boats and apparently knew my wife. Knew her the way the Bible says. Right, shyster?"

My hands curled into fists, and I took a step toward him, but Maya put out an arm to block me. "If you had treated her right, treated her as she deserved, she would not have sought out other men."

"Who are you to judge me?"

"Someone who loved her—as obviously you did not."

"Get the hell out of here!"

"We will go, but . . . ." She paused, making him wait for it. "We know what you did, and we will see you again."

"Are you threatening me, you little spic?"

Maya smiled, showing sharp little teeth as white as bone. "Is that the best you can do? I have been called much worse. No, I am not threatening you—I am simply telling you what is going to happen."

"That you'll see me again? Big fucking deal." He made a dismissive gesture toward me. "That goes for you too, scumbag. I know what you can do to me—nothing. Because I know what I know about you."

I started to raise my fists then and would have hit him as hard as I could, but Maya said, "No!" loudly enough for the few remaining people to turn and look at us. As I considered whether to obey her, she said, "Later" in a lower tone and blocked me again.

There was a long, tense moment when none of us spoke. Then Kingman said, in a guttural voice I'll probably hear again in hell, "Get the fuck out of here—both of you."

When we didn't move, he stepped close to us and added, "Now."

I looked at Maya to see what she'd do. She waited another few seconds and then stepped back. She looked at me and tilted her head toward the door, and I followed her out of the room.

I could feel Kingman's eyes boring holes into us all the way.

CHAPTER FORTY-ONE

We got in my car and headed back to the church. I could tell that Maya wasn't in the mood for conversation, but something was bothering me, and I had to bring it up.

"Look, what's this all about?"

She glanced at me, then stared through the windshield, saying nothing.

"Come on, tell me."

She still didn't anything.

"Damn it! Tell me. I think you owe me that much, considering the risks we're taking."

She turned back to look at me. "What do you want to know?"

"Why you've got this hard-on to go after Kingman. Why you're so determined to avenge Justine's death."

"What difference does it make to you? You have your reasons for going after him, and I have mine."

"Yes, but you know what mine are. I think I deserve to know yours."

She thought about that for several seconds. "All right, I will tell you. Justine was my half-sister."

It took a moment for that to sink in. "Your half-sister?"

"Yes. We had the same mother but different fathers."

"You don't look much like her."

"Please do not be stupid. A lot of full siblings do not look alike, much less half-siblings."

"So after your mother had Justine, she married someone else and had you?"

"No, it was not like that. Our mother was married to Justine's father but had an affair with my father."

"Did Justine's father know you weren't his?"

"Yes. He and our mother had not been sleeping together for some time, so obviously I was not his child."

"How did he handle the situation?"

She looked over at me. "You really are naive, amigo. He handled it the way most men would—he divorced her."

"And she married your father?"

"No, he was already married, and his wife did not want a divorce, so our mother was left with two children to raise by herself. She had little money, and neither of the fathers would give her any. Justine's father had to pay child support, but that was barely enough to feed Justine much less me."

Maya paused, probably remembering what that time had been like for the three of them. "So our mother sent me to live with a cousin of hers in Mexico." She pronounced the last word "Méjico."

"That woman and her husband treated me like their own child, and it was simpler for me to take their last name."

"So how did you and Justine become close?"

"I was always very curious about my half-sister. I knew her only through holiday cards and occasional phone calls, but to me, a little kid growing up in a small town in Mexico, she was worldly and sophisticated. So when I was eighteen, I went to live with her."

She looked out the window, seeming to watch the world going by outside but probably seeing scenes from her past. "Our mother had been killed in a car accident a couple of years before—hit by a drunk with no insurance and no money, so Justine could not recover anything from him. She was having a hard time. She had dropped out of school after studying art for a while."

"And . . . then what?"

"She was using drugs and using men too—using them to pay for the drugs and everything else. Not that she had much. But she was not a streetwalker—more like an escort."

"Or a sugar baby?"

Maya frowned. "Yes, I think that is the term although I hate it. My sister was merely doing what she had to do to survive."

"She could've gotten a job."

"Doing what? She had no skills, only her beautiful face and body. And I was going to community college, so she had to support me as well as herself."

Maya didn't mention the bad checks, the pawnshops scheme, or the prison sentence that Jack Greese had told me about. I was sure she knew all that, but I didn't ask her. Instead, I thought about Justine.

I didn't agree that she'd had no other options, but who was I to judge? I hadn't been there, hadn't been faced with taking care of a teenager while dealing with a drug problem and hustling to survive. I decided that, actually, Justine had turned out rather well, all things considered.

"Obviously she got past all that somehow."

"Yes. I married young, at twenty, and got an office job, so I was able to help her then. My husband got transferred, and I didn't see Justine nearly as often after that. But she got off drugs and married one of the men she had been seeing. He was an older guy, divorced and lonely. He may not have known about . . . Justine's other friends."

"Or maybe he knew and just didn't care."

"Perhaps. In any event Justine used the marriage to improve herself. She learned to dress more tastefully and act and even speak in a more refined way. She finally read those art books she had bought in college, and she started painting—it turned out she had talent."

"Yes, she did. I've seen one of her paintings."

"I have one, a beautiful landscape with two young girls shown in the distance, sitting in the shade near a river. You can guess who the girls are."

"Yes, I can.'

Maya wiped her eyes with her hand. "So now you have heard the whole story. Her husband gradually became depressed—maybe he did know about the other men—and killed himself. That is when she came to Kilmihil, then married Kingman. And after I got divorced last year, I decided to move here to be near Justine."

I remembered what Jack had told me about how Justine's husband might really have died. With Justine dead, probably no one would ever know the truth of that. *But it doesn't matter,* I thought as I pulled into the church parking lot, *she's gone and I'm partly to blame. I know it, and I know Maya knows it too.*

I wondered what Maya had planned for me. I was sure I'd find out . . . after we took care of Kingman.

CHAPTER FORTY-TWO

The next morning Chief Carruthers came by again. I was keyed up about what was going to happen that night, so I'd closed my office door to keep Kris from noticing. She buzzed me to say that the chief was there and wanted to see me.

I froze. I literally couldn't move for a couple of seconds.

"Pete? Are you there?"

"Uh, sure, sure. Please send him in."

I had just enough time to squeeze my eyes shut and open them again, trying—probably without much success—to plaster an innocent expression on my face. Then the door swung inward, and I saw Kris in profile. She gave me a look that seemed puzzled, even worried, and then stepped aside to reveal the chief.

For an instant I imagined myself in an old Western movie, the bad-guy lawyer or businessman being confronted by the incorruptible lawman played by Gary Cooper. But it wasn't a movie, it was real life, and no director was going to call "cut" and tell everyone to take a lunch break.

I've thought many times since then how much better it would have been simply to tell the chief the truth. The outcome would have been much the same for me, but it would have been better for everyone else involved. Not for Justine, of course—it was too late to save her. But better otherwise.

I considered that option as I showed the chief to a seat and asked Kris to bring us both some coffee. Asking for coffee was mostly to buy time, to decide what I would or wouldn't say. That was a mistake—if I hadn't had the extra time, I probably would have told him the truth. But those few seconds enabled to me to fool myself into thinking that I had still had a way out, a way to save myself from the consequences of my actions.

God must have been shaking His head at me then.

The chief and I sat and talked about the weather until Kris brought the coffee. She'd fixed mine the way I take it, and she brought the chief his with cream and sugar on the side. He told her he took his black, so she gathered up those things and left, closing the door behind her.

Chief Carruthers drank from his cup and put it down. "That's good coffee, Pete. Thanks."

"Thank Kris. She makes better coffee than I do. I don't know what her secret is."

The chief studied me for a moment. "One of the first things I learned in this job is that everyone has secrets. That's what I want to talk to you about."

If I'd been cold before, I went to subzero then. I drank some coffee to give myself time to think. What was he after? Did he suspect I'd had something to do with Justine's death? He hadn't seemed to when he'd interview me before, but maybe he'd learned something since then.

But if he had, from whom? Surely Kingman hadn't told him about Maya. And she wouldn't have said anything to him—at least not until we'd carried out our plan. Even then she'd take care of me herself, not leave me to the law.

I couldn't think of anyone else. Maybe someone had seen me after all—either at the Kingmans' house or after swimming ashore. That didn't seem likely, but I couldn't rule it out.

Chief Carruthers was still looking at me, obviously waiting for me to say something. I didn't know what would be safest, so I tried a joke. "My secrets are really boring, Chief. Not worth your time." I laughed, and he smiled faintly.

"Oh, I don't know, Pete. You're a lawyer, so you must know some interesting secrets."

"Yes, but those aren't mine, and anyway they're covered by attorney-client privilege."

"Not secrets you learned from someone who's dead now. Justine Kingman, for instance."

"I was representing her in connection with her divorce—her prospective divorce—but that's all."

"Why did she want a divorce?"

"She was very unhappy."

"Why?"

I paused. "Is this conversation confidential?"

"Yes. Of course I can't guarantee you'll never have to repeat any of it in court. It depends on what you tell me."

"She said Kingman was abusive to her—physically as well as mentally."

"And emotionally?"

"Yes, that too."

"So was she seeing someone else—another man? Women who want a divorce often are."

"She never told me about anyone else." Technically true but a lie nevertheless.

"Hmm." The chief sipped his coffee thoughtfully. "Do you think she would have if there had been another man?"

"Maybe. I can't say for certain. She wasn't my client very long, not even long enough for me to file her case in court." I'd started to tell him that I hadn't known her all that well, but that would have been difficult to say convincingly. I decided to try what seemed like a logical question. "Why do you ask?"

"If she'd been having an affair and Kingman found about it, that would give him a motive to kill her."

"I heard he has an alibi."

"He does. But he's a rich, powerful man. It's not that hard to hire someone to commit murder. I've known it to be done several times. Although it is hard to find someone who can do it and leave almost no evidence as in this case."

"You think that's what happened?"

"I think that's what could have happened. That's why I wanted to ask you about Justine, whether she was seeing anyone."

"Well, as I said, if she was, she never mentioned it to me."

The chief studied me again, longer this time. "And you—the two of you, I mean—were you close?"

I wondered how to answer that. Of course we'd been close—we'd been lovers, and if there's no way to get closer than that.

No, wait, I thought. There is one way: you can plot with your lover to kill your lover's spouse. That brings you closer. So close that only the devil stands between you, and he's a slim, slippery fellow.

I knew that from personal experience.

"You can't avoid being close with a client you're representing in a divorce proceeding. You learn too much about that person, the spouse, and the marriage. You have to play psychologist to a certain degree. That's why a lot of lawyers don't want to handle divorce cases."

"So you're saying you were close."

"Yes—professionally speaking."

He paused. "Just professionally?"

"Chief, you know there are rules against lawyers sleeping with their clients."

"Yes, I do. And I also know that those rules are frequently broken. Let me ask you straight out, man to man: were you sleeping with Justine Kingman?"

I forced myself to look him in the eye and say, "No, I wasn't."

He seemed to weigh that answer for a few seconds, trying to decide whether I was telling the truth. At the time I thought I'd convinced him, because he nodded and said, "Okay. I'm glad to hear that. Both for your sake and for . . . Sally's."

She must have told him about our dinner, I thought. She probably hadn't gone into detail, but apparently she'd said something about it, and the chief knew she wasn't inviting every guy in town over to her house.

"She cares about you, Pete. You must know that."

"Yes, sir. We've been friends for a long time, and I think very highly of her."

I could tell that wasn't the answer he wanted, but I didn't know what else to say. I'd screwed up and lost Sally forever, and I just had to live with that. There was no point in pretending otherwise.

"Then you'll be careful not to hurt her, won't you?"

"Yes, sir. I certainly wouldn't want that to happen."

"Good." He waited a moment, making sure he had my full attention. "Just be sure it doesn't."

He left then. I walked to the front door with him, neither of us speaking, and opened the door, letting in some of the morning's hot humidity.

He turned to look at me, those steel-blue eyes impossible to read even so close. He hesitated a moment, then held out his hand. I took it and we shook.

"Remember what I said, Pete."

"Yes, sir. I will."

He nodded and stepped outside. I closed the door and started back toward my office. I glanced at Kris and could tell she was intensely curious about the chief's visit. I thought I should tell her something so she wouldn't build it up in her imagination and gossip about with her friends.

"Chief Carruthers is looking into Justine Kingman's death. He's talking to everyone who spent a significant amount of time with her in the last couple of we weeks."

"You don't know what might've happened to her, do you?"

"She was my client—our client—in the preliminary stages of a divorce proceeding. That's what I told the chief."

"Does he have any idea what happened?"

"I think he has some theories but no proof of anything yet. We'll just have to wait and see how things turn out."

"I guess so." She turned back to her work, saying as if to herself: "That poor woman . . . what a horrible way to die."

Yes, it was. No one knew that better than I did.

CHAPTER FORTY-THREE

When Kris went to lunch I called Maya on my new phone, the burner I'd picked up right after hammering the first one to pieces. I'd given her the number when I'd dropped her off at her car, so she knew it was safe to answer the call.

"Hello."

"Hi, it's me."

"Yes, I know."

Hmm, I thought. *Pretty frosty.* Okay, she didn't have to be my best friend.

"The chief came to see me."

She didn't say anything.

"He thinks that maybe Justine had a lover and Kingman hired someone to kill her for that."

There was more silence, and I thought that perhaps she still wouldn't say anything, but then she spoke. "The chief is a smart man."

"Yes, he is."

"So is Kingman. He did not even have to hire someone to do it."

That stung—as I'm sure she meant it to—but I couldn't argue with her. She was right. And I guess that made me dumb . . . or at least dumb enough to fall into Kingman's trap.

Too dumb to save Justine.

But that night we were going to do something about the situation. That night we were going to spring a trap on Kingman.

"Did you call him?" I asked.

"Yesterday, just as we agreed."

"And?"

"I told him about the file and what is in it. I said Justine had been afraid he would find it, so she gave it to me for safekeeping."

"Did he believe you?"

"I think so," she said. "I read a few things to him—names, dates, places. He did not dispute any of it."

"Did he want to know where Justine had gotten the information?"

"Yes. I said she had hired a private investigator."

"I'll bet he asked who it was."

"Yes. I told him I did not know, but he guessed."

I waited, hoping she wasn't going to say what I was pretty sure she would say.

"He said, 'Greese, right? I played dumb and just repeated that I did not know."

Kingman's "lucky guess" bothered me. How had he come up with Jack's name so quickly? There weren't a lot of private eyes in our area, but Jack certainly wasn't the only one. It seemed unlikely that Kingman could have hit on the right person immediately.

So it wasn't a guess. Kingman must have found out somehow that Jack was looking into his business dealings. But not before Jack reported to me, giving me the information Maya had read to Kingman over the phone.

There was nothing I could do but plow ahead. "Then you mentioned the money, right?"

"Yes, fifty thousand dollars. He said he would have it for me tonight."

Maya's offer to give Kingman the file wouldn't have been plausible unless she'd asked for payment. "And he agreed to meet at his house—just the two of you?"

"Yes."

That was a relief. I'd wondered whether Kingman would insist on meeting Maya at some neutral site—maybe a dark parking lot somewhere. But I was sure he planned to double-cross her some way, and he probably thought he could do that better at his house than anywhere else.

I was surprised to find that I didn't care about the money—Maya could have it all, assuming Kingman really came through with it. I'd been tempted by the money Justine had offered me—true, a lot more than fifty thousand—but the only thing I cared about now was going to see Kingman and doing what we planned to do.

"Good. I'll pick you up at ten," I said.

"Why so early? I am not supposed to show up until midnight."

"Because I want to make sure that he's really alone."

"Oh. Okay, then." She paused. "If you want, you could come over earlier. I will fix us something to eat, and we can . . . relax."

Said the spider to the fly, I thought. I didn't think Maya would try for me until we were done with Kingman, but I wasn't going to bet my life on it.

"Thanks, but I've got some things to do. I'll see you at ten."

"All right," she said. "Be careful until then."

"You too."

"I am always careful, Pete. You should know that by now."

Without giving me a chance to respond, she said goodbye and hung up. I put the phone down and sat there, listening to the silence. Then I did some thinking.

Kingman wouldn't have liked learning that Jack was looking into his business affairs and . . . other things. He wouldn't have liked that at all. And he'd killed people who'd seriously displeased him. Jack had given me some proof of that, and Justine's death was more proof.

Or, as Chief Carruthers had suggested with respect to Justine, Kingman could have had it done. He could easily afford to hire a hitman. I'd heard there were former military men in the Norfolk-Virginia Beach area who advertised themselves as "soldiers of fortune" and were available to kill for a price.

I picked up the phone and called Jack. It rang several times, and then I got his answering machine. I hung up without leaving a message.

Then I scribbled a note to Kris, telling her that I might or might not be back that afternoon. I grabbed my keys, locked the front door behind me, and left.

CHAPTER FORTY-FOUR

I'd been to Jack's place only once, taking him home after a late-night poker game when he was too drunk to drive. That had been a few months ago—and of course it was graveyard-dark at the time—so I wasn't sure I could find the place. But after driving around the neighborhood for over half an hour, I came across what I thought was his house.

Townhouse, actually, an end unit in a row of houses that were so similar as to be almost but not quite identical. Most of them, Jack's included, needed painting and other attention that they weren't getting and apparently hadn't gotten in a while. Jack had once owned a single-family home in a fairly nice neighborhood, but after two divorces he was probably lucky to be able to afford this place.

The lawn looked like Jack—overgrown, almost shaggy, but just respectable enough to get by. The front door looked like Jack too—no name or number but three deadbolt locks, one on top of another and all warning would-be intruders to go somewhere else.

I rang the bell and waited. Nothing. I rang it again. Still nothing.

I glanced back at the car parked closest to the house. I didn't know what Jack was driving at the time. To help him with tail jobs, he traded cars a lot, but they were common models, all inconspicuous and souped up under the hood so that they were faster than they looked.

The light-gray, four-door sedan I saw could have been Jack's, but there was no way to tell for certain. So maybe he was home and maybe he wasn't.

I went around to the back. A wooden fence ran around the back yard, and the gate was—Jack being Jack—locked on the inside. The top of the fence was just low enough that I could climb over it, so that's what I did.

Then it hit me—I hadn't heard Jack's dog.

Jack had a German Shepherd named Max, and he said the dog was better than any home-alarm system on the market. I remembered how the dog had barked and scratched at the front door as I pulled Jack up the steps and fumbled with his keys. I thought some of the neighbors might come out to complain, but maybe they were used to the harsh yapping.

Max had shut up that night as soon as he saw Jack, but he should be barking now because Jack wouldn't climb his own fence. But he wasn't barking.

Maybe Jack took him for a walk, I thought. Maybe. But something told me that wasn't it—something hard and cold like a ball of ice at the pit of my stomach.

I eased up to the back door, wishing I'd brought my Glock with me. The screen door was slightly ajar, the aluminum handle broken, and I pulled it open, moving slowly so the hinges wouldn't squeak. The back door was also ajar, and I could see that it had been jimmied, perhaps with a crowbar. The fresh, raw wood to the left of the two deadbolts was chewed as if by some wild animal eager to get at what was inside.

I didn't want to go in Jack's house. I wanted to turn around and walk away. No, run away. Not look back.

But I forced myself to go in. I'm still not sure why.

I gently pushed on the door, standing as far back as I could. When I had the door about three-quarters open, I stopped and listened. I heard nothing. I waited for a full minute, but no sound came from the house.

I opened the door the rest of the way and stepped inside. The first thing I saw was Max. He was lying on the kitchen floor in a pool of blood so dark red it was almost black. The jagged hole in his chest showed me where he'd been shot. The size of the hole suggested he'd been shot at close range.

I could imagine Max barking furiously in the kitchen as someone jimmied the back door. That someone had apparently cracked the door and shot Max through the narrow opening, knocking him back to bleed out on the dingy linoleum.

Jack couldn't have been in the house then. If he had, he'd have come to see why Max was barking, and he'd probably be lying there next to his dog.

If I'd had any sense, I would have left. Maybe the shooter was still in the house. But there was no smell of gunpowder in the kitchen, and Max looked as though he'd been dead for a while.

I stood still and listened again. Nothing but the faint ticking of a clock on the wall. It was my fault if anything had happened to Jack, so I decided to see if he had . . . come home.

I slipped off my shoes, quietly found the largest knife in the kitchen, and tiptoed into the small dining room. Nothing was out of the ordinary except that someone had rifled through a stack of case files left on the table.

Had rifled through them quickly, it appeared. File folders and loose papers were scattered across the table and had fallen on the floor. I glanced at the folders and saw that most of them were labeled with the "last name, first name" of their subjects. I knew which folder the intruder had been looking for: "Kingman, Benjamin." That he—maybe she, but I doubted it—wasn't still there looking told me he'd found the folder.

And taken it with him of course.

"He" might be Kingman himself, but I doubted that too. Kingman probably wouldn't risk being caught doing what the intruder had done.

But . . . was there something else? As I slid my sock feet across the hardwood floor, moving closer to the little foyer, some instinct made the hair on the back of my neck prickle. I raised the knife—not that it was going to do me much good if the intruder was still around with his gun.

Bringing a knife to a gun fight. Smart—just like all the other smart things you've done since you met Justine.

I found him there in the foyer. He was crumpled on the floor, shot in the chest just like Max, but the killer had used at least two bullets on Jack. And unlike Max, he must have died quickly, because he'd bled very little.

Just to be sure, I touched his cheek with the back of my hand. Ice was never colder.

I could reconstruct how it had happened. The killer had forced the back door, where he was less likely to be seen than at the front door, shot Max, and then looked for the Kingman folder. As he was looking, Jack came home.

The killer had hidden in the dining room, let Jack get all the way in and close the door, and then shot him. Apparently he'd been willing to risk the noise of his shots—there weren't any neighbors on one side, and there was a good chance that during the day no one was home on the other. If he'd used a small-caliber pistol, there wouldn't have been much noise anyway.

I should have called Chief Carruthers and waited for him to arrive. That was my duty as an officer of the court. But he would have asked me a lot of questions I didn't want to answer—couldn't answer without incriminating myself. And I wasn't willing to do that. I thought I could still save myself.

Of course I was wrong.

CHAPTER FORTY-FIVE

I thought hard. What had I left prints on at Jack's house? Nothing but the knife, the door knob, and the door latch. I pulled out my handkerchief and wiped them off in that order.

Then I left, glancing around to see whether anyone was watching. I didn't see anyone, so perhaps no one saw me. I got in my car and drove away at a normal speed.

I figured I was a dead man. If Kingman had Jack killed because of what he knew, Kingman would certainly have me killed—I knew more than Jack had.

Was turning myself in the only way to be safe? Confess to the chief so that he'd lock me up? But Kingman might get to me even in prison. It's happened before. Lifers have little to lose from killing a fellow inmate.

No, the safest thing was to go through with what Maya and I had planned. I might have to deal with her afterward, but I'd take that chance. I'd already taken plenty, so one more wouldn't make much difference.

I didn't know what else to do, so I drove back to the office. I hadn't eaten lunch, but I wasn't hungry, not after seeing Jack lying there dead. Two friends of mine killed in just a few days, and I was responsible. Well, at least partly responsible. There was no way around that.

When I walked in, Kris looked up from her computer. She did a sort of double take and then stared at me.

"What's wrong, Pete?"

"What do you mean?"

"You're pale as a ghost. Did something happen?"

Just another murder. "No, nothing happened. Nothing's wrong."

"You sure?"

"Yes!" I snapped it out and instantly regretted my harsh tone. "Really, I'm fine. Just a little tired, that's all."

"Okay, you're the boss. But I think you should get some rest. You look like you've had a long week."

I gave her a weak smile, the best I could muster. "Yes, it has been a long week. Probably for you too. Why don't you knock off early, go have some fun?"

She glanced at the wall clock. It was only three-thirty. "There are still a couple of letters I need to finish."

"They'll wait 'til Monday."

She paused, looking at me again. "Pete, if there's something going on . . . I mean, if you're in some sort of trouble, you can tell me about it. You know I won't tell anyone else, and maybe I can help."

"Why would you think I'm in trouble?"

"Because I'm not stupid. I see—and hear—what goes on in this office. And I can figure what goes on outside it. Like with you and Justine Kingman, for example."

"She was just a client."

"Uh huh. She was a client but not just that."

"I think you have an overly vivid imagination."

"And I think you have a well-deserved reputation for chasing women. You couldn't resist a smart, good-looking woman, especially one with a lot of money, who was going through a divorce."

"As I said, you're imagining things."

"I don't imagine how you look at me sometimes. Like I'm an ice cream sundae. I'm surprised you haven't made a pass by now."

I didn't reply, letting her remark hang in the air. Sure, I'd been tempted to try to get Kris into bed, but I hadn't done it and was almost proud of that. I had damn little else of which to be proud.

After a few seconds she said, "I'm sorry. I shouldn't have said that. You haven't done anything out of line with me. It's just that I've heard some things, and I thought . . . well, it doesn't matter what I thought."

"There are people in this town who don't have enough to do, so they gossip a lot."

"I guess that's true." She paused again, biting her lip. "I meant what I said about helping you."

"I know."

"Okay. Then I guess I will take off—if you're sure about that."

"I'm sure. I'm going to leave soon myself."

She nodded and began shutting down her computer. I went into my office and sat, staring at the wall.

In a minute or two Kris appeared in the doorway. Instead of her usual smile she wore a frown, and her forehead was creased with worry lines.

"I just wanted to say goodbye."

"Thanks, Kris. Goodbye, and have a good weekend."

"You too." For a moment she looked as though she was about to renew her offer of help, but all she said was, "Goodbye, Pete."

She said it as if saying it for the last time, and I wondered whether it would be the last time. Maybe so.

After she left, the office was still and quiet. What was that phrase

Charles Williams used in a couple of his novels? "Intensely still." Yes, that was it. The stillness was intense, hanging over me like a heavy weight, making me almost afraid to move.

Of course, given what Maya and I had planned for that night, I had reason to be afraid. I wondered if Jack had been afraid, there at the end when he saw whoever had come after him. Jack was a tough guy, not afraid of much, but aren't we all afraid of death?

I was. I was honest enough, at least in that one thing, to admit it to myself. But I wasn't going to back out. I owed it to Justine—and to Bella—to go through with the plan.

I sat there, trying not to think but thinking anyway. Remembering the day Justine walked into my office in that white tennis dress, her face flushed from exercise, beads of sweat on her forehead. Her lovely forehead. Lovely like the rest of her.

But with evil on her mind. And in her heart—a heart that sensed I had enough evil, or at least weakness, in mine to help her. As I had helped her. Until I killed her.

If I'd had a gun at that moment, I think I would have put it in my mouth and ended everything right there. Sometimes I wish I'd been able to do that. But my pistol was on the boat, so I couldn't.

I sat there for a long time, watching the shadows inch up the wall as the sun lowered in the sky. I wanted to reach out and stop them, pin them in place so that time wouldn't pass. So that ten o'clock wouldn't come.

But I knew I couldn't do that. The only way to stop time is to stop yourself, and I'd already decided I wouldn't.

As I sat there, my stomach rumbled, and I realized I hadn't eaten anything all day. To have enough energy to what I had to do that night, I needed to get some dinner.

I thought about picking up some Chinese carryout and taking it to the boat, but then I realized it would be good for me to be seen in a public place somewhere. That wouldn't be a perfect alibi, but it would be better than nothing.

I decided to go to The Barge. It was one of my usual places, so there would be nothing out of the ordinary about my being there. I might run into someone I knew, but that would only strengthen the alibi.

I shut down my computer, picked up my briefcase (because that's what I always did), and plucked my coat from the rack. Then I headed for the front door, turning off lights as I went.

Darkness followed me.

CHAPTER FORTY-SIX

On the way to The Barge I stopped to gas up the car. I was thirsty, so I went into the shoppette to buy a bottle of ice tea. The man at the counter knew me by sight and spoke in a friendly way.
"Hot enough for you?"
"Yep—although I've seen worse."
"Me too. But it'll cool down after Labor Day. Say, how's your dad?"
"He's fine, thanks."
"What's he up to these days?"
"Not too much. Just enjoying his retirement."
"Nothing wrong with that. Looking forward to mine in a couple of years."
"Good for you."
"Next time you see him, tell him Bobby Slater said hello."
"I'll do that, Mr. Slater."
"And tell him he raised a polite son."
I smiled. "He'll be glad to hear that someone thinks so."
I gave the man a wave and left. As I walked back to the car, I wondered if I'd ever have a chance to give that message to my father.
By the time I got there, The Barge was about half full. The hostess gave me her practiced smile and, in answer to my question, said she could give me a table outside.
As we walked through the restaurant, I saw a few people I knew, none well. If we made eye contact, I nodded or waved but didn't stop to talk.
Everything was going exactly as I'd hoped ... until the hostess led me outside and I saw Sally.
She was with a man I didn't know, a good-looking guy, well dressed and about our age. They had drinks in front of them, but their menus lay on the table, so they'd probably decided what to order. They were smiling and chatting in a friendly way that suggested they were on a date.
Sally's dress confirmed it—black, hemmed above the knee, and cut just low enough for her pearls to lie against her smooth, lightly tanned skin. She looked lovely. Whoever the guy was, he was lucky to be having dinner with such a beautiful, smart, and charming woman.
I felt glad for Sally, glad that she was out on the town and obviously having a good time. But I felt sad for myself even though I knew I had no one else to blame for that feeling.

I turned my head so she wouldn't sense I was looking at her. The hostess showed me to a table that wasn't close to Sally's. As I sat, I looked at Sally again, and she didn't seem to have noticed me, so there was no need for me to go over and say hello.

I should have chosen a chair that would put my back to their table, but I didn't. Some voyeuristic compulsion made me sit sideways to them so I could glance at them once in a while. That brought me no pleasure—in fact, quite the opposite—but I kept doing it as their food arrived and they ate, still chatting pleasantly.

I had a martini before dinner and then another with my grilled fish with rice and asparagus—a light meal that wouldn't weigh me down later. I was finishing the fish when I sensed someone coming my way. I looked up and saw Sally and her date walking toward my table.

I stood and said hello to Sally, keeping my voice friendly but not overly warm. She kept hers the same way as she said hello and introduced her date. I can't remember his name—maybe Nathan something, a banker there in town. I hoped he realized he'd struck it rich with Sally.

She explained to him that we had known each other for several years and were often on the opposite sides of criminal matters. He smiled pleasantly enough, but his eyes were cold and gave me a hard look. I looked back at him, not caring what he thought.

Not caring about anything really at that point. Just marching down the road toward hell.

They stayed less than a minute. After they left, I sat and pushed the last bite of fish around on my plate for a while. I thought about ordering another drink but decided against it. I could feel the first two, but they'd only made me a little braver. A third might make me careless.

I paid the check and left a tip large enough for the waitress—a new person, one I didn't know—to remember me. Then I walked out to my car.

I checked the time—almost 7:30. Too early to go to Maya's and sit around with her while we made each other nervous about carrying out our plan. Plus I needed to get my Glock. The cool of the evening was settling in, so I put the top down on the car and then headed for the boat.

When I was about halfway there, I noticed that someone appeared to be following me. In the rearview I saw a pair of headlights that was never close but never quite went away. Maybe the other driver was just headed the same way I was. But I didn't think so.

Trying to find out, I drove faster but didn't lose those headlights. Then I slowed way down, but they didn't gain on me.

That answered it—somebody was following me. I thought I knew who it was . . . the same guy who'd gone to see Jack and left him lying the way I found him. A guy hired, undoubtedly, by Kingman.

I decided to lose him if I could. I probably couldn't outrun him—a professional hitman would have enough sense to drive a fast car—but I knew the back roads well. Probably better than he did, especially if, as seemed likely, he was from out of town.

I was coming up to a good place to try it. I sped up again, opening a sizeable gap between our cars, and switched off my lights. I looked for the narrow opening in the woods to my left and spotted it just in time.

Resisting the strong temptation to brake, which would have lit up my brake lights, I took my foot off the accelerator and slowed to a speed I thought—or hoped—would let me make the turn. I cranked the wheel hard, skidded some, and slid onto a narrow strip of cracked blacktop that probably didn't appear on some maps.

Tall pines loomed on both sides, so there was barely enough light to see the road. The shoulders sloped sharply down to twin ditches, so I knew I'd crash if I let a wheel go off the rough pavement.

But that would be better than ending up like Jack.

I maintained my speed until I was a hundred yards down the road. Then I slowed and risked looking in the mirror. Nothing but blackness.

So apparently the trick had worked. Whoever had been chasing me had gone on down the main road, leaving me there in the dark woods.

But what if he doubled back and found the side road? I did a careful K turn and headed for the main road, still keeping my lights off.

When I got there, I slowed to a crawl and edged up enough to look and listen both ways. Nothing. No car lights or sounds, nothing but the night sky shinning above me, the faint whish of the breeze, and the muted buzz of insects.

I pulled out on the road and drove back the way I'd come, staying right at the speed limit. I didn't want some cop to pull me over, wonder why I was pale and sweating, and ask me a bunch of questions I didn't want to answer.

I took a different route to my boat, hoping that the stalker didn't know where I was going. That seemed a forlorn hope—the location of my boat was certainly no big secret in our little town. But I had to go there—I had to get my gun. And then it would be time to leave for Maya's.

So a quick stop at the boat, hoping my friend wouldn't be there when I was.

CHAPTER FORTY-SEVEN

When I got to the marina, I parked in the darkest corner of the gravel lot, far away from my boat. I sat in the car for several minutes, looking out over the lot and the wooden piers beyond, trying to see anything out of the ordinary.

It appeared to be the normal scene. Two of the three pole-mounted security lamps were on—the third one had burned out a couple of weeks before, but the cheap, lazy manager hadn't gotten around to replacing it. In the pale, yellowish light they cast I could see a few cars and a couple of pickups that belonged to my fellow liveaboards.

It was darker out on the piers. Most of the boats lying motionless next to the pilings were dark, but dim lights shone through portholes here and there.

I didn't see anything unusual. But that didn't mean much—the guy could be anywhere. He could even be on my boat, waiting for me, gun in hand, the way he'd waited for Jack.

Then it occurred to me that the two situations were different. The shooter couldn't risk the noise of gunfire here. The sound of a shot would surely prompt one or more of the marina residents to investigate. No, he'd have to use a knife or a club, and that meant I might have some chance if he were on board.

That gave me a little hope for only for the few seconds it took me to realize that the hitman might have a suppressor. A gun enthusiast I knew—we have lots of them in Virginia—had told me they're not really "silencers" but do keep the sound of gunfire to a minimum.

That might be the real explanation for why he hadn't been worried about noise at Jack's place. If so, I wouldn't have a chance after all.

That was another risk I'd just have to take. Considering where I was at that point, one more wouldn't make much difference. And perhaps he wasn't on the boat at all. There was only one way to tell.

I slid out of the car and retrieved a flashlight from the trunk. The light wasn't much of a weapon, but hitting someone with it would be better than using only my hand.

I walked slowly toward my boat, scanning from left to right and back again and then glancing behind me. I was the only thing moving in the parking lot.

When I got to the boat, I stood on the pier, listening as I had before going aboard Kingman's boat. I heard the same thing I had heard then: nothing but the usual sounds of wind and water and the nighttime.

I waited two or three minutes and still heard nothing unusual. But whether the hitman was there or he wasn't, I couldn't wait any longer. If he hadn't already come to the boat, he would soon. And I wanted to be gone when he did.

I stepped down onto the boat, switched on the flashlight, and played the beam over the main hatch. It was closed, just as I'd left it, and appeared to be locked.

I went to the hatch and checked it, and, yes, it was locked. So I'd beaten the guy to the boat. Score one for my team.

I unlocked the hatch, went inside, and grabbed the Glock. I checked to make sure the magazine was full before stuffing the gun in my pocket. Then I locked the hatch behind me and started for my car.

I almost made it.

When I was a dozen or so yards from my car, I heard gravel crunching softly behind me. I turned and saw a tall, thin man dressed all in black. He had a gun aimed at me, a medium-caliber semiautomatic, and my speculation had been correct: there was a suppressor on the end of the barrel. The man was looking at me with a grim expression on his lean, pale face.

I wasn't sure where he'd come from. He'd probably driven into the lot while I was on the boat, spotted my car, and then hidden behind one of the cars I'd passed while walking to mine. If my car was there, he knew I was on the boat and would either stay there or, more likely, given our chase earlier, come back to the car. He'd waited to see what I'd do, and I'd fallen into his trap.

There was no way I could get my gun out and aim it before the man shot me. My only chance would be if the man did something careless, and he didn't seem the type for something like that.

As I stood there, frozen, the man smiled, and his smile was grim too. That sounds as though it doesn't make sense, but I think he smiled in anticipation of doing something he liked to do—killing.

"Drop that flashlight and turn around."

His voice was low and rough, like that of a heavy smoker. I let the light clatter onto the ground and turned, wondering if he was going to shoot me in the back. But then I realized this man would have no hesitation about shooting me face to face, so that wasn't why he wanted me facing the other way.

It was to search me. "Hold out your arms," he said, and I raised them.

He jabbed his pistol into the small of my back and ran one hand and then the other up and down my sides, shifting the gun so quickly I could barely tell when he did it. Of course he found the gun in my pocket and pulled it out.

"Well, well. How does that song go? 'Send lawyers, guns, and money'?" He paused. "That's right—'the shit has hit the fan'."

I sensed him putting my gun in his own pocket before he ran a hand over my chest and back. Then he grabbed my crotch. I think that was more to humiliate me than to search for anything, but, if so, it had the desired effect. I was ashamed and angry all at once, and I wanted nothing in the world so badly as I wanted to kill him.

I heard him take a couple of steps back. "Put your arms down and face me," he said.

I turned again and saw that same grim smile.

"Now we're going to see Kingman—he has some questions for you. But don't try anything cute or you're a dead man. My orders are to bring you in alive if possible but dead if not."

I didn't say anything. I was busy thinking about how to take that gun away from him.

"Do you understand?"

I nodded.

"Good. Now let's go to your car. You'll drive."

I walked toward my car. The man followed, staying back just enough that I couldn't twirl and hit him but close enough that he couldn't miss shooting me if I did something stupid like that.

When we got close to the car, he said, "Put the top up." That figured—he wouldn't want to tool around in an open car where people could see his face and perhaps spot the long-barreled gun he'd be pointing at me.

"All right." I unsnapped the cover that went over the convertible top when it was folded down and tossed the cover on the gravel. I wanted to open the trunk, but I was afraid that if I moved to do that, he'd be suspicious and wouldn't let me. But maybe this way would work.

I put the top up—easy and quick on a Miata—and, standing outside the car, closed the front latches that held the top to the windshield frame. "Okay, it's done."

He glanced at the cover on the ground and took a step toward me. "You just gonna leave that there, huh? Let your friends know something wasn't right when you left?"

"I just . . . ."

"Just nothing. Put it in the trunk."

I sighed to make him think he'd outsmarted me, but I felt a surge of hope. Maybe I'd outsmarted him.

Being careful to keep a scared look on my face—it wasn't hard to do—I picked up the cover, unlocked the trunk, and opened it. I folded the cover in my arms and laid it in the trunk.

As I did that, I used my left hand, the one farthest away from him, to pick up one of a pair of single-horn deck cleats I'd taken off the boat. I wanted to replace them with double-horn cleats and had removed them so that I could match their mounting-screw holes with new cleats at the chandlery.

The horns on the metal cleats weren't sharp, but they were pointed, and the weight of the cleat felt good in my hand. It I could hit the guy with the cleat, it would hurt and perhaps give me a chance to get his gun.

Or get shot. I knew that was the more likely outcome.

I wouldn't have much room to swing the cleat in the car, so I needed to make my move while we were standing there. I slammed the trunk lid shut and half-turned toward the guy.

"Look, I just thought of something. What if—"

"Don't think. And don't talk. Just get in the fucking car."

He motioned with the gun toward the front of the Miata, and as soon as the barrel wasn't pointed at me, I threw the cleat in his face.

The metal made a satisfying *smack* on his flesh. He yowled and put his free hand on his face. I sprang forward and did my best version of a karate chop on his gun hand. The pistol clattered to the gravel, and I punched him in the gut as hard as I could. He grunted and doubled over. Then I clubbed him on the back of the neck with my clasped hands.

He slumped to the ground, and I snatched up his pistol. As I stood there, wondering whether I should shoot him or just tie him up, he rolled onto his back and fumbled to pull my gun out of his pocket.

That decided things, and I shot him in the head.

CHAPTER FORTY-EIGHT

Even with the suppressor the gun sounded loud to me, but the sound must not have carried far, because I didn't see any lights go on or hear anyone call out.

I thought about taking a second shot, just to be sure, but from the awful way his head looked—the stuff of nightmares—I didn't think he could be alive. I put my fingers on his wrist and didn't feel a pulse.

I got my Glock and his keys from his pockets. Then I checked his gun's magazine. I didn't know whether I'd need an extra pistol, but having one with a suppressor could come in handy. There were five cartridges left—more than enough for the shooting I'd have to do.

I put both guns on the passenger seat of my car. Then I clicked his car key and saw lights flash on a dark sedan about halfway across the lot.

I got that car and parked it near his body. Then I put my hands under his armpits and heaved the body into the trunk, trying not to get blood on myself or my clothes. That was the heaviest lift I've ever done. Maybe the dead carry the weight of their sins. If so, that guy was carrying plenty of them.

I backed his car over the bloodstain on the gravel. No one was likely to investigate the car until the trunk started to smell, and that would take a day or two even in the heat. I hoped to be around to move the car before then, but if I wasn't . . . then it wouldn't matter.

I checked the time. I had half an hour before I was supposed to meet Maya. I got in my car and headed for the motel where she was staying.

It was the same place where Justine and I had made love once. I thought about that as I drove, and I found that Justine's face was becoming a bit indistinct to me. I kept getting her face mixed up with Sally's and even Maya's so that I was imagining a sort of composite of all three women.

I wondered if I was going crazy. Maybe I was. Maybe I had to be at least somewhat crazy to do what I was doing or even had already done.

Like shooting that guy in the head. I'd never done anything like that before. I knew it should have made me feel terrible, but it really just made me sort of numb.

I wondered how much weight I'd carry when I was dead.

I pulled into the motel parking lot and found the door with the number she'd given me.

I knocked lightly on the door, and she opened it instantly as though she'd been watching for my arrival.

She was wearing black pants that fit like a second skin and a low-cut red blouse that revealed the top halves of her swelling breasts. Her black hair, pulled back and done up with some sort of red fabric thing, accentuated the pale planes of her high cheekbones.

"If you walked down the street at noon in that outfit, you'd stop traffic."

"I will take that as a compliment. I want Kingman looking at me, not looking around for you."

"Good thinking. Smart as well as beautiful."

That earned me a smile, but she said, "Save it for later."

"If there is a later."

"You should not think like that. We can do this."

I wondered whether I should tell her about Kingman's hitman, what he'd done to Jack and what I'd done to him, but I decided she didn't need to know. And I still wasn't sure we were on the same side, at least not for more than the next few hours. As she'd suggested, we'd have to see what might happen between us later.

"Okay, I'll take your word for it. Should we head for Kingman's?"

She glanced at a wall clock. "Not yet. There is plenty of time. Let us have a drink first."

"I seldom turn down the offer of a drink, but we need to be sharp tonight."

"We will be sharp. I said *a* drink, not the whole bottle."

"All right."

She had bourbon—maybe she liked it or maybe Justine had told her that I did—ice, and a bottle of water. She made two medium-sized drinks and handed one to me. As she drank from her glass, I poured a little water in mine. Then we sat in the two chairs in the room.

"You do not like the taste of the bourbon as it comes?"

"Yes, I like it fine, but I like to sip a drink."

"I see. Like me, you try to be careful, to be in control."

"I screw up as much as the next guy. Look where I am tonight."

"We are where we should be. And we are going to do what we should do."

"You sound very sure of yourself."

"I am. Why not? Are you not sure of yourself?"

"Never. Well, hardly ever. I'm often unsure of things—what I should do, what I should say."

"But not with women, I think."

"No, I guess not. Or with my boat."

She smiled. "The two things that you love."

I thought about that. "Yes, I guess so."

She had some more of her drink. Then she put the glass down, rose, and stepped over to me.

"Here, try the taste now."

She leaned down to kiss me. She was right about that too—I could taste the bourbon on her lips. They parted, and her tongue, seeking mine, darted into my mouth. I felt her breath, bourbon-scented, warm on my face.

After a long moment she stood, and then I stood and bent to pick her up and carry her to the bed. But she stopped me with the palm of her outstretched hand.

"No, not now. We do not have time for that. Later we will."

I didn't say again that I wasn't sure there would be a later. At that moment a desire to take her ran through me like a strong electric current, making every part of me as rigid as iron.

For an instant I thought about brushing her hand away and throwing her on the bed. But I knew she was right: there wasn't time if we were going to carry out our plan.

She must have sensed what I was thinking. "And later it will be much better. We will have this night behind us and can take as long as we want. We can take forever if we want to."

I tried to say something, but that current was too strong, and I couldn't make my mouth work right. I waited a moment, tried again, and that time it worked. "All right. We'll wait. I suppose we should get going now."

She touched my cheek, and I thought I felt a little electric shock. I knew it was probably just static from the cheap carpet, but I wanted to think that perhaps there was a current running through her too.

Then I remembered that I'd felt the same thing when I first touched Justine. Maybe the sisters shared more than just some of their DNA.

As I was thinking that, she said, "Yes, we must go." She stepped over to the desk, picked up a manila folder, and slid it into a large purse.

The folder's contents were a near duplicate of the documents in the Kingman file that Jack had given to me. When I'd copied them a couple of days earlier—after Kris had gone home of course—I'd left out only a few things that suggested why Jack had been investigating Kingman.

Then I'd left the folder with Maya. That was the bait she'd used to get Kingman to see her, the bait for which he'd agreed to pay fifty thousand dollars.

We had to take her car—Kingman needed to see hers, not mine, in his driveway. I got the two guns out of my car and started for her passenger side.

She stopped me by holding out the key. "No, you drive. You can find the place better than I can."

"But you need to be in the driver's seat when we pull in."

"We can swap when we get close."

We're already close, I thought even though I knew that wasn't what she meant. "All right."

I unlocked the car and opened the passenger door for her. She gave me a brief smile as she slid in. "Justine said you are a gentleman."

"She didn't know me that well."

"Oh, I think she did. She knew the important things about you."

Well, she knew one important thing, I said to myself as I walked around the car and got behind the wheel. She knew I'd kill for her. Or at least help her kill someone. Yes, I supposed that was an important thing to know.

And Maya knew it too. That was why I was in the car with her and headed for Kingman's place. I just hoped it wasn't going to be a one-way trip.

The way the boat ride had turned out for Justine.

CHAPTER FORTY-NINE

When we were a mile or so from Kingman's, I saw a narrow farm-access road, dirt bottomed, on the left. I turned in, parked, and killed the lights and engine.

I looked at Maya. In the darkness, with her black hair and dark clothes, all I could see was her face, pale in the moonlight, and her shining eyes. Shining with fear or excitement? Maybe some of each. "You stay here. I'll go check things out and make sure he's alone."

"Let me come with you."

"No, you stay here. One person is less likely to be spotted than two. Plus if someone wants to use this road, you'll have to move the car. That's improbable, but it could happen."

"Really?"

"Sure. Anything *can* happen. If you do have to move the car—I mean, if someone gets a good look at you and the car—we'll call the whole thing off. So if you're not here when I get back, I'll know what happened."

"But then how would you get home?"

"Don't worry about me. Just remember what I said—we'll call it off."

"If we have to."

I paused. "Yes, only if we have to."

I left then, taking the hitman's gun with me, and walked down the road toward Kingman's place. To avoid leaving footprints, I kept to the pavement.

When Maya and I had first come up with this plan, I'd hoped the weather would be rainy on "the night." Kingman would have a harder time seeing or hearing me in the rain. But when we got to that night, I realized dry weather was better for us—fewer footprints and tire tracks.

I'd just have to try to be unseen and unheard.

As I approached Kingman's, I checked my watch: 10:54 p.m. That gave me just enough time to scout the place and walk back to the car before Maya needed to drive here.

I remembered the layout from . . . that night. When I thought about what Kingman had done to Justine, my actions didn't seem quite so sordid. But then I recalled what Hamlet said about "seems," and a wave of shame washed over me. I was glad my father didn't know what I was doing, and I hoped he never would.

I came up the driveway and moved around the lawn the way I had before. Because I'd already scouted the place once, doing it again was easier and quicker. But the house wasn't as dark as it had been the previous time, so I had to be more careful approaching it and peering through the windows.

Kingman was in his study. He was sitting at his big desk in a leather chair. A bottle of whiskey, a half-empty glass, and a snubnosed revolver were on the desk next to him.

There was also a fat envelope, which I thought must contain the money—or something that Kingman would want Maya to think was the money. But then I realized that Kingman probably wouldn't risk blowing the deal over a stack of ordinary green paper with a hundred-dollar bill on the top and bottom. No, he'd have a stack of real money.

Why not? He wasn't going to give it to Maya. If he gave her anything, it would come from that snubnose.

Across the room images flickered on a TV screen, but the sound was either off or turned down so low that I couldn't hear it. He didn't appear to be watching the program, whatever it was.

Instead he was staring moodily into the glass, and, I suppose, thinking about something. Justine? The whereabouts of his hired gun? How he'd handle Maya's visit later that night?

I didn't know. Maybe he was thinking about how he'd kill me if his man had failed to do it. Well, I wasn't going to give him that chance.

A full circuit of the house showed me that no one else was there. Or at least no one I could see. But if Kingman could hire one hitman, he could hire two. So maybe he had a bodyguard who was staying out of sight. If he did, I'd find out soon enough.

I hiked back down the road. As I got close to the farm lane, I looked for the car but didn't see it. Had the house won on my one-in-a-thousand bet that no one would want to use the lane that night?

I sprinted toward the lane's entrance. Still no car.

Then, as I came even with the entrance, I saw it parked farther down the lane than I had left it. I pulled out the pistol and, holding it down by my side, walked slowly up the car.

All the windows were down, and I saw Maya in the driver's seat. For a moment I thought she was asleep, but she heard or sensed me and turned her head toward me as I stepped up to her window. "Thank God it is you. I was getting worried."

"Why did you move the car?"

"I was afraid that someone driving by would spot it and then stop to investigate. So I drove farther in to make the car harder to see."

"All right. Did anyone come by?"

"A couple of cars several minutes apart. Neither of them slowed down as they passed."

"Good."

"What did you see at the house?"

"Kingman, sitting in his study and drinking. Probably thinking too—thinking about whether to kill you when you come in."

"I know. You did not see anyone else."

"No, but that doesn't mean no one else is there. It would be easy to hide from sight in that big house. The only way to find out is to go in."

"Then that is what we will do."

"Yes. That's what we'll do."

I slid into the back and lay down on the seat. I didn't want Kingman or anyone else to see me in the car.

Maya started the engine, raised the windows, and backed out slowly, keeping the lights off until we were on the road. We didn't talk.

She drove the mile to Kingman's. It seemed to take forever, but finally I felt the car make the turn into the drive, and then I heard the tires crunching over the oyster shells.

I resisted the urge to say what she was to do. We'd gone through the plan several times until both of us had memorized the steps. She was to park close to the house and go to the front door. Kingman should let her in. If he asked to see the file, she should take it out of her bag and show it to him but not hand it to him. If pressed, she could say that she had to see the money first.

The key thing was for her to get inside and distract Kingman enough so that he wouldn't lock the door. If he did lock it, she'd have to find some way to unlock it without his noticing. Our plan didn't allow for evidence of a break-in.

The car stopped, and she turned off the engine. In the sudden silence I could hear the engine ticking as it cooled.

I expected her to get out, but she didn't move. "Are you okay?" I kept my voice as soft as I could.

"Yes." She also whispered. "How about you?"

"I guess. As okay as you can be for something like this."

"Do not tell me that you want to call it off. Or do you?"

I thought about that. Part of me did want to go, to turn the car around and drive out of there. Maybe drive to police headquarters and tell them the whole story.

But another part wanted to go ahead. To do what Maya and I had set out to do. For Bella and Justine. And now for Jack.

For myself too, if I were completely honest.

"No. Do you?"

"No."

"Okay. Then we need to get going."

Without saying anything further, she opened the door and got out, taking her bag with her.

In case anyone was watching her, I waited until she was well away from the car before raising my head just enough to see her walk up to the front door. She rang the bell. Nothing happened for a several seconds. Then the porch light came on, and the door opened.

Kingman—or whoever opened the door—must have been standing well back, because I couldn't see anyone but Maya. I wondered if the person had a gun in his hand. Probably.

It was time to bring out the guns.

CHAPTER FIFTY

Maya went inside, and the door closed. I waited half a minute in case someone was watching to see whether Maya was alone. Then I pressed a switch to keep the interior light off, picked up both pistols, and eased out of the car.

I kept low and closed the door gently, making only a *click* that didn't carry far. Still keeping low, I ran to the side of the house and stopped to listen. I heard nothing but the night.

I eased onto the porch and up to the front door. I said a silent prayer and put my hand on the knob. When it turned I exhaled, surprised to find that I'd been holding my breath.

I shoved the Glock into a front pocket, raised the pistol with the suppressor, and used my other hand to push the door open as quietly as I could. I stepped inside, the thick oriental rug deadening my footsteps.

Now I could hear talking from some other part of the house. I followed the sounds toward Kingman's study. It figured he'd take her there—that was the room where he felt most comfortable. Plus he had booze in there—and guns. The booze and guns that were part of our plan.

He'd already been drinking, so we wouldn't have to try to force any whiskey into him. I'd shoot him with one of his own guns—using the revolver he already had out would be easiest—and make it look like suicide. There wouldn't be a note, but there would be a folder full of incriminating material that would have put him away for a long time, maybe the rest of his life. No one would want to face that.

We hadn't foreseen Jack's murder, but now we could use it to our advantage. I'd leave the hitman's pistol on Kingman's desk, and the cops might figure that Kingman had shot Jack as revenge for gathering all the dirt on him. Having that killing hanging over him would be another reason for the suicide.

I tiptoed down the hall that led to Kingman's study. Halfway there I felt something small and hard poke into my back. A voice said, "Stop right there and drop the gun."

That surprised me. I hadn't heard a thing. Another surprise was that I recognized the voice—a baritone, not loud but commanding and with a Tidewater accent.

Chief Carruthers.

I stopped, but for a moment I debated trying to twirl and knock the gun out of his hand. Then he poked his gun into me harder and said, "No, don't try it, Pete. I don't want to shoot you, but if I have to, I will."

So I gave up on that idea.

"I said to drop the gun."

I let go of the pistol. It bounced on the runner and then lay still.

"Take two steps forward. Just two."

I did as he said, and he scooped up the pistol. He put his gun into my back again. "Now walk into that room. Slowly."

Something, probably the chief's talking, had silenced the voices in the study. After another couple of steps I was close enough to the door to see Kingman standing by his desk, pulling papers out of a manila folder, but I couldn't see Maya. If I remembered correctly, there was a sofa on the other side of the room, and Maya was probably sitting there.

As I entered the room, I saw that my guess was right. Maya was on the sofa, her bag in her lap. When she saw me without a gun and the chief right behind me with two, her eyes widened and her face grew pale. I didn't blame her for being scared—I was damn scared myself. This scene wasn't playing out at all the way we'd planned it.

"You're right, Ben. He's in the blackmail scheme with her. I didn't believe you, but here he is." The chief's voice was almost normal, but I knew him well enough to hear a touch of disappointment.

"Of course I'm right." Kingman was standing in front of his chair with Maya's folder open before him, some of its papers scattered across the desktop.

He stared at me, hate radiating from him like heat from a stove. "Scarcelli is nothing but a bottom-feeding shyster, a rip-off artist who stumbled though law school the way he stumbles around this town. He's no better than his father, that old drunk in the shitty trailer."

"Okay, okay, there's no need for that. Pete, go sit next to the lady."

I walked over to the sofa, trying not to look as scared as I felt. I turned and sat, the Glock digging into my thigh. I didn't know why the chief hadn't frisked me. Maybe he couldn't imagine his daughter's friend Pete having more than one gun.

Kingman was still glaring at me. "And I'm right that he killed Justine."

"I know you said that, but what motive could he possibly have had?"

"They'd been having an affair, but Justine broke it off. He was afraid she'd feel guilty and tell me about it, and he knew what I'd do to him if I found out. So he drugged her and took her out on my boat. Maybe he planned the fire, or maybe he'd just planned to throw her overboard and the fire was an accident. Either way he killed her."

"Do you have any proof of that?"

"Yes, right here." He opened a desk drawer, took out some glossy prints, and tossed them, one by one, in front of the chief. "Look, photos of them having sex at the Riverside Inn. A private eye took them for me."

Chief Carruthers stepped closer to the desk. He glanced down at the photos but didn't touch them. "Which PI?"

"A guy named Jack Greese."

That was another surprise. So Jack had been working for both sides . . . . I'd thought he was more professional than that, but obviously I'd been wrong. That took away a little of my desire to kill Kingman, but there was still plenty left, especially with those dirty pictures spread across his desk.

The chief nodded. "Yeah, I know him. And I've seen some of his work over the years. Does their affair tie into the blackmail scheme?"

"No. This little tramp here must've cooked that up on her own."

The chief turned to Maya. "And who are you, ma'am?"

"Maya Martínez. I am not a tramp! And I am not blackmailing anybody. I just told Mr. Kingman that I had some information he might want to purchase."

"What kind of information?"

"Mostly about his business dealings. A few other things—personal things."

"I see."

When Chief Carruthers didn't ask her why Kingman would want to buy information about his own doings, I knew he understood what sort of information it was. And I also knew he could simply turn everything over to Sally and let her decide what charges to bring against Kingman.

But if it was that simple, why had Kingman arranged for the chief to be here when Maya delivered the folder? Why hadn't he just hired another thug to stick a gun in my back? Wasn't he afraid of the chief's knowing about that folder full of incriminating information?

The chief turned from Maya to Kingman, and I saw the look that passed between them. Then it hit me. Kingman wasn't worried about what Chief Carruthers would do with the file because he wasn't going to do anything with it. Except maybe burn it.

Kingman had something on the chief just as he did on many other people in town. Maybe Kingman had had Jack do a little digging on the chief. Or maybe . . . maybe it was as simple as a payoff.

Suddenly I knew how Chief Carruthers had paid for Sally's law-school tuition, for Rusty and all those riding lessons, for the house that looked bigger and more expensive than she could afford. The total probably wasn't a huge figure, certainly not for a man as rich as Kingman, but it was enough to put the chief in Kingman's pocket.

The realization hung over me like a black cloud. I'd always thought of Chief Carruthers as the one incorruptible man in town. But really he was down there with the rest of us, wrestling in the mud like everyone else.

"What are you going to do with them?" The sharp sound of Kingman's voice cut through my thoughts.

"Do with them? I'm going to arrest them of course, take them to the jail."

"No. They'll talk. I don't want that."

"It can't be helped. Besides, it'll just be their word against yours, and nobody is going to believe them."

"There's another way." He picked up the pistol from his desk.

The chief's eyes narrowed. "No, there isn't. You're not going to do that."

"You're right—I'm not. You are. These two prisoners are going to be shot while trying to escape. Let's take them outside."

"No."

"Goddamn it, Dave, I'm not asking you! I'm telling you! That's how we're going to handle it." He pointed the pistol at me. "Stand up, shyster. I'm going to make you pay for fucking my wife."

The chief had been holding his gun down by his side. Now he raised it slightly but without aiming it at anyone. "Ben, now I'm telling you. We're not going to do that."

Kingman turned toward the chief, and the pistol turned with him.

Then things happened quickly.

CHAPTER FIFTY-ONE

Maya scooped a hand into her bag and came up with her shiny little pistol. She didn't say, "Freeze!" or anything like that. She just shot Kingman in the belly.

A look of great surprise came over his face, and he slumped to the floor. The chief assumed a firing stance and aimed his gun at Maya. "Drop it, lady!"

He'd picked the wrong time and place to be chivalrous. Instead of dropping the gun, Maya shot him in the chest. The chief returned fire, and the heavier bullet from his pistol slammed Maya back against the sofa cushion.

Blood spurted from a big hole that must have been near her heart, and some of it sprayed onto me. The chief staggered, putting out his free hand for support but finding only air. He dropped to his knees, raised his pistol feebly toward me, and then fell onto the floor.

When the gunshots stopped ringing, the sudden silence seemed very loud and the room stank with the sharp smell of cordite. I looked at Maya. Her beautiful dark eyes were open but staring at nothing. Or maybe staring at eternity. She was clearly dead.

I got to my feet, shaking a little from adrenaline or fear or perhaps a combination of both. I heard Kingman sucking in air, so I knew he was still alive. I stepped close to him, being careful not to step in the pool of blood forming beneath him, and kicked his pistol out of his reach.

Next I checked on the chief. He was still alive—barely—and I knelt beside him.

"Chief? Can you hear me? I'll call an ambulance, get you to the hospital. Just hold on."

He clutched my arm, harder than I would have thought possible, and made a sort of awful gargling sound. Blood came from his mouth.

"You . . . you . . . Sally . . . loves . . . you be . . . good to her."

Then he died.

I knew because of the way the pressure eased on my arm and the way he went limp all over. I knelt by him for a little while—praying, I guess—and finally I stood.

I went over by the sofa and picked up Maya's little pistol from the floor where she'd dropped it. I turned toward Kingman and aimed the gun.

His eyes were open now, and as he watched me, they grew wide with fear.

"No, no," he said in a shaky voice. He had both hands over the wound on his belly, and he raised one, covered with blood, toward me. "No, wait, I have money. All yours if—"

I didn't let him finish. I shot him in the face.

He died instantly. Too quickly, of course, given how Justine had died. But it was over.

I wiped off the gun with my handkerchief, put the gun in Maya's hand, and pressed her fingers around it. The prints wouldn't be very good, but they'd probably be good enough, and she already had powder residue on that hand. I'd called Maya a few times, so I took her phone from her purse and stuck it in my pocket.

I retrieved the hitman's pistol from the hall and wiped it off. Then I closed Kingman's hand on the butt. When I let go, his hand opened, and the pistol lay there on his lifeless palm. He didn't have powder residue on him, but that was all right. The hitman had been dead for quite a while, so Kingman could have washed his hands in the interim.

Then, with the handkerchief draped over my fingers, I searched Kingman's desk. It took a few minutes, but finally I found what I was looking for—an unlabeled folder with a single sheet of paper in it. The paper had "Carruthers" written at the top and two columns of figures below that. The figures were dollar amounts and dates. None of the amounts was over ten thousand dollars, but they added up to almost half a million going back seventeen years. So my guess about the chief had been right.

I gathered up the pictures of Justine and me and put them in the folder from Kingman's desk. I pulled up my shirt, slid the folder into my waistband, and dropped my shirt down over them.

I left the papers Maya had brought. They helped to explain the killings. And if reporters got leaked copies of some of them or even just learned about the sort of information they contained, the press would have a field day. People love it when a successful but arrogant person is exposed as being corrupt. The Germans have a word for that feeling: "schadenfreude."

And then of course the police would be a lot less interested in pursuing an investigation into what had happened.

I also left the money where it lay. Although I was tempted to take it, Kingman's banker or broker or someone else might know he'd quickly pulled that much cash together and might wonder where it had gone. Then that someone might start looking for the money, and I didn't want it to lead to me.

Also, the money made the three-way shootout more plausible and implied that no one but the shooters had been in the room. So even though I'd gotten into this awful thing partly for money, I decided to get out of it without any.

Then I looked around the room, thinking about what I'd touched with my bare hands. Nothing but the two guns, and I'd taken care of both of them.

Something made me go back to the sofa and stand there for a minute. I forced myself to look down at Maya with that terrible hole in her chest. I put the back of my hand to her cheek and felt that it was already growing cold.

I wondered what Maya would have done to me if we'd been able to carry out my plan. At one time I'd thought she might kill me too, but that thought had faded. Perhaps we would have been close, at least for a while. I like to think it might have been that way. But fate had intervened.

I walked out of the house, stopping only to wipe off the knob on the front door. I got into Maya's car, drove it back to the motel, and wiped it down. Then I took the Miata back to the marina and parked in my usual spot.

I fished out the hitman's keys, drove his car to Kingman's place, and parked it in the driveway, close to the house. I wiped that one down too and left it there, unlocked and with the key still in it.

I hoped the cops would think Kingman had shot the guy and put him in the trunk. But I didn't really care what they thought as long as they left me out of it.

I started the long hike back to the marina. After I'd gone about a quarter mile I remembered a scene from an old black-and-white movie, a crime story in which a man had conspired with a woman to murder her husband. After they killed the husband, the man was walking down the sidewalk and suddenly realized he couldn't hear his own footsteps.

But I could hear mine. They sounded almost as though someone were following me. I even turned around once to check, but no one was there. No one but me. And my conscience, I guess. What was left of it.

Walking back took a couple of hours, and I had to be careful to duck into the woods whenever I saw a car ahead of or behind me. That happened four or five times, but I always managed to get off the road before the car got close.

I got back to *Law Lass* about four in the morning. The silver half-moon sailed overhead, making the ten thousand stars seem dim and pale by comparison. The air was still and so was the water. None of the boats showed any lights. I was exhausted in body and brain, wrung out by the night's madness like a dirty, wet rag.

I stepped onto my boat as quietly as I could without—in the unlikely event that anyone was watching—seeming furtive about it. I unlocked the hatch and went below.

I didn't risk turning on a light. I hid the folder under my berth and then groped for the bottle in the warm darkness. After knocking over a couple of plastic glasses, I found it. I twisted the cap off and drank deeply from the bottle, the whiskey burning a path down my throat. I drank again, feeling the warmth start to spread in my empty belly.

I thought of Kingman then, gut-shot and head-shot and now burning in hell if there was one. I thought there probably was—I was close enough myself to smell the sulphur. And to see the devil grin.

It was a nasty grin that made my skin crawl as though I'd seen a rat—no, dozens of rats, all coming toward me, their sharp yellow teeth barred and their red eyes shining.

Yes, it was a nasty grin, and I drank until I couldn't see it anymore.

CHAPTER FIFTY-TWO

The next morning—late the next morning when I finally got up—my head felt as though someone were banging on the inside with a hammer. I took three aspirin and drank water like a camel. I didn't feel like having breakfast but decided that, to avoid suspicion, I'd better stick to my usual routine.

I got cleaned up, went out and bought a copy of *The Kilmihil Chronicle*, and continued on the Captain's Café, where I sat at the counter and ordered scrambled eggs, turkey sausage, and coffee. While I waited, I read the paper, but there was nothing in it about the four dead people at Kingman's place.

Marge brought my coffee. As she refilled the water glass, she said, "Heard the news, Pete?"

I was afraid to ask but knew I had to. "News about what?"

"About the chief. And Mr. Kingman. A woman too, but I don't know her name."

"No, I haven't. What happened?"

"They're all dead. Shot to death. The maid found them this morning."

I tried to look shocked. I guess I managed it well enough, because all she said was, "Yeah, I know—a horrible thing. I wonder what happened."

I shook my head. "Who knows? Maybe the police can figure it out."

"Maybe. I'm sure Sally Carruthers is just devastated."

Sally. I'd been trying not to think about her, but that comment forced me to. I imagined her lying alone in bed or sitting alone at the breakfast table and getting a phone call from a police officer to tell her about her father. How he'd been killed. I imagined how she must have cried—probably was still crying. The two of them had been close, and this wasn't something Sally would get over soon—in fact, she'd never get over it, not fully.

And it was my fault.

"Yes. Yes, I'm sure she is."

"Poor thing. Now she's all alone in the world."

Marge gave me a look that implied I should do something about that, but I pretended I didn't know what she meant. When I didn't say anything, her expression turned to one of impatience, and I'm sure she was thinking that all men are idiots. Or at least that I was.

I didn't disagree with her, so I still didn't say anything. She must have sensed I wasn't in a mood for talking, because she brought my breakfast then and left me alone.

I ate silently, pretending to read the paper, but really I was thinking. How long would it be before a cop came to see me? To ask what I'd been doing that Friday night? A day? Two days? How long would I have to wait, my nerves stretched as tight as a drumhead, before I got that tap on my office door, the boat's hatch, or even my shoulder?

"Mr. Scarcelli, we need to talk to you."

Then it would all be over. I didn't think I could lie well enough to fool them, and if they got suspicious and started looking for evidence, they could probably find some. They could certainly find my fingerprints at Kingman's, for example. Not from last night but from when I'd visited Justine there. And the motel clerk might remember us. Perhaps other people had seen us together.

That's what I thought as I sat there, mechanically eating my breakfast while feeling frozen inside.

But I shouldn't have worried. I got away with it.

Oh, that state cop came to see me—the one who'd been there before with the chief. He asked me whether I knew anything about the business at Kingman's, and I said I didn't, nothing but what had been in the news. Then he asked me if I knew anything about the death of Jack Greese, and again I said I knew only what the news had reported.

He asked me if I'd ever hired Jack, and I said that I had from time to time like a lot of other lawyers in town. When he asked me if I'd hired Jack to check on Kingman, I readily admitted that I had, that it was a common tactic in divorce matters.

I even gave him a few documents I'd taken from the Kingman file Jack had brought me—documents that hadn't been in Maya's folder. Those papers had been subject to attorney-client privilege, as attorney work product, when Justine was alive, but the privilege had ended with her death, and I didn't want the cop digging into me any more than he already was.

He asked me about Maya and the guy in the car trunk. I said I'd met Maya when I'd run into Justine in a restaurant but didn't know anything about her except that she was friends with Justine. I said I didn't know anything about the guy in the trunk.

He seemed satisfied and left after telling me not to go out of town for a while in case the police had more questions. I said sure and walked him to the door. That seemed to end things with me as far as the police went.

For the next few months I stuck to my usual routine, sailing on the weekend when the weather was fine and working during the week. I went to see my father once in a while but otherwise didn't socialize with anyone, especially not Sally. I went out of my way to avoid seeing her.

The only thing out of the ordinary was that I didn't date anyone. For the first time in my adult life, I turned into a monk.

Kris even kidded me about it once. "Pete, I can't believe you're not seeing someone. You must be spending time with some lucky lady on the sly. I should warn her about you."

"Let's just stick to work, okay? I think we know too much personal stuff about each other."

A hurt expression came over her face, and she pouted for the rest of the day. I finally had to apologize.

"Look, I'm sorry. I didn't mean to be so curt. I'm just kind of focused on work right now."

"Forget it. You're right—we shouldn't be in each other's personal business."

After that Kris was always professional—in fact, her job performance improved—but she became a bit cool toward me. Also, she started dressing more conservatively for the office although for Kris "conservative" still meant "hot." I told her that she was doing a good job but otherwise didn't say anything about the changes.

Maybe because I was paying more attention to work, I won the biggest case of my career. I'd been representing the estate of a woman, a nurse, who was killed by a drunk driver as she was coming home from a late shift at the hospital where she worked. She left behind her husband and three young children.

The man who hit her had been convicted of drunk driving a few years before. This time he was in a company car, and it turned out that his employer hadn't bothered to check his driving record before giving him the car. So I went after the employer as well as the driver himself.

Both of their insurance companies knew that a jury would be very sympathetic to the husband and children, especially given that the driver had pleaded guilty to the criminal charges and gotten six years for them. The court was going to let him wear regular clothes, not an orange jumpsuit, at the civil trial, but that wouldn't have helped him much.

So on the afternoon before the trial was to begin, the insurance companies settled for close to the policies' coverage limits, a total of almost seven million dollars. And I got a third of that.

Although people sometimes sneer at personal-injury lawyers, that win got me a lot of good publicity. I came off as the defender of the little guy—or in this case a hard-working nurse, her husband, an electrician who was an Army vet, and their children, two girls and a boy, all three of whom were visibly devastated by the death of their mother. The insurance companies were right—the jury would have crucified the drunk driver and his employer.

So for a couple of weeks afterward people came up to me and congratulated me on beating the insurance companies and getting a big win for the nurse's family. The money wasn't going to bring her back, of course, but it would make things a lot easier for the family she'd left behind.

I started getting a better class of clients after that, and the other lawyers around town treated me with more respect. I wasn't the Oliver Wendell Holmes of Kilmihil, but neither was I the bottom feeder I had been.

I was so busy enjoying my new situation that I didn't realize it wouldn't last long.

CHAPTER FIFTY-THREE

Then one day Trey Marston phoned me. He started by congratulating me on the drunk-driving case. I thanked him but said I'd just been lucky.

"I think it was more than luck, Pete. You handled that case very well. A lot of lawyers would've taken a lower offer and settled sooner, not risked going to trial, but you were ready to roll the dice and take the case to a jury."

"Well, I thought we had a pretty good case."

"You did, but we never know what a jury's going to do. They probably would have found the driver liable, but who knows what the award would have been? Maybe less than what you got—maybe even a lot less."

"Could be. Anyway, I appreciate your kind words."

"Sure. By the way, I wondered if you'd like to apply to join the country club? I'd be happy to sponsor you, and I can get someone else to be the required second sponsor."

I thought about how I'd gone there soon after I met Justine, how the guard had known right away that I wasn't a member.

"Thanks, Trey, but I'm not sure I'd fit in. I don't own a single polo pony."

He laughed. "Come on, Pete! We're not stuffy. Just some golf and tennis, drinks by the pool, that kind of thing."

Then I thought about how badly I wanted to be a member, at least if I thought the other members would accept me as one of them. My father wouldn't understand—he'd sneer and call them a bunch of goddamned stuffed shirts—but I knew I wanted to join if they'd have me.

"Okay, I'll think about it."

"Good. I'll send you an application. The dues are actually pretty reasonable—not that you have to worry about that now!" He laughed again to take the edge off his reference to money.

We got off the phone then, and I sat there thinking. Joining the country club . . . something I'd always wanted. I imagined myself driving an expensive car—I could afford one now—to the club, tossing the key to the valet, and strolling up the front steps of the clubhouse.

Then I wondered what it would have been like to be there with Justine. Drinking dry martinis with her in the cozy bar on a Saturday evening, saying hello to people we knew, and then enjoying a gourmet dinner in the formal dining room, her bright eyes even brighter in the candlelight.

Or sitting by the pool with her in the late afternoon, sipping something tall and cool. Admiring how she looked in her swimsuit, her shapely yet slim figure something no woman her age—and damn few younger than her—could match.

Then it hit me. Six people were dead because Justine had walked into my office that day in that little white tennis dress. Because she'd seduced me—not that I'd resisted much—and drawn me into her scheme to kill her husband. Well, he was dead, all right, but so was she. And Maya . . . Chief Carruthers . . . Jack . . . even that nameless guy who'd come after me. All of them dead.

Suddenly I remembered a line I'd read somewhere: "food for worms." I struggled to recall where it was from—maybe someone's epitaph? It didn't matter. The line was true, and its truth was all that counted.

It was mid-afternoon, and we were busy in the office, but I wanted to be by myself. I told Kris to take the rest of the day off, and she never disagreed when I said that.

After she shut down her computer and got her purse, she stood in the doorway, giving me a strange look. It was sort of puzzled and sad at the same time.

"Are you all right, Pete?"

"Sure, why not?"

"You just seem a little . . . down. I thought you'd still be on cloud nine after our big win."

After I'd given Kris a fat bonus from the proceeds, she'd started referring to the case as "our" win, but I didn't mind. She had played a role in it, and I was glad she was proud of what our little firm had accomplished.

"Sure, it was great." I didn't hear any sarcasm in my voice, but maybe Kris did.

"It *was* great. Is the high just wearing off for you?"

"Yeah, I guess so. On to the next case."

"Sure. Okay, boss, I'll be going."

"Have a good evening."

"You too."

She gave me some more of that strange look, and then she left. I sat there for a few minutes, not doing anything but breathing, not even thinking.

I was tired of thinking. I'd done all the thinking I wanted to—more than I wanted to. God, was I tired of thinking.

In fact, I was tired in general, mentally and even physically although I hadn't exercised in a while. Not unless you call lifting a whiskey glass exercise.

And tired emotionally. Regret was like a big rock that I carried with me all the time, a boulder I could barely lift but could never put down. Regret that I knew would never leave me.

After a long while I did what I had known for some time I was going to do. I picked up the phone and called the police.

The woman who ran the little office answered. I told her who I was and asked to speak to Andy Barrett, the former sergeant who'd been appointed as the new chief. After a few seconds he came on the line.

"What can I do for you, counselor?"

"Nothing, Chief. Except listen."

I started telling him the whole story, beginning with the day Justine walked into my office. When I got to the part where we discussed killing her husband, Barrett stopped me.

"Hold on, Mr. Scarcelli, I have to read you your rights. And if you want to talk, to tell me all this, we need to do it in person. I'll send a couple of officers to pick you up, okay?"

"Sure."

We hung up, and I sat there again, looking around the office as if trying to memorize it. I knew I'd miss the office—my comfortable chair, the oak desk, the pictures sitting on the furniture and hanging on the walls. I'd enjoyed practicing law in that office, feeling that I was in charge of something I'd built myself, something worthwhile.

I'd done it to make money, of course, but I'd helped people too. At least I like to think so. But in the end I guess I just wasn't good enough.

For a long time, most of my life, I'd thought I was a better man than my father. What was he now but an old drunk who lived in a dirty trailer and bored people with sea stories that probably weren't true?

Sure, he was all that, but at least he'd never murdered anyone. Or, as far as I knew, even seen it done. I'd done both. And for what? For nothing. I didn't have Justine. I didn't have half of Kingman's money. I didn't even have Maya. And now I'd never have Sally even if I hadn't decided not to inflict myself on her.

I had nothing. Nothing but the years of time that stretched out before me, an endless ocean of time.

The cops came then, a man and a woman. I didn't know either of them, and we didn't talk much. I got my suit coat off the rack and locked the front door behind me. Then we drove to the police station.

Barrett had called the commonwealth's attorneys, and one had come over to his office. He was a young guy who looked like he hadn't yet graduated from college, much less law school. But then I'd begun to notice that people his age looked younger to me every year.

Barrett read me my rights and asked if I wanted to make a statement. I said I did. Barrett switched on a recorder, and the two of them let me talk, not asking any questions.

The young prosecutor took notes, but Barrett just looked at me, watching my eyes. Carruthers had trained him, and I thought Barrett would be a good chief. I hoped he'd avoid making the mistake Carruthers had even though I'd destroyed the evidence of that and didn't say anything about the payoffs in my statement.

It took about half an hour to tell it all. When I finished, I stopped talking, and the room was silent for several seconds.

Then Barrett cleared his throat and looked at the prosecutor. "I guess you have some questions for him."

"Yes, I do."

The prosecutor skimmed through his notes and then started asking me about specifics. Exactly when did this happen, that happen, and where? That sort of thing. I answered the questions, and the prosecutor took notes.

That went on for another half hour. Then the prosecutor looked at Barrett and nodded.

Barrett looked at me.

"You're under arrest, Mr. Scarcelli. For murder, conspiracy to commit murder, and blackmail. There will probably be some other charges too." He looked at the prosecutor, who nodded again.

"Sure, I understand."

Barrett called for the two officers who'd picked me up. They took my belt and shoe laces and put me in a holding cell. I was the only person in the cell.

When the cops left, they closed the door and locked it behind them. That made a distinctive metallic *clang* that had a ring of finality, a sound that somehow signaled the end of something.

That sound echoed in my head for a long time.

CHAPTER FIFTY-FOUR

They didn't have to try me. I pleaded guilty to all of the charges, even to a couple I didn't think were justified. But I knew I was going to prison for a long time anyway, probably for life, so I didn't care.

I didn't care about anything at that point. Well, only two things. I knew I had shamed my father, and that was another thing I regretted. He came to the jail once to see me, but neither of us had much to say, and he didn't stay long. I asked him not to come back, and he didn't. I think that was best for both of us.

The other thing was that I didn't want Sally to be involved in my case even as an observer. I dreaded the thought that I might see her across the courtroom at my sentencing. Might see pain in her lovely face.

I should have known she wouldn't have anything to do with it. My public defender, another guy who looked barely old enough to shave, told me that he'd heard Sally had recused herself from every aspect of the case. Because her father had been at Kingman's house that night, her boss was willing to let his best prosecutor stay completely out of it even though they hadn't charged me with murdering the chief.

So another prosecutor argued to the judge that I should get life for killing Justine and Kingman and for my many other heinous crimes. I'm sure that if Virginia hadn't abolished the death penalty, he would have argued that I deserved execution instead. The judge—a new one I hadn't appeared before—listened impassively, not asking any questions.

He listened just as impassively to the public defender argue that a long prison sentence—long but not life—was adequate punishment, given that I'd never committed any other crimes, had killed Justine by accident, and had shot Kingman—who might have died anyway—in self-defense. That last claim was a stretch, but the judge let him make it, again not asking any questions.

The judge said he would rule in three days, and I spent those days staring at the walls of my jail cell. Somehow I was able to turn off my brain and not think. Although I barely moved and slept ten or twelve hours a day, I was more tired than I had ever been in my life. I felt as I thought soldiers must feel when they've been through a hard battle—one they lost—and are waiting to learn what they enemy is going to do to them.

Sometimes the enemy shoots them in the head, and I wished that would happen to me. But I knew it wouldn't.

The judge gave me forty-two years, meaning I might get out in thirty-six, assuming I behaved myself. Still, that was a long, long time. I had to face the fact that I'd be an old man before I got out—if I lived long enough to get out.

They sent me to Sussex II State Prison, a fairly new lockup southeast of Petersburg. That was a break—I'd been afraid I'd go to "the Onion," Red Onion State Prison, a supermax facility out in Southwestern Virginia, right on the Kentucky border.

The Onion was said to be—and undoubtedly was—the toughest prison in Virginia. Although many of the prisoners were kept in isolation much of the time, the word would have gotten around that I'd been a lawyer, and one of my fellow prisoners probably would have shanked me because he hated the public defender who hadn't gotten him off or the prosecutor who'd put him there—or both of them.

I don't think I'd have lasted long in the Onion.

Sussex II is all right. It's no "country club" prison, but it isn't brutal. After I stood up to the first two or three guys who tried to back me down—I got lucky and put one of them on the floor, moaning with pain—the other inmates left me alone.

The prison has a good library, as prison libraries go, and at first I spent a lot of time reading. Then the staff asked me to teach reading and writing classes to the guys who can barely read—there are a lot of them—so now I do that for a few hours each day.

Toward the end of my first year someone asked me to help with his appeal, and it was something to pass the time, so I agreed. The next thing I knew I was helping several guys with their appeals, and between that and the teaching, I stay busy.

I haven't worked on an appeal for myself. I'm where I deserve to be, and I'm not going to do anything to try to change that.

After I'd been here about three years, my father died. He drank himself to death and, apparently, died in his sleep. No one found him for several days. The postal carrier noticed that his mailbox was full—unusual because he didn't get much mail—and phoned the chief's office.

The cop who investigated told a reporter for *The Kilmihil Chronicle* that the "death scene was one of the worst I've encountered." I didn't think they needed to put that in the paper, but they did. My dad didn't leave me much, and what little he did went into a victim's fund.

Sally came to see me not long after that. She was the first visitor I'd had in prison although Kris had written to me a few times until she must have figured out that I wasn't going to write back.

I didn't have to see Sally, but when they told me she was there, I decided to talk to her for a few minutes. That may have been a mistake.

She looked just the same if a bit tired. I thought she was probably working too hard. She smiled when she first saw me, but she stopped smiling when she saw how much prison had aged me. It does that to you— as though the knowledge of all those years to come behind bars weighs on you and makes your body run toward the day you might get out.

She asked how I was doing, how they were treating me, that sort of thing. The prison staff monitors all such visits, so I kept my answers short and neutral. She could tell I was holding things back, but she didn't press me about it.

She asked whether I'd heard about my father, and I said I had. She said she'd made sure he got a decent burial and a headstone. I told her to let me know how much the funeral and headstone cost, and I'd try to find a way to pay for them. She told me not to worry about it.

I asked her how she was, and she said that she was very busy, that she had a lot of cases on her desk and handling them helped take her mind off her father . . . and me.

I didn't have anything to say to that. I just looked at her, knowing it might be the last time I'd ever see her.

It was. She left after fifteen or twenty minutes, and I didn't hear anything else from or about her until I read in the paper that she'd married Trey Marston.

In one of her letters Kris mentioned that Trey divorced his wife after he learned she was having an affair with the tennis pro at the country club. Sally and Trey married a couple of years later. Trey is a good guy, and I think he'll make Sally a good husband. And, of course, he is a lucky, lucky man to be married to her.

A lucky man. I could have been that lucky man, but I wasn't. I wasn't good enough for Sally, and I'd know that even if she hadn't. Maybe she'd realized it when I went to prison. If not then, she must have figured it out when she came to see me. For her that had probably been like finishing a book she never wanted to read again.

So here I am, in this cold, impersonal, concrete labyrinth. Far from the sea. Far, far from the sea.

It's taken me a year to write this story. I've done most of that late at night when things get quiet, and I'm left alone with my thoughts. The thoughts I try not to think during the light of day.

As I said at the beginning, among the many things I miss are the tang of saltwater and the cries of gulls. Sails billowing against bright sky and hulls carving through dark water.

I stare into the darkness that comes to surround me, shutting everything else out, everything but the beating of my heart. My heart from which all of this came—my lust, my avarice, my willingness to kill.

And as I stare into the darkness, the long, slow darkness that lies ahead of me, I hear a strange sound of mirth. A low chuckling that makes my skin crawl and the hairs stand on the back of my neck.

A strange, terrifying, awful sound of mirth.

I hear the devil laughing.

THE END

More hardboiled action thrillers by

TIMOTHY J. LOCKHART

Smith
$15.95

"Smith — just Smith - is a tough as nails killer, a secret operative and tough fighter, and Timothy J. Lockhart makes this adventure a compelling must read."
—Gary Lovisi, *Paperback Parade* & *Hardboiled* magazines

Pirates
$15.95

"...with bullets zinging and baddies converging from all sides, it's anyone's guess who will make it alive out of Lockhart's gruesome, exhilarating adventure."
—Nicholas Litchfield, *Lancashire Post*

A Certain Man's Daughter
$15.95

"...an enjoyable hardboiled read with snappy dialogue and a touch of humour."
—Paul Burke, *Crime Fiction Lover*

Unlucky Money
$15.95

"Lockhart's style is bare bones narrative. Just the facts in a linear investigation... future Wendy Lu books will be quite interesting..." —*Men Reading Books*

In trade paperback from:
Stark House Press 1315 H Street, Eureka, CA 95501
griffinskye3@sbcglobal.net   www.StarkHousePress.com
Available from your local bookstore, or order direct from our website.

www.ingramcontent.com/pod-product-compliance
Lightning Source LLC
LaVergne TN
LVHW010203070526
838199LV00062B/4482